BELVOIR'S PROMISE

SUSANNA M. NEWSTEAD

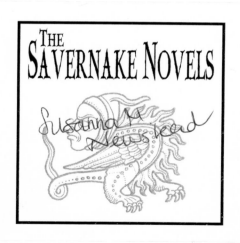

THE SAVERNAKE NOVELS

Susanna M. Newstead

PASTMASTERY PRESS

Acknowledgements

This book has been 40 years in the making and so there are many people no longer in this world, whom I must thank, not least my father who instilled in me my love of history. I must also thank my English teacher Mr. Hawkes who all those years ago told me I should write a book...and would.

I must thank my husband Stephen for putting up with all the years of research and for reading with a critical eye, every word I type.

I thank Valerie Drew for being my companion on many fact finding trips and for her wonderful photography without which the covers of my books would pale into mediocrity.

I would like to thank Eileen Enwright Hogdetts for her help and advice on publishing.

Other people and organisations have contributed their vast Mediaeval or other esoteric knowledge, namely, the archives of Marlborough College, staff at Devizes Museum, the Wiltshire Archive, Rich Price, Nick Baxter, Steph Woodhouse, Toni Louka Fernandez, Sarah Thursfield for her expertise on costume and the White Horse Bookshop of Marlborough who obtained some strange books for me. I thank David Ives, professional anthropologist, for being such an unstinting support and helpful critic.

I thank Matthew Ryan for creating the most wonderful cover and putting up with my whims and the many friends worldwide who have read and proofed my manuscripts.

Lastly I thank Bonnie Taher and Gill Whatmough for their help with the manuscript of Belvoir's Promise.

ABOUT THE AUTHOR

Susanna, like Aumary Belvoir has known the Forest of Savernake all her life. After a period at the University of Wales studying Speech Therapy, she returned to Wiltshire and then moved to Hampshire to work, not so very far from her forest. Susanna developed an interest in English history, particularly that of the 12th and 13th centuries, early in life and began to write about it in her twenties. She now lives in Northamptonshire with her husband and a small wire haired fox terrrier called Delphi.

TITLES IN THIS SERIES:

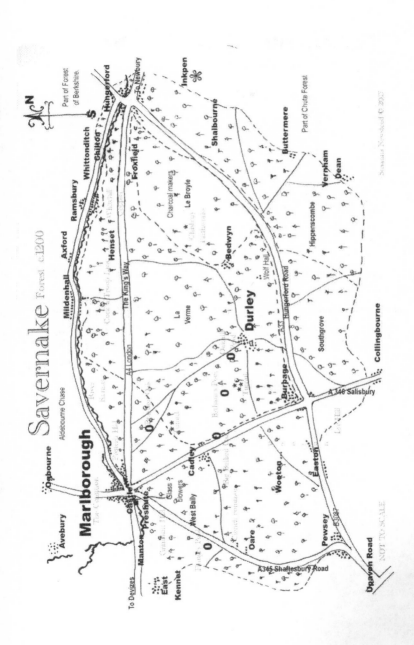

Savernake Forest c.1200

Durley Village c. 1200

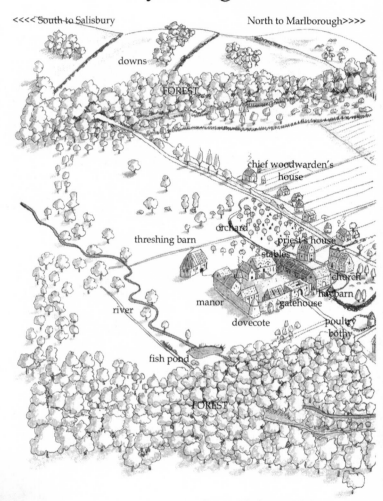

<<<< South to Salisbury

North to Marlborough>>>>

downs

FOREST

chief woodwarden's
house

orchard

threshing barn

priest's house

stables

church

manor

haybarn

gatehouse

river

dovecote

poultry
bothy

fish pond

FOREST

Susanna M. Newstead © 2017

Durley Village c. 1200

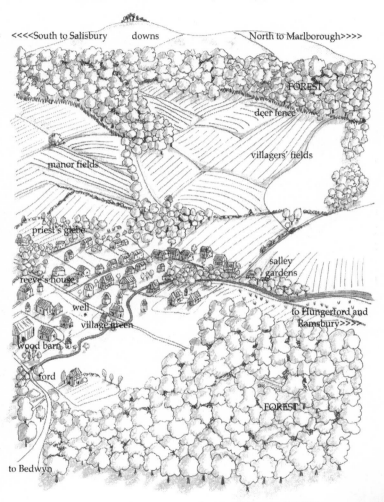

Susanna M. Newstead © 2017

Chapter 1

"**S**TAY or I will kill him". A knife is pointing to the side of the servant's neck.

"Back, for he will do as he says," I cry. "I have reason to know it." The man gestures with his free hand to my two nearest guards and they come pliantly into the middle of the room, leaving the door free. The other two guards stand behind him, short swords drawn. The felon will not go that way. The villain crosses the edge of the space and is almost past the fire, when the two wolfhounds left in the room to keep me company, rise up as one and with an unearthly growl, leap on him. He is unprepared for this and steps backwards. As he raises his arms to ward off the bared teeth, the young lad he had by the throat slides down and scrabbles on his hands and knees away from the fracas.

The knife flicks towards the dog's face, Gog I think, but Magog's teeth have already bitten into the felon's wrist and the knife clatters uselessly on the floor. The murderer screams and steps back again, falling over the stone hearth and into the fire turning to save himself as he goes.

The flames, which have been desultorily licking the almost burnt out logs, flare into life with the new material to catch at; the hood of the man's clothes which have fallen over his head. The man tries to turn over to rise to his knees but the heavy wolfhounds ravage and tear at his back and shoulders, pushing his face into the flames.

The rest of the cloth begins to catch fire. I notice his hair begin to smoulder. He screams incessantly. There is a terrible smell of charring flesh and hair.

All this happens in an instant and I am powerless to prevent it. My limbs are as heavy as stone.

The dogs snarl and tear, rip and gouge. Neither of them seems to mind the flames which lick at the man's body from underneath them. I frantically search the room for something to pour onto the flames but we have drunk every drop of liquid and no water is to be found in any bowl or pot. Not even the chamber pot has anything in it.

The man is by turns, whimpering and crying, screaming and yelling curses. He pulls off, with badly burned and ravaged hands what is left of the smouldering and smoking clothes and rises to his burned knees. The dogs push the felon over again and with one movement Gog deftly goes for his throat. I see what was left of the miscreant's devastated face as the dog fastens his teeth and rips. The noise the man makes is prolonged; a high pitched scream falling to a bubble and a gasping, with a sobbing, that was no sobbing for there is no throat to sob with. The dogs back off snarling and growling, sensing the job done.

The man is writhing on the ground, blood pumping from his wounds. His eyes, or what was left of them, are staring at me. It seemed to take an age though I suppose it is only a few heartbeats and then suddenly, the life goes out of them.

***

"Oh…Oh…! Is it you scribe? Did you just bang the door? Have I been asleep? You put the fur over me you say. I felt you do it, I think. I have been asleep and dreaming haven't I? I always dream of that terrible moment. It's as clear in my mind, even after all these years, as the pointy little nose on your face.

That one and no other. Ah well, perhaps I will cease to dream of it once I have dictated my tale to you, my scribe. Let me catch my breath."

***

They tell me I am dying. Pah! Doctors! What do they know? In my life I have known only one doctor worth anything and he has been dead these twenty years. I do, however, feel a cold creeping up from my feet to my flanks, despite the hot stones they have placed there. They have heaped me with rugs and furs but I feel chilled and light and my body is floating. Perhaps they are right. My spirit is as heavy as the oaken bed on which I lie. No, do not misunderstand me scribe. I am not afraid of death. Death is not a thing I fear. It is but a longer sleep than that into which I have fallen a ten thousand times in my long, long life and how can I be afraid of sleep? No - I will go to sleep but not before I have lifted from my spirit something which I have kept secret some forty years or more. I must tell it. I must lighten my soul. God knows, for he has heard my supplication, my prayers and watched over my penances and will judge me accordingly at the end. If I must suffer in purgatory, so be it but I will not be condemned for eternity. He knows.

I must attempt to be more lucid. God has heard my secret and so now, I must write it down for all to hear.

***

"Come closer scribe...closer, so that you may hear me clearly. My voice can be weak and I will not tire myself unduly with shouting. Now write this down for me."

***

That I, Aumary Belvoir, Lord of Durley, once Warden of the Forest of Savernake, friend of kings and king of friends, knowing that the sands of my life are trickling fast away, do wish to set down for all to know, a truth of my life. A truth concerning the death of the boy Duke Arthur and of another death, closer to my family. This is a secret I have kept almost life long. For the good of my soul I shall tell it now. Those whom it would hurt are long dead and there is now no need for silence. I have kept faith with my King and my friend. For those of you too young to remember, you will know, for your tutors will hopefully have told you so, that the old King Henry, second of that number, had four surviving legitimate sons, Henry, Richard, Geoffrey and John, strong sons of a strong king. But we know what happens when too many strong flavours are thrown into the pot: they fight for supremacy of the broth. Henry then Geoffrey went first to their maker, Geoffrey leaving a young son Arthur, Duke of Brittany. Now you all know how the others squabbled. It is the stuff that tavern songs are made of. Old Henry died a broken, sad and disillusioned rag of the man he had been and we all know who we got next. Poor, vain, foolhardy, fighting mad Richard. The country hoped for better things but the devil dresses his servants in the most angelic robes, (Christ, I of all people must know that). Tall, brave, handsome and warped - oh not just in that way - it's said he preferred the contents of the breeches to what lies under the skirts, though it was never proven. (God will judge him and I pray he is merciful to the sodomite, if sodomite he was.) It is said that Richard was vain, greedy, juvenile and selfish; his cranium filled with deeds of daring and valour leaving no room for kingcraft. Now! I hear you cry - in what way was he different from his father?

Yes, Henry was greedy and selfish but greedy for England's sake and selfish for the good of his peoples and empire, which stretched from the north of this island to the shores of the Atlantic sea. Everything that man did - and he was a great monarch - he did for his kingdoms. Richard did only one thing for his country, besides beggaring it and stripping it naked: he got himself killed and John, young Lackland - clever, wily, hard working, hard playing, hard bitten - John was crowned king. Poor unfortunate John, the youngest of Henry's sons, most beloved of his father, whose only crime, at first, was to follow a golden legend and inherit a mess. Yes, he mismanaged, yes he was foolish but John was my liege lord, my choice, my friend. John loved Marlborough, my childhood home and spent time there both as a young man and as king. We grew close together as two stems from one tree bole, though John was my senior by eight years. I looked up to him I suppose. Yes, John was my friend, for ill and for good.

And it was for John my sovereign and friend, that I would keep this secret almost to my grave.

"Moisten my lips with water a little and I'll go on..."

Now you have had a lesson in history, all you young things who are ignorant of our present king's sire. The names may mean little to you but it is important that you understand, for my poor John, (God rest his bones at Worcester) had been dealt very poor dice and has been badly used by the chroniclers, by the tellers of tales and the writers of so-called truths. I had already cast my die when the old king was alive. I could see what the crows would do once the body of England was dying - oh yes - I knew what France was plotting. We all did. I was young then in the spring of 1191 but I thought I knew where I must place my trust. I knew that if I wanted to see my manor pass to my grandchildren, I had to keep peace with the man who would probably, if he lived, win in the end. The power of the old king was extinguished and the new King Richard was off on Crusade. Doubtless, he was a sun that was too bright to burn long anyway and I could sense, somehow, that John's power was waxing. I chose John. He cared about England, I thought. The castle at Marlborough, John's castle, became a magnet for anyone who thought himself aggrieved by William Longchamp, the man whom King Richard had left in charge of the country. He was an unpopular governor. A Norman by birth, he had little love for the English people he ruled, indeed he affected to deplore them. His imperious ambitions had alienated everybody and, as happens often with little men thrust into the path of power, he eagerly prodded his family members into positions of influence. The barons taunted him as a jumped up jack-in-office. Even the clerks of the administration could not abide him.

I spent time with men who thought as I did, that John and not Arthur of Brittany should be next King of England.

With the belt of knighthood new around my waist and with manhood nudging me into action, I rode off in search of adventure, excitement and Count John as he was then. I found him in the castle at Marlborough, made common cause with and melted into the pot of the dispossessed, disgruntled and the disappointed; younger sons with nowhere to go, nothing to fight for; older men sick of Richard and his disinterest in his country and men in between fearful for their French properties. Of course, we all know what happened. Richard sent wily old Walter of Coutances, the Archbishop of Rouen to restore order. Things deteriorated and John was beaten for a while, his star momentarily blotted by a cloud. I was dragged home by an irate - a very irate father who beat me, locked me up and starved me and no less did I deserve, for my father was a king's man... whichever king was on the throne and that king was now an absent Richard.

My father was Geoffrey Belvoir, an enormous straight backed, whale bodied, black avised man with a jaw like a mastiff's and a voice to rival Thor's thunderbolts.

I liked him and he liked me, until then. Now, for a while he watched me, had me watched, spoke to me rarely and spoke of me in whispers. My mother's brother William Labarge, who was more tolerant of the young, succeeded in convincing him that I was youthful and stupid; that time would mend me and my foolish bid for power was but the stirring of a martial character yet to be revealed; and that I had been led astray by older men.

How wrong he was. Still, peace was restored and my father strode about our estates like the colossus he was, with me at a respectful distance and life went on as normal.

Until that fateful day in April. We never ever thought that he could die. He would go on forever and the world around him would die. He was as permanent as the rocks of the hills themselves. To think of the manor without him was as absurd as the forest without the trees. Nevertheless, a few days after his forty-sixth birthday we found him, a great mound of a man, slumped at the bottom of the hall steps. His breath was still in him, though it came in snatches and the left side of his mouth was awry in a permanent sneer.

It took four of us to carry him to his bed, for he was a full head taller than any man on the estate and the fit had taken all the strength from his muscles so that he was as weighty as a dead beast in our grasp. We wiped the dribbling mouth, chafed the cold limbs and straightened the still right arm with its claw like hand. He moaned as we laid him down and his eyes rolled in pain. We suspected the fall down the stone stairs had broken some ribs, so we dared not move him again.

Towards nightfall, they called me up to the solar from the hall.

Haha! How ironic all this seems now. Except now I lie here and you sit where I stood.

Geoffrey Belvoir lay on his piled furs dribbling into his fine linen pillow and fretting the edge of the coverlet with his good hand. The useless arm was crooked over the counterpane and I saw him try to lift it as I entered. Our priest, Benedict of Cadley, pushed me forwards.

"Sir Geoffrey has asked for you."

I remember asking, "Has he spoken then?"

My uncle nodded. "He wishes to make his peace with you, Aumary - go forward."

I stepped to the side of the bed feeling weak and lonely. "Father...it's me, Aumary. You asked for me."

The black brown eyes flicked open. They seemed to be more deeply sunken than usual and the skin of his face more pale, with a tinge of blue. His lips were blue. His hair and beard with just a trace of grey at the temples, normally so black, seemed even blacker framing that ghostly face. He struggled with his tongue as if it were too large for his mouth. He grimaced, teeth clenched, one side drawn down in a sneer that was no intended sneer.

"Aumary....I am dying"

"No sir…you're…."

It was such an effort for him to speak distinctly that my protests faded and I listened, my ear almost pressed to his cheek, to hear the whisper more clearly.

"I am going…and I leave you the manor and the forest…."

This I already knew.

He took a deep breath and moaned again at the pain of it, "You must look after your brother." Now his words were muffled and mumbled, slurred with spittle but they were quite clear to me. "You must look after your brother."

I was seventeen years of age, my mother had died in my third year. I had no brother. No sibling at all, but I did not argue. The fit has addled his brain, I thought; he is talking gibberish. I nodded, trying to calm him.

My eyes strayed to the other side of the bed. My uncle William was watching me carefully. He nodded once. My father breathed deeply and there was a little more force in the voice suddenly, "I want you to swear….."

I would have sworn anything to keep him alive, to have him restored to health.

"Yes…yes…." I looked up.

I must have worn a quizzical expression because there was our manor priest staring straight at me. His eyes were bright and bold, then he too nodded. "Listen to him, Aumary. He tells the truth." My heart flew to my Adam's apple and pounded there. The noise in my ears was deafening but above it I could hear my father saying, "They….will bring him….to you. He is twelve years old. He is your true brother, Aumary. I married his mother two years ago…." The rest was a bubbling cough.

I straightened up. Father Benedict leaned over my father but the good hand, still strong, pushed him away and with renewed strength, the old deep voice came back to shout, "Bring me the Bible."

No one spoke. I heard small feet pattering out of the room, gone, I suspected, to fetch the Bible from its resting place in the private chapel at the other end of the hall.

Time passed. I tried to quiz simply, with my eyes, my uncle William and the steward of our manor, Piers of Manton, the other man present. Both were men of influence here but neither would speak to or acknowledge me. All was silent save the stertorous breathing of Geoffrey Belvoir.

Eventually the pattering feet returned and the Bible was lifted from its box. Benedict took it and laid it reverently on an embroidered cloth which covered a tall chest standing by the wall of my father's chamber. He reached over, took my arm and led me to the Bible, pressing my hand down with force.

"It is what he wants," said Father Benedict.

I pulled my hand away. "But I don't......"

"Swear on the Bible, Aumary. Swear by all the saints you know that you will take care of your brother." My face must have screwed up in puzzlement for father's eyes, hitherto focussing fuzzily, suddenly hardened into dark orbs and pierced mine almost painfully. I reached the bed in one stride.

"But why...I don't know him..Why do…..?"

The good hand rose up and gripped mine.

"He is a minor and as such vulnerable. He has been my favourite this past year since..." He sighed "He needs a guardian. Look to him." He dribbled again and sucked in breath. My heart stopped... on oath...it did.

"Swear!"

The priest reached for me once more and placed my hand again on the Bible.

"Repeat after me..."I, Aumary Belvoir do solemnly swear before God........."

And so I swore.

Later that evening they showed me what they had done. Underneath that Bible, underneath the cloth in a small box atop a pile of other things, was a reliquary. My great grandfather Ivo had brought it back from the Second Crusade, from the Holy Land. The hair of St. Margaret they said, in a tiny decorated gold box, no longer than my middle finger. I had sworn on a holy relic and would be damned out of hand if I ever reneged.

Some while after, my father died and I became the Lord of Durley and, if I were confirmed in it by the King, Warden of Savernake Forest.

And that oath became Belvoir's Promise and the cause of much woe.

Chapter Two

"Close up the shutters! There's a gale blowing and I am not yet ready for my soul to depart. Close the window please! Now where was I? Oh yes."

At the top of a tower on a blustery spring day, screwing up my eyes against the sunlight, raking the horizon for the first sight of my surprise sibling. The household was in mourning. Long faces were compulsory about the manor but mine was longer than anyone else's. If truth be known, I did not want a brother. I had been an only child for so long that the thought of another child of the blood draining my father's affections, made me hate him before I had ever set eyes on him and he only a child of twelve. However, I had my consolation. I was now Lord of the Manor of Durley and the King's ministers had seen fit to confirm me as his warden in the forest of Savernake.

It was what I had been brought up to do. This brother of mine was a minor, conceived out of wedlock; I could not call him 'bastard' though I would dearly have loved to, for his mother had in truth been married to my father some few years but he was a younger son and as such had no claim on anything. Everything was mine. But I had to recognise him as a Belvoir. I had sworn an oath on my immortal soul. I had loved and revered my father and could not cross him, even in death. I had seen the newly executed painted scenes high on the chancel wall of our little manor church. I knew what hell looked like; I could feel the pricking of the little devil's forks, I could sense the heat of the fires of hell, smell the sulphurous breath of the Horned One. I know what happened to a forsworn man, a man who swore a solemn and holy oath before God and then when God was looking the other way, broke his promise. No, God is never too busy to see into a man's heart and my heart had been clean when I made that oath. I did not want to burn in hell for all eternity.

"See...see what just thinking about it can do to a man. Why I'm burning up... open the shutters...let in some air. It's stifling in here!"

I remember I had just decided that I must do as I had promised and care for my unlooked for sibling, when my sun dazzled eyes picked out a fluttering on the horizon, a greenish flicker on the blue distance. Five riders, three men in dark colours and one other on a light coloured horse, (of course, my uncle William on his favourite) and a smaller pony bearing someone that seemed at that distance to be all gold.

They dipped out of sight momentarily as they reached the track which led to the gate and reappeared fanned out in a line, clear of the trees. I was gripped by a burning sensation in my belly. I know it was jealousy. I sure that my father had not meant the words he had spoken, for when one is dying, one perhaps says things one doesn't mean. The mind is not to command and he had not been in command of his tongue either.

Why do you look at me like that, scribe? No. No. I have not had a fit, no stroke. My mind is fine..JUST WRITE and keep your thoughts to yourself! There is nothing wrong with my mind...yet.

Now I knew that it would be gross discourtesy not to be at the hall steps when the lad dismounted but I wanted to see him before he saw me. I wanted to have that advantage, so I ran along the palisade to the wooden tower which was all that served as our gate house then. I looked down on him as he passed beneath me and into the manor yard.

By one of those quirks of fate that can change one's history in an eye blink, a noisy magpie was circling above cawing wildly. It had been noisily flitting from branch to tower, from tower to fence post all morning, so I paid it no heed but the lad on the grey pony tossed his head up quickly and fixed it with bright brown eyes. It shit on him. As his gaze took in the bird he saw me perched on the parapet and our faces must have been open to each other. If he had cared to, he could have seen curiosity, jealousy and fear and loathing all at once in my look. In his I saw only innocence and I was suddenly deeply ashamed.

I ran down the steps and bounded ahead of the party to slide into place beside my steward Piers, my reeve Walter and the priest Benedict.

The lad threw his leg over the ears of his pony and deftly landed on his toes, laughing and scrubbing the bird lime from his shoulder with his gloved hand. He made some small joke with Uncle William who had ridden the few scant miles to Collingbourne to fetch him.

Never in my life had I seen a more beautiful creature.

He was as fair as a May morning. As fair as I was dark, with a cap of shining hair like spun gold. His eyes were a rich nut brown and the whites were the perfect blue white of the newborn. His skin, as taut and white as a new sheet,bore two cheeks as pink and soft as a girl's. The early morning sunshine bounced from him, haloed from his hair and his light coloured clothing and all the while those deep dark unfathomable eyes watched me. I was reminded of an angel I once saw in a painted book. They tell me brown eyes in one so fair is a sign of rare beauty. My eyes too, are brown but more as you would expect for my colouring is black. Then... I am what I am. I am what I seem.

I thought, "This is no son of my father."

Geoffrey Belvoir was as dark as a December morning, large boned, huge handed, broad shouldered, dark skinned. This creature is all opposites. Compact, delicate and as light as Apollo. I remember thinking, as we made a pleasant nonsense of the ritual greeting, giving the kiss of peace on both cheeks, bidding the party enter the hall to take refreshment, seeing to the disposal of baggage and servants, I remember thinking, "this is an impostor. My father has but one son of the blood, Aumary Belvoir and that could not be disputed, for I was as like to my father as Castor was to Pollux.

This youngster gripped my arm and I was treated to the brown look. No - here was a son of the blood for Geoffrey Belvoir's eyes stared back at me, long, cold and unblinking as if risen from the grave, not yet a settled mound. My heart fell to my boots. No, I could not dispute it. Robert Belvoir was my brother.

No wait...we climbed the steps and I dipped my head as I had learned to do since I had outgrown the door and cracked my forehead a few times. No, not a true brother, only a half brother. I was beginning to feel better. Son of my father, yes, but not of my mother. He was only my half brother. My heart began to climb again to its usual resting place. Therefore I was only half bounden to look after him. Again, NO! It could not be. I had sworn an oath to God. I wish to God he had not heard me.

We were still exchanging niceties as we sat down to eat together. Now I had leisure to watch everyone carefully. The party had consisted of my brother Robert, my Uncle William and two men at arms, for the roads were still unsafe and it was wise to travel protected. They had been dismissed at the dais steps. The fifth man was, I learned, a Breton by birth, who had been engaged by the mother's household as tutor to Robert. Quimper was a small, undernourished man with an intelligent but ratty face and a skin as clear as a baby's, drawn tight over sharp bones. The bones weren't the only things sharp about him, for his eyes missed nothing. They darted to and fro like a snake's tongue sensing the air, suspicious and uneasy. I was beginning to feel good about myself again. No, I had made a promise to a father I had loved and respected, sworn an oath on holy relics and the Bible. I would keep my promise to look after my little brother; after all he was young and inexperienced. The priests tell us that what is on the outside is a reflection of the goodness within, so Robert, by his looks, must be an angel.

A little later, I was sitting eating, toying with my food. My left hand neighbour, Uncle William was too busy in conversation with the tutor Quimper to eat or to pay me attention, so my eyes strayed with an odd fascination to my silver-pale brother who was sitting a little way off to my right. I'm sure, I said to myself, that he's a good enough fellow and even as I watched him eat, he smiled at me and that smile, swift and charming, melted all that had gone before. And then an instant later something happened, something so insignificant, so commonplace, that I had begun to doubt I had really seen it, except for the lingering sense of disquiet which stayed with me.

All through the meal, yea even before a bee, one from Father Benedict's hives, newly out with the spring flowers, had been knocking its head against the horn in the window behind my head, fooled by the spring sunshine flooding in through the opening. I had been aware of its buzzing and had meant to tell the good Father to rescue it from fretting, but it had been pushed to the back of my mind, for I had more pressing matters. Tired and weary of searching for the outdoors, the little creature fell to the table with a small plop. Everyone's head was turned away down the table where a superb jelly had just entered on a large plate. There was much stamping and whooping, for I had made sure that a good feast should welcome our new family member. I had known what was coming so didn't turn with the others but for some inexplicable reason I turned to watch Robert.

Robert was watching the bee approach him on its back, skidding closer helplessly like a skater on ice, its little legs heavy with spring pollen. Its eyes must have been dazed by the lamps that burned brightly day and evening in the hall. Robert's eyes hovered over it. The bee righted itself at last, smoothed down its wings and preened its legs. Before it could gather itself for a leap into flight, Robert, smiling faintly, brought down the handle of his eating knife and with a deliberate knock, crushed out its little life.

It was nothing more than that. No one else saw it. He picked up the tiny carcass, still thrumming, between his forefinger and thumb nail and with a look of distaste, dropped it into the rushes of the floor.

I turned away and shivered though it was warm in the hall. I told myself not to be so girlish for it was only a bee. But I had seen the look in those dark brown eyes and what I saw made me foolishly afraid.

***

So Robert came to live at the manor of Durley in the Savernake and all was almost as it had been before. I was still considered a minor and so must have a guardian until I was 21. I was an orphan. The right to manage my affairs and even arrange my marriage, (though in truth that had been organised years before by my father), belonged to my feudal lord. That lord was the King and so I could do little without the great lords about the King must debate the issue. However, affairs were managed with Walter Reeve's capable help, with the astute eye of my uncle William cast over matters and with my steward Piers' strong hand on the tiller of the boat that was the estate and household of Durley.

Early spring moved into a wet early summer and we made long and difficult work of cutting the hay, for the days were dark and the skies threatening. The swallows returned to the barn and their old nests and began to repair and build. We brought in our sheep from the downs, to shear, for wool was an important source of revenue for us.

Robert was closeted with his tutor for much of the morning and then for a few hours each afternoon, Tom the manor's wool factor would teach Robert all the dull business of our wool trade-buying and selling, the keeping of the records and accounting, in addition to the managing of his mother's thread business. All this Robert took to readily, with a greedy intelligence and a willing heart. Indeed he was very amenable, cheerful and polite and liked by everyone.

We had decided amongst us that he must have a definable role and the manage-ment of these businesses seemed as good as any for the youngest son. My father had settled monies on Robert and that was enough for his needs but as he grew we realised he needed a more settled place in the hierarchy. As I grew to know him, I began to ask questions about his former life.

He was, it seemed, the son of a lady of Collingbourne village, a widow whom my father had first seen at the wool market in Newbury, as she oversaw the disposal of her wares, for she was a spinster - one who spins wool into thread.

"She fair took my breath away with her beauty," said my Uncle William "and more than that, she took away your father's heart as sure as it was her own."

My mother and father's marriage had been an arranged one, as many are. They grew to a fondness and a respect but there was, as far as I knew, little love in the match. I never supposed it mattered. But there was no doubt my father had loved with all his heart this bright, golden woman from Collingbourne and eventually made her his own.

"It was not my mother herself who did the spinning, you understand. But when her first husband died leaving her alone with no kin, she took on his business." Robert had told me after some encouragement.

This was no mean endeavour for a woman; it was a goodly affair of many workers scattered over the countryside around the village and within.

"She oversaw this with a great business acumen and in a short while she'd in-creased the profits twofold. She wasn't just beautiful, you know, but possessed of a clever mind. That's what father said." I winced at his use of 'father'; it was still a raw wound for me.

Quite apart from falling for the lady's charms, my father had seen a superb busi-ness opportunity: our wool and her spinning industry and they had fallen in togeth-er, in more ways than one. A little while later Robert was born and two years later, they married secretly. The whole affair must be kept quiet though, as my father had no permission to marry whomsoever he wished, without the

King's say-so. There could have been great upheavals at the time were it known, for King Henry the second of that name, was jealous of his patronage and had ideas for everyone under his thumb - even to marriage, all naturally to feed his own advantage. Richard, our Lionheart, was a different creature. What happened in England was of little interest to him, until he needed money for a ransom and then suddenly things became more interesting to his counsellors. Richard might have been approached for permission to marry and that would have cost my father dearly no doubt. However when Richard was imprisoned, things changed. Taxes were levied to fill the coffers required to buy back Richard, our noble, chivalrous sovereign and all eyes were turned hungrily to businesses.

Our manor was no exception. We paid our dues and much of it came from the business of thread made by Matilda of Collingbourne. Only my maternal uncle, William and my father and the priest Benedict had been privy to the secret and those who worked in that industry, seven or so miles away. I had no idea, before Robert came, that we had such business interests. No idea that I had a brother who would one day perhaps, manage the wool, carding and thread side of our workings.

It suited me...the manor and the forest were mine.

I had wondered why, two years back, my father had become morose, ill tempered and prone to bouts of melancholy. I had thought it was the old problem, a stomach rupture which plagued him now and again, especially when he over-ate or ate those things he knew would do him harm. We jollied him along. I know now that it was then that his precious Matilda had died of a lump in the breast and he was distraught. The business was quietly taken into ours officially and no mention was made of Matilda.

"Father couldn't bear to speak of her," Robert said sadly. "I had none with whom I could grizzle or gripe. There was even a time when father would not see me be-cause I reminded him of her."

I felt for him then, a little lad, alone but for tutors and factors and guardians. Lonely and friendless. I patted him on the back... "Well, Rob..." I said, "it is all changed now."

It never occurred to me to ask why my father had waited until his death bed to free this beautiful, bright butterfly of a boy and bring him home to the rest of us, why he had been kept away almost hidden, in Collingbourne.

***

It was a few weeks later that things started to happen. I stroked the bony, pale head in front of me.

"Good dog Samson, you'll be well 'ere long." But I knew in my heart of hearts it was not to be.He lifted his muzzle to me as if it was as heavy as tree trunk, that swift, bold clever dog who could course over the downs after hare, or dart in and out of the forest trees in search of game with as much speed and ease as a maiden plaits her hair. The reed like tail quivered and was still. Samson was my favourite hound, a tall lymer and my constant companion. No more loyal a creature ever lived, none more biddable and affectionate to me. I had others, naturally, but this one I had chosen...why no - he had chosen me and I allowed him freedoms no other dog was granted. He never abused them.

Samson was three years old when my brother Robert came to us. Lithe and ath-letic, quick of brain and almost human to me, this dog. I would reach down and there would be Samson's head, like a stick I could lean on. My rangy, strong boned, right arm. A tall dog, pale in colour like old straw with a black muzzle and pure brown intelligent eyes that could guess, before you had even made the deci-sion, what it was you wanted of him. I loved that dog dearly.

Now the black muzzle was flecked with foam and the brown eyes were dim and unfocussed. He lay on his right side, panting. I remember asking my houndsman, "Can we do nothing for him, Plum?"

The man was so called because of a red mark in the shape of the fruit, which disfigured his face. He was a veritable wizard with dogs and horses and I trusted him.

"I have never seen anything like it, sir," he said. "In all my years. I have no idea what it is. Must be something he ate but you well know he don't eat only what we give him. He's a good lad...he don't go foraging. Why should he?"

"He's been eating grass for a while now," said Uncle William, "I've noticed him. Trying to make himself sick but it never works." He rubbed his short coarse grey beard with a stubby fingered hand. "And now....this." I'd noticed this grass eating too.

As if by signal, poor Samson began to retch, his ribcage tensing. He rustled in the straw of a quiet stable where we had put him and then was still again. Nothing but foam emerged from the lips. The breathing became faster.

"Can we make him sick? Can we get him to drink salt water?"

Plum shook his head. "I've tried it m'lord...just comes back but nothing else. Water in - water out and he hasn't pissed properly in two days but he's shitting terrible he is. Black stuff. He's fitting too....bursting he is."

I rose from my knees. "Watch him carefully. If there's any change..." I left the words hanging. They knew to fetch me. And why. As I turned to leave, I noticed Robert leaning against the doorpost of the stable.

"Is he no better?" he asked as he straightened up and fell in alongside me as I walked with a slow step to the hall. I suppose I sighed. "No.... I don't think it will be long."

"Shame, he was a good hound and you love him."

"Aye...the best."

"Do they know what it is...why he is dying?"

"No."

"Do we need to be careful of the other dogs then?"

"Why's that, Robert?"

He shrugged and the long pale hair dropped over his shoulders like a girl's. He flicked it back. "Well, if he has eaten something, perhaps the rest will......"

"We shall watch everything from now on most carefully," I said. "Everything they do, everything they eat. Plum will take great care. We shall see if we can isolate that thing which has done for poor Samson."

They called me an hour before vespers. I knelt in the straw by Samson's side. My right hand was out of the dog's vision, my left stroked his head. His long whip-like tail, despite his sore state, rose and fell once.

"Run free my great friend," I said as I as gently as possible eased the sharpened, the very sharp knife, between Samson's ribs and up into his great, full heart. "You go to pave the way for me." He shuddered once and then lay still. There was very little blood.

My Uncle William laid a hand on my shoulder as I cradled the dog's head.

Had I been alone I would have wept.

"I have lost my best friend," I said.

And I meant it.

"Aw, Don't snivel you silly boy....'tis a long time off now. Go trim your pen or something. PAH! What's that? Dogs don't go to heaven? What utter rot. Then I shan't go either."

***

In the middle of July when we were all so busy with checking and treating the sheep for scab, Robert came to me and asked if he might take a greater part in the running of the demesne. I squinted up at him from my knees where I had been looking at a ewe's feet.

"What would you have us give you to do? You are yet a boy and you have your studies and the wool." He didn't bridle at that as I expected but gave me that sweet smile of his. "How old were you when you did more than clean father's boots and polish his helm, as a good squire should?"

I stood. "We have no father now for whom to do those things." I ran my dirty arm over my filthy and sweaty forehead. "What would you like to do?"

He gave that girlish shrug, the bright hair falling over his brow and sticking to it, for it was one of the rare hot days of that year.

"I have been here a while now and I just think there are things I might do to help. You know."

"I'll think of something I suppose" I told him.

I meant it at the time but life went on and it was a while before I could give him a thought on the matter, for, within a sennight, something else happened to claim my attentions.

In the good weather of August when we were many of us out in the fields bringing in the wheat and were much taxed by time constraints, Piers, my steward, with his usual good sense of organisation, had the younger girls of the manor bring out the customary ale, onion, cheese and bread for the dinner meal.

They came, the girls, with their baskets and panniers, trooping up the hill to the head of the main field where we had all congregated in the shade of the hedge, to eat and sup. We set to for it was hungry and thirsty work and I was not one of those lords who sat in comfort in the shade of my hall whilst my workers toiled. I toiled with them. They laughed to see it, but I was willing and able and in those days, strong in arm and back. Stripped of my shirt I had become as brown as a filbert. I sat with them.

At once, our joking and good natured banter was interrupted. Robert came run-ning down the hill, shouting at the top of his voice.

Many of us jumped up and ran up to meet him, though I was late rising.

His face pink, his eyes wide like a girl's with belladonna, in shock, trembling, he managed to say,

"Come quick...it's Piers, he has fallen. He's hurt."

I ran then as I had never run. We found Piers atop one of the hay carts. It seemed Robert had seen him miss his footing on the walkway surrounding the manor walls and stumble over onto the cart, which with others was waiting by the wall to be emptied and stored before the threshing could begin.

I was in the act of climbing up onto the cart, puzzled why Piers did not rise, brush himself down and laugh at his clumsiness.

What was he doing up there in the first place?

"Piers, Piers, why did you...?" I sank into the stooks of wheat.

Piers lay on his back, gulping like a landed fish. Blood trickled from his mouth. His eyes were stark, pained and frightened.

I yelled, "Fetch the priest QUICK!" for I knew we had but moments to save his soul.

I leaned forward, the stooks shifted under my weight. There was the culprit.

That morning someone had broken a wooden shaft of a hay fork. Easily done. We had thrown it aside and reached for another. Not carelessly, you under-stand, for the tines are lethal and we had stuck it in the ground a way off, ready to be collected by our tool smith and mended. The fork had indeed proved lethal, for there it was sticking into the back of my steward; into his lungs and out of his chest.

Somehow the fork had travelled to the manor courtyard in the cart and become embedded tines up in the wheat. Poor unknowing, unfortunate Piers had fallen on it. I would have stripes on the back of the man who left it there. I lifted Piers' head.

"The priest is coming," I said, hoping to give him a small crumb of comfort in his dying moments. He closed his eyes.

Then he said at a whisper, "Robert."

"I am here, sir," said my brother, climbing up onto the wheel of the cart.

Piers shook his head frantically, bucked suddenly at the pain involved in such an action; his lips drew back in a grimace, air escaped from...I know not where. He lay still, blood trickling from his lips.

It was too late for the priest's intervention.

***

The fork was taken as deodand, that silly tax which says the thing that causes the death must be forfeit. The coroner was informed. It was his right to pronounce cause of death. It was deemed an accident, death by misadventure. My steward, a man I had known all my life was dead in an instant. I was lost. I sat in the hall alone. What had Piers been doing up on the wall walk? The puzzle went round and round in my brain. Who had left the fork there? No one had owned up...no one meant for Piers to fall foul of it but someone had left it. Another puzzle for my tired brain, whence could I procure a man so knowledgeable about the estate, so well versed in the running, so clever with it all? That man, I realised would have to be me. I trembled.

That day I think I became a man.

***

Now we shall come to my bright lass...my cherub, my little bird and the light of my life.

"What are you sniggering about you, mucky minded scribbler? Just you make sure you get this down absolutely right or I shall see you starved of your dinner.

*I know how you love your food! Oh yes - don't think I do not. You'll be tightening
your waist cord three knots 'ere long, you mealy-mouthed pen scraper."*

I had now reached the age of nineteen and I had been betrothed since the
age of nine to a neighbour's daughter. She was now seventeen and of an age to
marry. I had not cared much when, all those years ago, she had been promised
to me. She had been an awkward, boyish creature, no prim fine lady in the bud
and I had liked her instantly as one small boy takes to another, to chase and climb
and run and swim.

She had grown into a lively young lady, quick witted and sharp, still
freckle-faced it was true, but it had been after all almost a love match and I was
not displeased with my lot.

In the spring of 1193, eighteen months after Piers' death, I was as pleased as
I allowed myself to be, as I rode off on Bayard my favourite roan, to meet Cecily at
her father's manor in Bedwyn to be married in the private chapel there by Father
Godfrey. It was one of those spring days which songs speak of. Calm, sunny but
not hot, green bursting forth from every bough, birds chirruping from every
bush, flowers decorating the wayside, their little faces straining up to the sun.

With me rode William my maternal uncle, who was a tower of strength
to me and who since the death of Piers, had spent more time at Durley than his
own home in Marlborough town. My sergeant at arms rode beside me, (though
truthfully did we need such a titled man)? Hal was a small stocky chap with a great
beard almost to his navel and a taste in clothes as bright as a jay's. He was however
a good man in a fight as the roads through the forest were still not as free of lawless men as we would like. Richard Marshall, my senior groom accompanied,us;
John Brenthall my chief woodward and bringing up the rear, Robert, riding a
beautiful grey, as befitted his own colouring, which I had seen fit to bestow on
him on his name day. He had grown a little in the twelve months or so and had
outgrown the pony he had ridden when he first came to Durley.

We rode down into a steep coombe where the forest thinned and scrubby
bushes gave way at last to rough grass. Then passed two or three assarts clinging
to the very edge of the forest and came out into the sunshine, to an open common
and towards the village of Bedwyn. We rode slowly and with dignity through the

forest and a few folk round and about cheered, knowing what was afoot. We turned at last on a lane known as Harepath. Congrye's manor lay to the north of the road but as we approached the path a solitary horseman came riding towards us.

Robert, drawing close to my elbow, exclaimed under his breath, "Mind yourself brother Aumary, for unless I am much mistaken it is your father in law who rides to greet you." I sat up in the saddle. I had known this man almost all my life but now I felt myself, unbidden, redden up to the roots of my hair. After today, Master Toruld Congyre was to become my good-father, my family. We noticed he had a fine falcon on his fist.

"Aumary...well met. We were just out trying my new bird."

"A fine creature, sir," I seem to remember saying, for want of something more sensible to say.

"The rest are over towards West Court, come.....we'll catch them up." And he wheeled in beside our party. The Durley contingent swiftly fell in behind us.

The track was clear and easy to follow and the conversation turned from the sport of ordinary folk to the sport of kings - The Crusade. I trod most carefully for I knew that Master Congyre's politics were a little blurred around the edges, as were my own, if truth be told. Nevertheless I wanted nothing to mar the day, least of all a petty quarrel over absent kings.

"I'm almost beggared. Took all my plate - even my altar candles, must go without. I've not a sconce left to put'em in. Blessed ransom! Why couldn't the bloody emperor just keep our cursed Richard?"

"Ours too," I said faintly amused. " But surely now the ransom is collected, it can be paid and the King can come home and things can return to normal."

The older man sucked his teeth.

"Richard cares nothing for this country. He'll be off again, mark my words. Then something might be done about the abysmal mess he's left behind."

"Hush sir," I said with a laugh. "This is treason you and I are talking."

"If it's treason, then it's damn good sense," said my almost father-in-law.

We joined the main party and embraced warmly before making off in the direction of Congrye's hall. Conversation now turned to the price of wool and the quality of the clip to be expected this year, for we were now in a more mixed company and words had to be chosen most carefully. No one knew when one's innocent word might be overheard and turned to evil.

***

What can I say about my wedding, my marriage to Cecily Congyre? Neighbours had gathered for we had many friends in common. In such a place as the Forest of Savernake, where everyone knew everyone else's business, weddings were a great source of entertainment, no matter whose.

The day passed in a haze of embracings, kissed cheeks, whirling dancing, rau-cous music and much food and drink, though I, being conscious of my duty that evening, tried to stay as sober as I was allowed. Through the haze, I saw many happy faces, smiling friends and neighbours and I felt proud that I, a young man of a mere nineteen years could attract such a gathering to his nuptials. Of course had I been less in my cups I should've seen it was more for Master Congyre and Mistress Cecily that the throng was so happily employed.

Cecily. My bright, sweet girl. A chaplet of flowers decorated her lustrous copper hair. She was dressed in a gown of sky blue and over it a bliaut of palest blue, decorated with small applied blue flowers and silver wire ribbon embroidery at the neck. I had never seen her look so womanly but there she was - my friend, my young wife-to-be, fresh, smiling and happy. We stood in the private chapel to make our vows before God and the assembled people. The little private chapel was full to bursting, even outside folk were gathered, straining to listen through the door and the small windows high in the wall. It was relatively dark in the chapel but outside the sun shone as fiercely as spring would allow. When we emerged from the gloom, the light blinded us temporarily so that we shook our heads in laughter and squinted into the crowd before us.

All was movement, colour and humming conversation. Into this came the definite hooting of a tawny owl.

Not once but thrice.

The whole party came to a standstill. Women looked from face to face. Men frowned. Then one old dame (God rot her) mumbled quietly into her beard but for all to hear, "When the owl calls in the day, unlucky the bride who weds in May."

They shushed her quickly but the damage was done. Other older women, you know the sort, all creased and lumpy faces and hairy chins, started to join in with other pronouncements; the bride would be barren, the groom would sicken and die, nothing good could come of such a union. I laughed. I looked across to my bride who was at my fingers end, her delicate hand raised over mine.

Cecily seemed unperturbed save for a slight gnawing of her underlip.

I raised my voice....

"Good people, tis but a tawny owl disturbed from his sleep by our junketings. Pay no heed. We are not such dolts as to be afraid of owls are we? We are modern men and women. No, superstition has no place here. Let us go and feast." And that was that.

You will have heard far too many tales of weddings and the eventual bedding of the knight and his lady so I shall gloss over those details. You don't need to know. I remember it well. We giggled ourselves through most of the night, I recall, and rose the next morning to take up the reins of our new life.

"What's wrong with you boy? You look like a fish in a keep net!

Did you really expect me to go into lurid detail of the wedding night?

Shut up your jaw and write like I have paid you to do! Saints alive! These clerics nowadays! Whoever thought that young men could be celibate and only slake their lusts with singing and praying...and yes writing too, needs to fall through a bawdy house roof!

Now. Have you got all that? Do I need to go back and say again? Good."

Spring turned to summer. Again we took in the hay, again we harvested our wheat..a good crop this time. There would be no loose belts this year, no loose teeth either. I realised that with Cecily's arrival at Durley, my task had been lightened for she took on the running of the house, as she had been brought up to do and was a quiet and capable presence about the manor. I rode easily on her back as cygnets do a mother swan.

"No...scrap that sentence.....I can see it's set up a snigger in you and so it will in others no doubt. Scrub it out I say!"

***

Day turned to night, weeks to months, the year turned. It was now 1194, the King had been released and, as my father in law had prophesied, he had taken off again intent on the reconquest of Normandy. John had been forgiven his latest misdemeanours and had taken to heart the warning from Philip of France; "Look to yourself, the Devil is loose."

On his way to Normandy to lick his wounds from his latest disappointment, John stayed with us for a short while, knowing as he did, our loyalty and friendship was his alone. I think he felt particularly bitter for he spoke about it being his mother who had urged him on and then that she had withdrawn her good wishes towards him and backed her favourite, Richard. It was ever so with him. John had been the last Plantagenet child and we knew that he felt an afterthought, a surplus child to mend the marriage of Queen Eleanor and King Henry. He did not mend it. No, we all know, for the chroniclers tell us, how the wedded pair quarrelled violently and at last they fell apart with great savagery and Henry had Eleanor locked up.

John swore to me then that he had truly thought his brother dead in far-flung lands, on some crusading path. It was as much a surprise to him, as to us all, when the ransom was demanded and we knew him to be alive, though I do not, with hindsight, think I can completely believe him.

As far as I know he remained loyal to Richard thereafter (there were a few little altercations between them) but once these difficulties has been dusted over, they remained friends of sorts, I think. Poor John, he did take to heart, take so hard, any rebuff of this sort and would fall into such a melancholy only a trinket (he was most fond of beautiful jewels) or two could shake him from it.

We sat late into the night, a few of us, chewing over the fat of the world as we knew it, no longer having to pick our words carefully for we knew we were all friends here. One major thing had changed and we could all see what it meant for us. John had been proclaimed heir to the throne. Arthur of Brittany, Richard and John's nephew and Geoffrey Plantagenet's son, was no longer in the race.

John smiled into his wine when we congratulated him, shaking his head. It was only until his brother had got a child on his new Queen Berengaria, he said.

Then, he would be John with few prospects plain and simple again. John Lackland.

I remember there was quite a lot of guffawing into ale cups that evening whenever there was the mention of Richard's marriage and the likelihood of an heir. Rumour had it that Richard had not seen (and so not cohabited) with his wife for quite a while and she had perforce, made her way to England through tempest and storm, fire and flood, alone, dispirited and neglected. It was the way of their marriage. She was to be so neglected the whole duration of their wedded life. There would be no heirs.

It was almost as if, that evening around the fire in the hall at Durley, with our bellies full and our ale cups brimming, we knew this was to be a truth.

We had forgotten one amongst us though, whose loyalties were not to be taken for granted but that is for a later telling.

***

Richard's marriage may have been no marriage at all, but mine most certainly was. Cecily brought me much joy. Besides being my helpmeet and confidant, she was a capable mistress of the house and of my heart. The longer I knew her, the more I loved her. Those were good years.

I remember one year in particular when we were about to go and gather the meadowsweet and rushes from the river, for new floor covering in the hall and chambers, a job we did every summer, Cecily summoned all to the courtyard and gave out the allotted tasks. Carts would trundle the few miles to the river bank, where folk would fan out, cut the reeds and the clean smelling meadowsweet from the banks, pile the bundles into the carts and trundle home again, tired and hungry but happy with a none so onerous task done and almost a holiday feel about it.

I was not going that year; sometimes I did for a day out, for I had other tasks to complete at the manor. This was one thing that the reeve could oversee easily and Cecily had decided to go for the sheer fun of a day in the open air away from our own four walls.

They would travel from Durley through the forest towards Marlborough, down Cock a Troop Lane, finding the least steep gradient down the hill and then journey East parallel to the River Kennet where they would stop to rest and eat and then begin the task of cutting. Late afternoon, they would return the same way.

Time passed. Then a great commotion at the gate drew me to the courtyard from my office, where I had been poring over manorial books. Unlike many gentle born men I knew, I had been taught to read and write; my father insistent that, despite trusted servants like Piers, the man at the top had to be conversant with everything written about his holdings. "How else will you know exactly where you stand, if someone is defrauding you?" he used to say. Even so, sorting manor records was not a task I relished; I was bored and tired.

One cart had returned, half full of meadowsweet, and on it my sweet Cecily was lain with a rough blanket over her. She neither moved nor spoke. Her eyes did not open to see that she had arrived home. I thought her dead.

The woman who travelled in the cart with her, Joan the laundress I think, climbed down from the cart bed.

I lumbered towards them like a drunken man but others had their mistress gently in hand and they one by one lifted her so carefully, supporting her head as they went.

"Oh God," I thought, "She has broken her neck."

She was dripping here and there and there was weed in her hair and head cloth and trapped in her clothes.

"No. Let it not be so," I heard myself say. "No, don't let her have drowned."

They smoothly manhandled her up the stairs and into the solar with me following, crying,

"What happened? Tell me what's happened."

It did not occur to me then, that if she had been dead, they would not have taken such terrible care of her.

They laid her on the bed and then began the fussing of the women, the exiting of all the men, except me, Robert and my reeve Walter.

Before I could speak, Walter said,

"We have sent for the surgeon from Marlborough. He's on his way. We had thought to take her there to him, since we were so close but he wasn't home. Fletch ran all the way there to be told the man is at Kingstones, setting a broken bone. I sent a man on there to fetch him here. I have also alerted Father Benedict and I sent a swift horse to her mother and father. They will be here 'ere long."

I think I nodded. He had done well. We were not so far from the farm at Kingstones and her kin must be informed. I swallowed; so must the priest. How I hated that thought.

"What happened?"

I picked up her limp hand and felt for the throb of her pulse. It was there but weak. I began looking her over for blood or injury but her womenfolk shooed me away. They began to carefully undress her of her wet outer clothes, trying not to move her too much and pile her with blankets. I gestured that we should go out and we all landed at the end of the hall in a group, joining those who had walked home with her but who had not made it up to the solar, by virtue of their lowly status.

They all stood before me with eyes downcast. The reeve spoke first.

"Mat, tell the Lord what you saw."

Mat Fisher, his head downcast and with a sob in his voice told me what he had seen.

"We was all strung out along the bank. It int very deep there where me an the mistriss was, but there's a few pools wot come and go and its quite boggy. I was busy with me hacking when I heard a strange sound, a kinda buzzin you know, like the whine of a bug. Then I heard a little thwack. I din't know where it come from." He looked up at me at last. "I din't see Mistress Cecily then. She was a few strides, perhaps ten, away from me - then she weren't."

What did you do then?" I asked him gently.

"I dropped me knife and started to search the bank. Then I finded her all floaty in the water, face down and I screamed enough to wake the dead to judgement I did."

I looked to Robert; he nodded.

"That's when we came running from all sides and helped to get her out."

"You saw nothing, none who should not have been there?"

They all shook their heads. There was a chorus of "No m'lord."

They were all as perplexed as I.

The surgeon arrived a short while later. He too was perplexed until, lifting Cecily's head without its head dress now, on to a clean pillow, and pulling her long hair from her face, he found a small almost round bruise on her temple surrounded by a tracery of fine blue lines.

"I've seen other instances like this," he said. "Tiny injuries to the head which seem small and insignificant but which can, in some cases, kill. There are no bones broken, no real outward damage but the person remains unconscious sometimes unto death.The damage is to the brain matter beneath the skull. Small but significant and unseen."

"Could this have been inflicted when she fell?" I asked, trying to make sense of it all.

The man threw back his head and stared at the rafters for an instant. "There was nothing there by the bank, on which she could hit her head, I'm told. And why the wound to the temple? If we fall we naturally fall forwards or backwards. We put out our hands to save ourselves, do we not? See......" He lifted both Cecily's palms to me, "Nothing, no scratches, no bruising, no mud even. She did not have the time to save herself. I think the bruise to the temple is the thing which has done the damage, the thing which made her fall."

Downstairs, I ran my hands through my hair and looked round the assembly. Did anyone have any idea what could have done this? I had collected together all those who were on the riverbank, and those who had remained with the rush carts. Twenty six people stared up at me as I stood on the dais and told them that their mistress was sorely hurt and asked had they anything that might be useful in explaining of how or why this had happened.

One youngster of about nine or ten, clinging to a man's hand at the back of the hall, was nervously jigging from foot to foot, staring up at his companion. I might have missed his expression, but the father, one of my woodwards, had noticed too and pushed him forward a little out of the throng of people.

"Jos has something to say m'lord, though he be but a child...I think...."

I cut him off, "Speak freely Jocelyn, we are listening." I jumped down from the dais and approached them. A corridor opened up as folk parted before me.

Jos was obviously frightened and backing away, began to gabble.

"Slow down and speak carefully. You will not be punished for anything you tell me and I will not be angry if it proves to be nothing." I smiled. I had never felt less like smiling in my life.

"Sir," said Jocelyn very quietly, "from what me ma says, the lady has a blot on her head, don't she?" Ah yes, his mother was one of Cecily's house workers, one who had helped when the doctor arrived.

"I seed its like before, last year when we was keeping the crows from the fields, me and Phil....at seed sowing time, Phil Wheelwright."

I nodded. I recalled the young lad, son of one of the manor workers.

"He got one too sir, on his leg. Near breaked his bone. It were a stone sir. He were lucky."

"A stone?"

"Yessir....I....din mean to do it, it were an accident but he got in the way." The child was almost crying. "I din do it sir...I din hurt the mistress..no sir.... Why would I? I din have no stones with me." I appealed to his father for sense.

"They were scaring the crows from the fields at seed sowing last year, my lord" he said "And little Phil well - he was just bein' a bit silly and right as my Josh flung his stone, he got in the way with his capering about and squawking at the birds. The stone near broke his big leg bone."

"A stone?" I was feeling dense...and then suddenly, I understood.

"No Jos, you are not to blame."

The insect-like whine, the small thwack.

Someone had deliberately flung a stone, a small round pebble, a stone from a sling shot, at my wife and viciously brought her down, as David had Goliath. This was the first time I felt the hidden evil present in my home and I shuddered at the thought. Durley was no longer the place of safety it used to be.

Chapter Three

IT was four days before my Cecily stirred. Her body went on working as normal and she had to be cared for as a babe in arms but her mind was far away in some unknown land where I could not reach her. The doctor had said, though nourishment was important, water was the most important thing of all and we had to get that into her above all else.

We tried a cup to the lips, a spoon, I even tried taking it into my own mouth and 'kissing' it into her lips but it trickled away or she coughed it up again.

At last clever Tom Herder, the wool factor, who had worked his way up from a humble shepherd in my father's time, came in with the answer. A fine hollow stem of some water plant, cut and dried with which he had coaxed orphan lambs into feeding, was put to use. I watched as he sucked up water into the stem, then quickly barred the top of it with his thumb, gently inserting it quite a way into Cecily's mouth and then, as he released his thumb, the water would trickle down her throat and she would swallow as if she herself had taken the sip. It was a magic I had never seen before. And so this went on for four days.

Naturally she grew a little thinner. When she awoke she would be happy about that for she had always said that she was chubbier than she would like to be. I liked her so. To have my Cecily back with me again, I would have taken her stick thin and in her shift!

It was my time to sit with her, in the evening when all tasks were done. I remem-ber lolling by the window looking out on the evening glow, hearing the swifts screaming at their supper of high flying midges. I chattered on, as I had done every evening since the accident - no, I cannot call it that, can I, since her attempted murder? I chattered on about things I had done, the things we would do when she awoke, silly inconsequential things. About how her mother has been sitting with her all day, sniffing into her spinning. About how her friends had come for a peep at her, how young Jocelyn, who seemed to have taken it to himself to take news of any development back to the rest of the more lowly folk of the manor, had come and gone, with a downcast look and a, "Oh...no change then...?"

The roundels of the goat beard, a fluffy headed dandelion type of plant that grew around the manor, were floating hither and thither on the evening breeze. Amazingly ,some of them had stayed intact and were winding ever higher in the courtyard, like little fairy balls of gossamer on the heated air. A few of them had made it whole, through the open window of the solar to settle, or to break apart on the furniture or the rushes.

Inevitably my eyelids grew heavy and I ceased speaking. I was nodding onto my chest when suddenly there was a voice beside me. One of the large desiccated goat beard flower heads had settled on Cecily's top lip, just under her nose and with her gentle breathing, had begun to be sucked in on an in breath. She raised her hand and brushed it away. Her eyes opened and she said, "Stop that Aumary....you are tickling me."

I laughed then till I cried.

She came back to us slowly but she had no recollection of the day at the River Kennet at all. To the end of her life, she bore the unseen scars of that episode, for she suffered ever after with megrims and would sometimes drift off in an unbidden daze and stare into space for an hour. She would always come back with no idea of where, in her own head, she had been and she would laugh and carry on with her tasks as if nothing had been amiss. Her memory too was impaired a little. She would forget small things that she had hitherto known as well as the lines on her palm, as if the blow had driven them from her head.

No matter. She was almost the old Cecily and I loved her nonetheless for it.

Her father had taken it upon himself, in anger at hearing the tale of the slingshot, to making inquiries around the manor and even further afield about that day, in an effort to find the culprit. There had been no hue and cry called at the time. Perhaps we should have been fined for that; but it would have been useless anyway. We had no idea what we were looking for then. Congyre drew as much a blank as had my servants and I. We could only think it a cruel prank played by someone unknown who had moved on. A vagrant, a lawless man, a wolfshead, who, seeing a pretty young woman unprotected and vulnerable by the riverside, let loose on her his anger at the world.

Master Quimper, Robert's tutor, we discovered, was quite competent in herb lore. He had made quite a study of the properties of plants for medicines for he was a man who loved to learn and to know things and then happily pass them on and he brewed with his own hand, a special concoction of willow bark and valerian which helped Cecily at those times when her headaches became too much to bear. He was the quietest member of our household, one whom you would pass by and not really notice. He was a softly spoken man with a jerky nervous manner, as if he felt his actual presence was an affront to you. However, he had a prodigious mind and a knowledge of things which seemed far beyond the ken of ordinary folk. Had he lived elsewhere, he might have become feared as one of the devil's minions. Durley Manor was enlightened, modern. We feared no such superstitious nonsense.

Life went on. The effects of the hot summer, as if it had been foolishly and grudgingly given, was taken away by a warm wet autumn and a bone hard middle of winter month which locked up the land, not so much with snow but with frosts and ice and cold winds enough to cleave a man in two. We celebrated Christmas and then the first Sunday after Twelfth Night marked the end of the festivities, when the plough was taken from its shed and manhandled to the church at Durley village to receive the priest Benedict's blessing. The next day the lads of the demesne dragged it round the manor and all the houses of the village, cracking their whips and singing loudly to drive away the evil spirits. (Oh, if only that could have been true - you see, we had not quite thrown off superstition after all.) It was Plough Monday and the year's work was to begin again.

It was on this day that Cecily told me I was to become a father. My happiness was complete. The whole manor and village rejoiced.

***

Spring came back to us. The moorhens built their nests by the crack willows. The chiffchaffs returned to their favourite trees and the star shaped stitchworts flowered again in the meadows and along the river, prolifically at Stitchcombe on the very edge of the forest and for which that village had been named. John, the chief woodwarden and his team, started the job of clearing the ditches and repairing the hedges. Off went the team of foresters to patrol the forest, check on the boundary markers, scour the woods for fallen trees, inspect the state of the common clearings within the forest space and the ditches and fences which had been erected to keep the deer within a particular area. They also made note of the whereabouts of other game therein and took a couple of men at arms with them, generally to make a lot of noise which would hopefully frighten away the less tenacious lawless men who might have camped in Savernake over winter. We did not want any further trouble and we had much to do.

We all had our allotted tasks. Robert had proven himself, time and again, able and possessed of a good mind, calm and sure at the jobs given to him. We relied more heavily on him now for the wool and thread side of our business and he never once grew overwrought with it all.

Then, a full three months before the day she should be brought to bed, Cecily was delivered of a girl child, stillborn, in the early hours of the morning of June 7th 1196.

It was a blow to us both. It often happened said my mother-in-law. First babies rarely came to full term. There would be others. We were young.

Christmas came and went. We dragged in a huge yule log for the central fire and decorated the hall with holly and ivy.

Indeed it wasn't long after that, that Cecily, a big grin on her face, told me once again, that she was to be a mother. I should be a father on St. Lawrence's day.

It was soon to be Robert's seventeenth birthday. He had grown taller and filled out and if anything, was more beautiful than he had been as a young boy. He drew the admiring looks of all the girls, both lowly and gentle-born. Even the old dames clicked their tongues and fussed over him, fluttering their eyelashes and heaving their bosoms as if they were girls of fourteen again.

I laughed to see such sport. His golden hair had lightened even further with the summer sun and his skin was fair still, though not unfashionably so, with a light summer tan. His smile was as charming as ever. That lovely smile was now be-stowed upon me that day in December, when I gave him, as his name day present, a wolf hound puppy, four months old, one from my own breeding bitch, Alceste, who had been a gift from a Norman-Irish cousin.

He was in heaven and he spent every available spare moment training the dog, whom he called Bran after an ancient God of Britain, so that he could bend it to his every whim.

We had special dispensation from the King, those of us in Durley Manor, whose personal property it was, to hunt in the forest now and again, so that we should not become poachers and incur the wrath of the justices in eyre.

As he grew Bran became as good a tracker as his dam and a fine dog for the game, tall and powerful, yet docile and affectionate in the right hands. If Robert had his wish, the dog would have slept with him in his bed, on the hall floor but I, at Cecily's instigation, banished all dogs from the hall at night (for reasons of cleanliness) and they, no matter who their master; manor man or visitor's, slept in the kennels with the other dogs.

All other dogs in the neighbourhood had to be permanently on a leash and declawed, as was the law of the forest, to protect the game. Any dog found poaching was killed and its master felt the full rigour of English Forest Law. The law was harsh. It became even tougher as time passed.

As a result, more men were driven to crime as their livelihoods were taken from them or they became destitute. We drove masterless men from the forest several times. It was not a job I relished. I tried to exercise a little restraint but had to be wary lest I be accused of neglect of my duties and fined. I had to be seen to be doing my duty and so some men must end up in the bowels of Marlborough castle, detained for unlawfully killing the deer, picking up firewood for all green wood belonged to the King and all fallen wood to me; or hiding out there illegally after fleeing from the town and some misdemeanour.

Midsummer brought us fence month, when forests everywhere were in 'defence' so that the does and the new born fawns should be free from disturbance. No one could move freely in the forest at that time, save those who had an absolute reason to be there.

Midsummer also brought the fun times. The maypole was set up in the middle of the village, and we caroused and danced, ate and played games and I must say I proudly became the village champion at fox and geese - a game of cunning played out on a large piece of grass on the village green with real people as counters.

Then at last on the feast of St, Lawrence, August 10th 1197, my son came lustily into the world at four in the morning.

We had all been banished to the hall, the men's side, to drink and play chess, to gamble at backgammon, or doze and yes, worry. I could not eat my supper, though I had eaten nothing all day, for Cecily had retired to the solar earlier in the morning after the breaking of her waters and I was sore afraid for her after the drubbing she had taken that time on the riverbank. We did not speak of it, or if it was mentioned it was in hushed tones and away from my ears. Would it go hard with her because of it? I need not have worried, for she was young and fit and Geoffrey (we named him for my father, naturally), came into the world with a cry that woke his father and maternal grandfather from a fitful slumber on not so comfortable benches at one end of the hall, where we had decamped to be away from the mess of men who normally slept there.

Once fully awake, I bounded to the steps and took the stairs two at a time but did not manage the whole flight, for there came Evisa, my lady mother-in-law, from the top step, with a wriggling thing wrapped in a fine linen sheet and looking for all the world like a curled, wet, red poppy bud. I descended backwards as she followed carefully. The eyes of the little creature creased up, the triangular puppy-like mouth yawned, and Geoffrey Belvoir took a gulp of Durley air and bellowed like a bull calf.

I took him in my arms, as is the tradition, for a man must take his own child to acknowledge him. In some households the child is lain on the floor in the rushes and the father must pick him up to claim it as his own. But as I have said before, we are a modern family. We have no need of such rituals.

I showed him round then, for naturally all had been woken, as proud as a magpie with a new jewel. He was my jewel and from that moment on, I loved him well.

***

That year ended in a hard and long January and February and we were all affected by it. The wolves, which usually stayed well away from us, crept closer and we could hear their howls echoing through the forest at night. No man was allowed out on his own to work or travel. The poor rangy beasts which we glimpsed through the trees, stalking us as we moved about our business, examined us warily with sad, jaundiced eyes, too afraid of man to attempt an attack but driven by their bellies to think about it constantly.

Our sheep were folded in special pens on the downs and were guarded day and night by our shepherds. They too had dogs, scrawny long-haired things whose only thought was the will of their masters and the good of the sheep and lambs. As they rarely strayed from the fields, they were exempt from the declawing law. They were usually a good enough deterrent to the wolves and truly, up on the downs, we were rarely bothered by them.

However one bitter February night, a few of the shepherd's lads came running to the manor and banged vigorously on the barred manor door to be let in.

Their streaming flares had been seen half a mile off by the nightwatchman Wyot Gatekeeper and I had been fetched from my warm bed to meet them in the hall. The wolves had been closing in all evening, they said, on the pens and the shep-herd's huts and more men were needed to scare them away. As hungry and tena-cious as they were, the beasts were still frightened by man and fire.

A party was organised. My uncle William, who was staying with us, was to lead them. Robert would go too and many men bedded in the hall, knowing that their livelihood and their prosperity was tied up in the sheep of the hills, not least the mutton in their bellies of an evening meal, gamely put up their hands and donned their winter cloaks to follow.

Some of the larger dogs were fetched and taken on a leash too, for they would be good support if needed. It wasn't the first time in my life we had had to do this but it had not been necessary for quite a few years and, yes, men were prepared to go and defend our property from these black monsters.

I wish to God I had not stayed behind that night.

It was towards the small hours of the morning, the blackest, coldest time when it is said, the soul is hunted by the devil and man is at his most vulnerable, that those of us left behind heard the baying of the wolves and the answering howls of one or two dogs and it made us shudder. I returned to my soft bed and my warm wife and the blood at last came back to my feet after pacing the hall in my indoor shoes, a few hours. I slept, and was woken almost at first light, by an insistent banging on the solar door and a yelling of my name.

I scrambled from the bed. Cecily sat bolt upright, holding her hand to her brow against the glare of the night candle I'd hastily grabbed from its plate.

"What's amiss now?" she said. "Surely the men are due back soon? The wolves won't hunt in daylight, however dark the day."

But a different kind of wolf had hunted that night and had brought down prey as easily, it seems, as water flows through open fingers.

At the solar door I barged into Walter and I caught him by the cloak or he would have tumbled down a few steps. "What is it?"

I lifted my candle. Lights were streaming into the hall from the open stair door as men entered, booted and cloaked, rubbing their hands, removing woollen gloves and stamping their feet. I looked for Robert. He stood stock still at the foot of the solar stairs, his beautiful brown eyes red with cold, his nose running. He shivered and looked away and I followed his gaze as through the door, carried on a cloak borne at each corner by the wolf guard, was uncle William. One swift look told me he was dead. No man could survive those wounds and live.

Men crossed themselves as the four cloak bearers with their burden came fully into the hall and laid it down with its bloodied corpse before the fire.

I was dazed, blinded. I remember sinking to my knees in the rushes beside the body, and the keen uprush of blood to my head with grief and anger, made me hot and red faced.

"What in the name of all that's holy?"

Robert was suddenly standing at my right side. "We should fetch the priest," he said with his usual calmness. I looked up at him, gripped his arm and pulled myself up to stand over him.

"EXPLAIN!" I shouted.

My lady wife had just then opened the solar door. I heard it open as she stepped out and turned to close the door behind her. She looked down quickly at hearing my raised voice, taking in the scene some fifteen or so feet below her.

I rarely raised my voice to any man but I am ashamed to say I shouted at Cecily now, "Go back, wife, and tend to our son."

She nodded once and slipped away.

I steadied myself and gestured to one of the men to fetch the priest, as Robert had requested. Then I took a deep breath, swallowed my grief and said again,

"Explain."

There had been, he said, a great confusion of folk up on the hills. There was no moon and the light from the flares was sparse as one moved from one patch of firelight to another through total darkness, except for the main fires burning brightly near the pens and the shepherd's huts. They heard the wolves and had decided to fan out with the flares in groups of three for safety. One to hold the torch, one to be eyes and ears and one with a drawn weapon, to fight if need be and to surround the pens and huts of the herds; but all the while keeping each others' flares in sight.

They saw but a few wolves and mostly the beasts kept a distance from the extra men. All seemed to be going well, for the beasts had drawn off from the brighter areas into further darkness. Suddenly and without warning, one lone wolf had sprung as if from nowhere and had pinned William to the ground. Robert was some feet away and the third man even further off, though both were there fairly quickly after, when they heard the snarling and yelling. The wind had been knocked from William's lungs, Robert heard the exhalation and the thud as my uncle hit the ground. Uncle William had had no time to draw a weapon it seemed and the creature that attacked him was fearless and bold, a large specimen. Robert, who was holding the flare, managed, to trip on some hidden obstacle and drop it in surprise and out it went like William's exhaled breath, leaving them in complete darkness. However before the light went, he saw the wolf.

The tale was then taken up by the third man in the group that night, Colmar, who was the manor's chief cook.

"Master Robert's dog Bran was on the wolf in a trice, m'lord. We could hear it snarling and fighting and suddenly there was no noise at all and I heard Master Robert cry "Enough" and we made for where we thought they were lying." He shook his head.

"The wolf must have made off, sir, down into a combe where the air was blackest and one other from another group came running with a new torch and we lighted the lost one and..we found....we found..." He tailed off and rubbed his face with a trembling hand.

I reached for his shoulder and squeezed. "I know what you found."

Robert drew a shuddering breath.

"The wolf bit into his face and tore William's throat. It wounded Bran on the shoulder I think and because of Bran's defence of William, made off before we could throw or use a weapon. I think I managed to get my knife to its flanks, well there was blood on it so... Besides we were frightened to hit William. It was so dark...and so quick, so dark, there was no way we could see and we didn't expect the wolf to turn and fight."

"Where is Bran now?" I asked.

"He too ran off probably after the wolf. He'll be laid up somewhere licking his wounds, no doubt. I wish he'd return so we can see the damage." He tailed off, a catch in his voice.

"We shall go out when it's light and look," I said.

Meanwhile I had another death to report to the coroner and a well beloved uncle to mourn.

"It's almost dawn, let two of you ride into the town for the coroner and then, when he has pronounced, we must make William's body decent for burial."

I took comfort in all the organisation that had to be done then. It was later that the whole sorry tale took root in my mind and I could grieve for a man who had been as good as a father to me.

The priest came and went. I remember thinking, how many more of my strength-ening bastions would be taken from me? The coroner (who lived not five miles from Durley,) made haste from his warm pre-dawn bed, for he was William's friend of many years and would not tarry over this task. Having summoned his twelve jury men and viewed the body, he did indeed pronounce the death accidental. The women took poor William's ravaged body to wash and cleanse it.

I would not allow Cecily to join with the women's side in this job though she begged me; I would not want that she saw the poor man in death as he was then, ripped and slashed. I knew she had been very fond of him.

She came to me a little later though, with a tear in her eye and a puzzled expression.

"The women want you to go to them. They have something to show you, Aumary."

I blinked. "Where have they taken him?"

"To one of the spare rooms on the northern side, the one we use for guests when we cannot accommodate them in hall."

The women parted before me in silence as I walked solemnly in on their ministrations a few moments later. Two pans of reddened water showed where they had been cleaning William's wounds and countless rags browning with old blood were thrown onto a plank table in the corner. There was that iron tang I knew to be blood, mixed with something more spicy and pleasant. The oils with which, I suppose, they had anointed him. William lay, naked but decently covered to the waist with a linen sheet. I remember thinking how gaunt he was and how the hair on his chest, once thick and brown, was now grey and thinner, amongst the scratches and bite marks.

I drew in breath "What do you need of me?"

Old Joan, the priest's housekeeper, who lived in a bothy close by the walls of the manor, stepped forward.

"We would just like to show you this, m'lord" she said. I followed her and she gestured for one of the other women to help her turn the body a little.

The wounds on the neck were ragged and the column of his throat was torn, al-most from ear to ear. The face was a mass of bites and scratches. The left ear was torn off and hanging and there had been some effort to push it back in place. The women, no doubt, would strap it up before long. She took up a candle and pulled me closer.

"It might not have been seen amongst all these wounds, m'lord," she said "but Old Joan knows what she is looking at. Bites from teeth, scratches from claws, yes. Force applied here to pull out the throat and tear the blood lines. These a wolf or a dog does. But this....," and she pointed with a horny black nail. "This sir, is the work of man."

I peered at the narrow and now clean slit about two inches wide which went up into William's neck; into his chin on the left side. Joan, without any squeamishness, inserted her finger and pulled apart the skin flaps.

"Joan knows a knife wound when she sees one. Christ knows, begging my blasphemy sir, I've sewed up enough knife wounds in my time."

The world reeled and I turned and was suddenly, quite sick.

"No, my young scribbler, don't you go smirking into your cowl. It was not queasiness on my part and you must not think it so.

I had seen enough death and destruction, even at that young age and was not prone to fits of biliousness at the sight of blood. It was the shock. The shock of suddenly realising that we had a murderer amongst us and one who could slip a knife into an aging wool merchant as easily as he would carve his daily bread with his eating knife."

Though my mind was in turmoil, I knew immediately what must be done. The coroner must be informed again and the verdict on my uncle must be re-examined. First I had to secure the manor. I called all those who had been on the hills that night to the hall, saying nothing of why and hoping that each man still had the weapon with him which he had borne out there in the dark of that night. Quietly I asked Hal of Potterne, the man charged with security and safety on the manor and my man at arms, (I kept two further men at my own expense billeted at the castle of Marlborough, against the time when I might ride out to fight with my king, in addition to those men of the village who would ride with me to war), to lock Durley Manor against any who might be tempted to flee. I felt vulnerable, betrayed, disgusted. I knew not whom I could trust but I knew I could trust Hal. He had been asleep in the hall by the fire all that night and had not been on the downs.

The men came shuffling into the hall, some complaining, some yawning and rubbing their eyes of sleep, others simply bemused. It had been a hard night but they knew that rest was a luxury they were not to enjoy that morning.

I tried to radiate a confidence I did not feel, an authority I had no spirit for. Jumping up on the dais, I set my feet wide apart and thrust my thumbs into my belt, as I had seen my father do when he was contemplating a tough task and lifting my head to look down on the assembly I said, as loudly as I could,

"One - amongst - us - here, is a murderer."

They all, to a man, looked up at me at that and there was complete silence.

"Every man will submit to an examination of his knife. If you carried them tonight out on the hill but do not have them now, you will be required to fetch them, under supervision. Those who carried no edged weapons, quarter staffs and the like will be asked to prove this by virtue of the word of his neighbours and his tithing, that he indeed did carry no sharp weapon. Is this clear?"

And so the search for the weapon which killed my uncle William was begun.

I saw a difficulty almost at once, for there were several knives of a common manufacture made in the town, all of the right type to have done the damage and one of imported manufacture. Five men had knives of the right type, Walter Reeve and Robert Belvoir, Colmar the cook, Hugh the pigman and Stephen Hawknose. No knife bore traces of blood.

Each man was questioned by me and by Hal of Potterne as to his movements that night. We compared notes later. All stories tallied. All accounts were the same. There was not so much as a chink of light, not a tiny gap into which we might insert a fact or two to push a man into confession.

Master Quimper spoke to me later that morning. I knew him also to be totally innocent for he too was not on the hill that night but bedded in his usual corner by the kitchen fire. He wanted to help, he said. Far be it for him to tell me, the lord of the place, what to do. He wore his usual self-deprecating manner, but what we needed to do, he said, as the Roman lawyer Cicero had pointed out apparently, was examine motive, means and opportunity. Cui bono - who benefits? We fell at the first hurdle: motive.

All that day we searched the hills and the manor for a murder weapon which might have been discarded or hidden. The coroner who had eventually returned after a few hours; (he had gone to Devizes to conduct an inquest into a drunken brawl which had gone wrong) was once again summoned. A man had been de-tained there, he said, and would hang no doubt, for that crime. Would we ever bring to justice the evil heart that perpetrated our own deed? It was growing dark again when he rode in at last.

He too peered into the fatal wound on William's neck and his face was a picture of anger as he straightened up.

"We will hush this for the moment and I will not convene another jury now," he said, "but I agree - it is murder."

We bedded him and his servants down in the manor that night for it was too late to ride to his home in Ogbourne, on the other side of Marlborough town. We spent the evening in conjecture and contemplation of the crime, until our heads ached and our bellies roiled with it.

William Labarge had been much liked, even loved and we could find no enemy, uncover no fact, invent no story which would account for the murder of so well respected a man of Marlborough. Nor could we understand how the crime could have been planned. No one had known that William was to be out there almost alone in the darkness that night. Were we dealing with witchcraft, that someone had known before we knew ourselves that it would be so?

That night I dreamed of wolves. Big slavering yellow teethed wolves. Each beast had a human hand and every one bore a knife like the one which had killed my uncle.

That day too we had sent out a small party to scour the hills for Robert's dog Bran. It was late in the afternoon when he was found, curled up under a bush in the river valley. Sadly, it was Robert who found him. I would not have wished that on him. Bran's head had been crushed by what looked like a large bite. There were wounds on his body, about the shoulders and neck, where he had fought and lost, ragged bite marks and deep scratches. Robert brought him home over his saddle, no easy task, for the animal was stiffening with rigor.

Over and over Robert berated himself for his stupidity in dropping the flare and his inability to act quickly enough to save William, his lack of control of Bran, who had run off despite, he said, commands to return and leaving the wolf to escape. We buried Bran with difficulty in the frozen ground with our other deceased canine companions and life went on. Uneasily, but life went on.

The wolves never returned.

Chapter Four

The weather gradually turned, although it was fully March before we could say that spring had come at last. All was slow starting. The winter aconites of the forest floor, usually early flowerers often pushing up though January snows, were late appearing and long in leaving. The ground was frozen for periods of time and farm work was delayed. The women sat, twirling their distaffs, the men whittled sticks, repaired tools or made toys for their children, glad to be out of the cold winds.

I spent some time at the castle for there was building work taking place there and I was interested to see how the masons worked.

The work there, set me thinking about improvements I might make to Durley Manor and so, when the first phase of castle work was almost at an end, I approached the master mason, Phillip Carver and asked him to wait on me at Durley on a day which suited him, to discuss my ideas.

He rode into Durley on a blustery April day, his pack pony laden with the tools of his trade for he had uprooted himself and was now en route to the west country where he was to work on another large project, a cathedral at Wells, I believe. Masons were peripatetic. They travelled where the work was. Some groups stayed together, others drifted off singly. Philip told me he could call on seven or eight good men for any work we might be likely to undertake. It took me almost all morning to explain what I wanted. He laughed at my eagerness, curbed my enthusiasms and we thrashed out a plan and a reasonable costing for updating the manor, which had seen no real improvement since my grandfather's time.

Stone was ordered and wood was granted from the forest around us, for although the trees grew on my land, I held the manor from the Lord Marshall. He was keeper of the castle and the largest landowner in the area, (save the Earl of Salisbury) who was ultimately responsible to the king, for the forest was the king's own property, and I had to seek permission.

Work began on the hall, on the manor walls and on the kitchen which was very outdated and too small for our needs now.

Colmar the cook complained bitterly about the upheaval and the disruption to his routine but still managed to feed us all. He grew sullen and bad tempered and would come to me at least three times a day with a tale of woe. It was when I told him that he should have a proper fireplace with a chimney that he perked up a little and I heard less of his gripes after that. I had seen one of these new inventions at the castle and so wanted to impress my wife, who hated the wood smoke from the raised fire, which stood centrally on a bed of stones, billowing about the hall. I would install one new fireplace in the communal hall, one in the solar and one in the kitchen. The smoke was vented to the outside by a flue which went up the outside wall of a building and thence through a hollow column, up into the air. No more smoky airs and if built and cared for properly, the fire would warm the whole place, not just those nearest to it, I was told.

Colmar was as pleased as a dog with two bones when I told him that his fire would be the grandest of these and that all modern appliances would be installed for him to use: a spit turned by a small dog (there were plenty of those at Durley); ovens to each side for baking, heated by the central blaze, space for hanging meat to smoke and a hearth upon which he could cook all manner of things, in pots and crocks.

He went off, rubbing his hands together with glee, to celebrate with a drink or two. I never saw him alive after that.

Later that day, Cecily came to me and told me that a whole barrel of burntwine had gone missing from the stores. She had been in there looking for something else, down in the undercroft and it was definitely not where it was usually stored. Cecily was a good housekeeper and she knew to the last inch of salt, how much of everything we had at every season. Puzzled, I went with her to look. Sure enough, there was a gap on the rack. The small barrel was missing. We had no pilfering on the manor. All men were well fed and had a generous allowance of ale per day. In good times we all shared in the bounty. The burntwine was used in small amounts for it was prodigiously fearsome stuff, for cooking and preserving and in medicinal receipts. One sip and you felt as if your throat was on fire. You grew to a drunken stupor very quickly on this volatile drink.

I couldn't imagine that any of my own people had taken the drink but did wonder if the stone workers and builders, whom we had taken into the manor, might be responsible. After all, we did not know them well.

I was just going off in search of my master builder when he came running at a trot, around the corner of the building which housed the privy, the latrines.

"M'lord..." He stumbled to a halt. He took off his coif and screwed it into a small bunch in his hand. I steadied him.

"You look like you have just seen one of your apprentices ruin your work, Phillip," I joked but I could see, too late, that I should not have jested for he was indeed, very upset.

"No, my lord." He made an infinitesimal shake of his head. I almost counted this man my equal. He might have been a tradesman but he was a master at that trade. I might have been a lord but what was I really but a tradesman of sorts, a servant of the crown and his junior by some twenty years or more?

"Tell me - what's the matter?" The problems which had beset the building works (there were just a few), came to my mind and I started to wonder which one had reared its head today. "Have we a problem shoring up the south wall again?"

"No, my lord." He swallowed, "It's your cook. I have just found him at the back of the privy wall. He is stone dead, sir."

We found Colmar slumped between the privy wall and several large boulders which had been cut and stored ready for the rebuilding of the main gate-way, hitherto made mostly of wood. He was tucked quietly in a gap between, wrapped in his outdoor cloak and sitting, his legs outstretched before him, his head hidden in the shadow of the large blocks of stone. I called his name, struggled into the gap and pulled him by the shoulder. He fell forward with a reek of spirits, a reek so strong it took my breath away.

"Saints!" I cried "Dead..maybe. Dead drunk, more like."

I grabbed hold of his boots and pulled him out.

More reek of spirits followed this operation.

"I think we have found where our burntwine has gone," I said almost to myself.

Phillip Carver knelt by the supine cook.

"No, I was right. He is dead sir. Dead of drink I think."

"Can you see the cask, 'tis but a small one?" We cast round but there was no sign of the offending container.

"Where the drunken man is, so should his drink be." I said. "He cannot have drunk it straight from the cask. There must be a bottle or a pitcher, or..... You were working in the kitchen Phillip, when did you last see Colmar there?"

Phillip replaced and adjusted the coif on his head and stood again. "About a short while after noon, the sext bell was ringing in the hall chapel, I remember."

I shook my head "He would have been very busy then with the preparing of the food for the afternoon meal. Colmar would never have left everything in the air to go off and drink himself into oblivion, on my burntwine."

I searched the body, looked carefully at him. There really was no sign of the burntwine save that terrible smell. There was no doubt he was dead though. Colmar knew the peril of too much strong drink taken over a short time. As far as I know, he had been a good man for his ale but this? Was I just being over cautious? I was beginning to have a terrible suspicion. Again a rider was despatched to the coroner. We were unlucky for he was from home again and was likely to stay that way for a few days. He had gone up into the northwest of the county on some quest, Chippenham they said. We would have to keep the body until he returned. So, I thought to have the town surgeon look at him for I was sore afraid that the wine had not been the death of him.

"If you saw him after sext Phillip and we find him now, an hour or so later, he had taken a great deal of drink in a very short time. He would be bound to know what it would do to him and the container must be with him. No man gets this falling down drunk, nay unto death and then calmly disposes of the thing which killed him. It's not possible. It must be here somewhere."

But it was not. I sent for Johannes of Salerno. We took Colmar to the mortuary, a round structure built into the corner off the northernmost walls. The doctor didn't arrive until almost that evening. Meanwhile I'd had the body stripped, looking for wounds or injury. Nothing. Colmar's clothes though reeked of spirit more than his mouth, almost as if he had been doused in it.

"We shall be in trouble with the coroner for moving him," I said to Phillip. "But what could we have done? Left a dead body for all to see as they made their way to their daily ablutions?"

The doctor, the same who attended Cecily all that time ago was a bright and thorough man. I liked him greatly. He was not one for silly remedies or procrastinations to increase his fees. He looked the body over with painstaking care. He examined the hands, the mouth, the eyes. He sniffed the mouth. Then he sniffed again.

"Can you find me a small dish or pot?"

One was procured and with a small spatula which he kept in his box of instru-ments, he teased something from Colmar's mouth. It was a small sliver of a plant; it looked like a piece of root and it had been stuck in his teeth.

Phillip became a little uneasy at this. This to him, he told me later, was rather a desecration of the poor dead man but he could see the sense in it and remained silent at the time.

Finally, the doctor took us out into the fresh air. The smell in the small mortuary, built to house only one or two bodies at a time, not four men, three alive and one dead and reeking of drink, had become over-powering.

He turned his gold brown stare on me, his brows drawn together and pronounced.

"It is not brandywine. It's poison. Aconite I think. I would say quite a lot of it. It's almost impossible to detect. The person usually looks like they have died of asphyxia. I'm only making a guess because I have seen it before. A few years back in Salerno, a wife was accused of murdering her husband and it transpired she used Aconitum. I saw the results of a large dose of it. The reek of the spirit disguised the smell of vomit and the foaming you often get when this poison is ingested. I am surprised he didn't void his bowels as well...they usually do." He was so matter of fact, I heard Philip, just a little behind me, take in a hissed breath and felt him cross himself.

I went back into the mortuary and fetched out Colmar's cloak. I stretched it out to the fitful sun on the ground before me.

"See..the stains - some are old, yes but there are patches, many patches, as if something has been poured over him. I gathered it up again and sniffed. It was still a little damp. "It was my good brandywine I think. We were meant to think he had drunk himself to death."

Phillip had recovered a little. "Yes, but why would Colmar be out in his cloak when he should be hot and sweaty in his kitchen preparing our meals? It doesn't make sense."

The doctor smiled then.

"You have yourself another murder, my young sir," he said.

***

I took the doctor in to the hall determined to get to know him further. I knew he lived in the town and that he had come there a few years ago from Oxford. We had had no need to call on his skill until Walter's quick thinking had caused him to come to Cecily's aid. I had no doubt that his care had saved her life.

He was about twelve years older than I. Tall, muscular for one who was not a fighting man, though something in his bearing told me he had been. He had shoulder length brown hair, scrupulously clean and shining, which he always wore tied back in a queue and was clean shaven. His eyes were an amber brown, clear and direct of gaze. I liked that.

I pushed a jug of the best wine in his direction and indicated that he should sit.

"I thought you and I should talk, Johannes," I said "It seems we are of like minds."

He looked up then, the wine cup to his lips. "Aye, we think alike there's no doubt. I would say we are of alike mind, my lord."

"It was good of you to come to us tonight. I did not know what to do when I found the coroner was away and we could not get the body of Colmar looked at and a decision made by a jury. The next best thing I thought was, to ask you for your professional opinion."

"I am flattered that you hold me in such esteem, sir."

"I do indeed. I have no doubt that I owe you a debt for bringing Cecily back to me."

"I did very little" he said, "and I was paid handsomely, for which I thank you. There is little one can do in cases like that. I have seen - though I have never performed it myself, a doctor relieve the pressure on the brain of a patient very like Lady Belvoir; a blow to the head, a swelling of the tissues, fluid building up. A small hole was drilled into the skull and the fluid drained. They call it trepanning. It worked. Remarkable. The patient was good as new in a short while. He would most certainly have died had it not been attempted."

"Have you the skill do you think, to do such a thing?" He pondered this for a while. "I studied seven years at the medical school in Salerno in Sicily, from whence I take my name, though I was born in Oxford. There is no doubt it is the most advanced school of its kind, owing much to the Arab world and ancient knowledge trickling from Egypt. I have seen things there that would not be believed here in England. Yes, I would have attempted a trepanning should I have thought it a wise move. But such things here in this country, can be considered dangerous magic. I do have to tread carefully and quietly if I want to continue to practice here."

"We move forward by small and secret steps, Johannes, in this world. Knowledge is often held back by ignorant people who believe that they have the right to suppress it."

"The Church is no friend to the surgeon, my Lord Belvoir," he said.

"No, no, that I know." I drank.

"So your birth in Oxford and your seven years in Salerno, what came in between? I think I can detect the slight swagger of a soldier. No, no I do not mean swagger do I?" I chuckled. "Though something in you makes me wonder if you once wore a sword and used it."

He laughed then, a light, tinkling suppressed laugh.

"I made a poor soldier. Yes, as a young man. I did not want to be a parchment maker like my father, though I did not know what I wanted to do. I was lured away, as many are, to the continent by the promise of fame and fortune. I travelled, I walked. I foolishly for a while enlisted as a mercenary. I found, though, to my dis-gust, that I had no stomach for soldiering.

Eventually, I fetched up at Salerno in Sicily, starving and ill and was taken in and brought back to health. I stayed, at first, as a lowly servant at the medical school there. After five years, working my way through the school of doctoring, I was per-suaded to follow King Richard to the Holy Lands. Whatever I thought when I set out, I think maybe I believed I could do some good with doctoring. It was not a good decision."

"You took the cross, were with King Richard? In Palestine?"

"Aye, and what a fiasco it was. I got to Cyprus and saw some fierce fighting there, sadly not with the infidel, but with the poor inhabitants of that island. Foolish and pointless. Richard and Phillip were regularly at each others' throats by then. All the leaders were bickering. There were constant outbreaks of fighting between rival groups. Eventually we managed to move on to Acre and to drive Saladin away."

"You have seen some action, my friend."

"But none of it meant anything grand, for we never got to the holy places. We never recovered Jerusalem as we had vowed. They turned tail and came home. And then Richard got himself captured." Johannes laughed at himself "By then, after the release at Acre, I had left them to their folly and made my way back to Sicily. I developed dysentery and ended up cared for again in my own medical school by those who had taught me. It was like being lost in these dark woods of yours and then coming out into the light of a clearing. They persuaded me to finish my studies and I am heartily glad they did. So yes, I once was a soldier of sorts. I had enough funds with my spoils of war and I vowed to use them wisely. It was the best seven years I can have spent, albeit broken up, and the best use of that blood-tainted money I could think of."

He stared into his wine cup, remembering those times, I supposed and musing on how the wheel of fortune turns us up and then down and gives us a good shaking for our pains. He said so. I smiled.

"We are glad that you came back to England and fetched up in our little corner of it."

"I came back a relatively wealthy man. Not bad for a young nothing, the son of a Saxon seamstress and a parchment maker. Back in Oxford I found that my parents had both perished. A type of sweating sickness had taken them apparently. Ten years away and everything had changed. I tried to set up practice but ha! The town was no longer the one I had left and I found myself pilloried and ostracised. They remembered me as a ragged Oxford urchin and to them I had grown too big for my boots. Oxford is not a place for new ideas. The old guard there do not want new blood, new ways. That is why I do not use my father's name, Aldate, but take the name of the place where I began again, where I was re-invented. I packed up then and three years ago came to Marlborough. I have not regretted it."

"We are very glad you did. We are honoured to call you a friend." I offered him my hand. He grasped my arm and smiled that warm brown-eyed look which crinkled the corners of his eyes.

And so began my lifelong friendship with that remarkable man, Johannes of Salerno.

I slept fitfully that night. None of us felt much like eating anything and you could see folk at supper that night, testing the ale on their tongue for a strange taste or smell before they drank. I drank wine as I had a little good French wine in my cellar. I needed it. I had the kitchen searched for any foreign material. The doctor, had told me what to look for: a purple plant, a pretty purple plant, with a hood like a turned over cowl and spikes like horns, deadly even to touch. Every part of it poisonous and so much more if the poisons were concentrated from the plant. Of course we found no such thing, not a trace.

I lay that night staring up at the underside of the bed canopy and going over it all in my head, whilst Cecily slept beside me. She was now carrying our second child and needed her rest. How could I protect those I loved and cared for? I had singularly failed to do so, so far.

I turned over also in my mind what Johannes and I had discussed that night over a pint of good wine; the death of my cook.

I thought about what Master Quimper had said. Motive.

What on earth was the motive for the murder of poor Colmar? Had someone taken umbrage at too much gristle in their broth? I threw that thought away as unworthy.

I had reported the murder of my uncle William to the sheriff and now I would have to do so with Colmar's untimely death. It was the sheriff's job to search out felons, not mine, though I would have been happy to devote time to this, had I had the leisure and any idea how to go about finding the murderer.

Eventually as the sun was almost coming up over the eastern wall, I slept. Thankfully, this time, I didn't dream.

About this time, when I was on the way to the carpenter's barn, outside the walls, to talk to him about the making of some fencing, I heard a muffled screaming coming from the poultry woman's bothy. I smiled; so a young pair at their coupling, I thought. Then I recalled that the poultry woman was a mature widow of forty with a plain only daughter of about thirteen. Neither, I thought would be so engaged in the middle of the day.

I was about to pass by; none of my business I said; when I distinctly heard a girl's voice cry out,

"No sir please... I can't... I don't....The plea was then cut off and a voice I recognised said,

"Hush girl, your wriggling only serves to add to my lust. I will have you. Stop wriggling."

I pushed back the leather panel which served the bothy as a door.

The girl was lying on her front with her kirtle pushed up almost over her head. She was struggling and crying quietly into the straw on which she lay. There between her outstretched thighs, leaning over her on his knees, was Robert, his chausses and braies round his ankles. I might have smiled and quietly disappeared but for the fact that he held her down with such force that it was clear she did not wish for this amount of intimacy.

I pulled the leather curtain back more fully and stepped onto the beaten earth floor.

"Robert, rape is a crime for which even a well bred lad like you can be called to account. Especially when it's on my manor and with one of my servants who is unwilling. Let her up."

He turned on his elbow then and gave me that deep brown stare. "She's willing enough - or she was a moment ago."

"Not now."

He stood, adjusting his clothing and the girl scrambled, sniveling, in to the straw bed piled up at the back of the building.

"Go, I'll speak to you later," I said.

Amazingly and with nothing to say, he left.

I waited a heartbeat or two. "Has this happened before?" I asked.

The girl shook her head and wiped her nose on her wrist.

"Did you encourage him as he said?"

Her eyes widened. "I only....said....."

"Did you lead him to believe he could couple with you as a man and wife do? Or did you say him no from the beginning?"

She shook her head, "He's so handsome and I thought.....m'lord"

"You cannot lead a man to lust and then decide you don't want to go through with it, girl." I shook my own head. "Admittedly, he should not force you if you change your mind but make sure before you enter into the bargain that the thing is what you want to do, absolutely. If it isn't say no as forcefully as you can. If a man forces you then, as the Master Robert seemed to be doing to you, it is rape and will be judged as such. No matter who they are."

She began to cry. "I didn't want to do that my lord...not that. My ma says I mustn't and I'm a good girl sir, really."

"Make sure you stay a good girl." And I left.

***

A short while later I ran Robert down to the stable where he was grooming his horse, rather vigorously I thought. I stood in the door with my arms folded and waited for him to acknowledge me. It took him a full few heartbeats. He knew I was there, there was no doubt but he'd made me wait. Eventually he turned, a wisp of straw in his hand.

"I suppose she told you I forced her?"

"No, she said very little actually. I think she was blinded by your charm, Robert."

"Then you believe me when I say she led me on...?"

"I believe she thought it would be fun to have a kiss and a cuddle in the straw with a beautiful young man who led her to think, mayhap, he was in love with her."

"Pah!" He threw away the straw. "I never said I loved her. I wouldn't. She knew it was just a roll, a bit of fun."

"It will not be fun for her if she falls pregnant, Robert. Oh yes, we are kind to our lesser folk on this manor. If they have children out of wedlock, we acknowledge them, help them out. We don't turn on them, 'tis true. You of all people should know that."

His brown eyes flared as I had never seen before and then, white and pinched round the nose and mouth he said, "If I have bastards, I will acknowledge them."

"Good. See that you do. I have no quarrel with a man taking his pleasure where he fancies. What I despise is forcing without consent. That I will not tolerate, whoever it is doing the forcing."

His face was suffused with blood, he was angry now. "I did not force her."

"No. I intervened, I think"

He took a step towards me. "I would not have...."

"No? It looked otherwise to me."

I turned to leave. "Have you never been led on by a girl, till your blood is up and you cannot help yourself, then?" he spat.

I stood with my back to him, in the doorway. I didn't turn to look at him, for I was disgusted with my little brother, little no longer.

"No, I have the control you seem to lack. Besides, my bedding was always with absolute consent. I have never, I think, taken a girl against her will," and I walked with a straight back and a head held high out into the yard.

"I will tell no one," I threw back at him.

"You looked shocked boy. Surely you did not think that I had never bedded a girl before I was wedded? How else are we to get the practice, eh? I may be old and shriveled now but I was once young and lusty. Oh suit yourself."

***

My daughter was born on a beautiful spring morning in early April when the sparrows were chattering in the eaves of the solar and the sparhawk was hunting them with silent intent. I was standing in the courtyard, looking at my new walls, when I saw the raptor gliding silently towards the bevy of sparrows feeding on insects in the paving cracks. Suddenly, all chatter ceased; there was total silence. The birds, as if by an invisible signal, flew up in a cloud and disappeared into the elder tree by the solar window. Into this silence came the cry of a newborn and I knew I had another child.

We called her Hawise for it was a good Norman name and I wanted my first girl child to carry my Norman blood forward. I promised Cecily that she should chose the next and that she could have a Saxon name should she wish.

She was a pretty thing with huge blue eyes which turned a lovely shade of green as she grew, and copper hair like her mother, though when she was born she was as bald as an old monk.

"Scribe. Please don't tell her that I said that. She's a fearsome woman now and liable to take offence and the last time I saw her, her hair was plentiful. She might visit me soon, if I don't die before she gets here.

Where was I? Ah yes...now this is a very important piece of my narrative and so pay great attention."

It was soon to be my name day. I am not one for celebrations of this sort but my wife had decided that this year we were to have a gathering of friends and family, colleagues and workers so that we might show off (this naturally was the real reason) our newly completed building works. The walls were done, the gate-house all but a few blocks finished. The chimneys were installed and the kitchen (God rest the bones of Colmar who would have loved it) was extended and with every convenience a cook could desire. Our undercook had been promoted and he was do-ing well in the job. I wondered idly one day, if he had done away with Colmar just so that he could step into his shoes. Just as quickly as the thought arose, I discarded it, as unacceptable.

Fine gifts were coming into the manor from those who could not come in person, to the feast, but who had been invited.

Johannes sent a barrel of Gascon wine, much appreciated by all those who drank the fruit of the vine.

There were foods of all sorts from kind people whom I knew in Marlbor-ough and further afield. Someone sent me a beautiful bolt of dark blue cloth, enough to make a new tunic and Cecily set to quickly with needle and thread to make and decorate it, so that I could wear it at my name day feast. (I suspected this was a bribe from some merchant intent on screwing a better price from our thread business, but I will not say it's so.)

That very day, came the most beautiful gift presented in a silken cloth bag of exquisite colour. The saffron and green shot satin of the bag glowed like the sun on moss and I would have been very pleased with just that. With it was a small piece of parchment and on it, in a clerkly hand was written. 'From John'.

It simply appeared on the hall table that morning and none could say who had brought it in. We made many inquiries but drew a blank. I picked up the bag and weighed it in my hands.

"So what do you think, Robert?" He was in the act of pouring himself some wine and peered at it over the chair on which I was sitting.

"Not money" he said "No jingling. Um maybe...um jewellery? Yes, John likes jewellery."

"It's heavy enough" I said and handed it to him. "Feel the weight of it." He took it then.

"Hmmm. Gold do you think...? Like the gold of the bag. No, it doesn't feel like that." He lifted it up. "Shall I?"

"By all means," I said. "I have opened far too many presents today." He was standing behind me, so I could not see what he did but I heard his indrawn breath and "oh" and turned to see what had impressed him so.

In his hand he held the most beautiful glove I had ever seen. It was exquisite pale cream leather with gold and beaded work on the cuff and embroidery with fine silver wires. Certainly the gift of a king. I stared at it.

"Oh my!" I remember saying "That is a gift to rival all gifts...except I hawk infrequently and only with my father-in-law's birds. I have no birds myself. I suppose he means for me to take up the sport. More expense then. Oh what one must do when one aims to be a cultured knight." I laughed and took a swig of my Gascon.

"Let me see," I said. I turned it over and over in my hand but did not try it and then gave it back to Robert. "It's a mite too small for my hand I think."

"Try it."

"No, no, you try it for me." He thrust his fingers into it and then snatched them out again just as quickly with a "God's blood, the seamstress has left a needle in it. Ouch!" And he sucked on his thumb.

That evening he grew very feverish, took to his bed and took no part in the festivities, and by the following morning he was ill enough for Cecily, looking very worried, to say that we should fetch the doctor from Marlborough, for she thought that if we did not and it carried on as it was, Robert was like to die.

Chapter Five

Robert's thumb had swollen to almost twice its normal size and Doctor Johannes was called. He lanced the small prick in Robert's thumb, opening up a larger cut which extended almost the whole length of the thumb from tip to root and drained a deal of pus. He was, he said, of the school of thought that a wound must be kept clean with boiled water and dry and free from pus. Many of his fellows, he said, violently disagreed with him on this but he would defend his ideas with the success rates of his patients' survival. Such body fluids, others said, were desirable and promoted healing but Johannes believed this to be a falsehood. How could something so foul smelling be beneficial? He also believed that a wound must be, as much as possible, open to the clean air. Poultices of honey and some concoction of herbs were applied daily but often Robert's hand was left with nothing but a light dressing. Gradually the thumb returned to a more normal size. Each day after, though in truth the original wound had been small, this remarkable doctor would scrape the new thumb wound where the poison had entered and he had enlarged it, with a scalded knife until it bled again. This encouraged the body to grow new tissue and amazingly, the wound healed. I have never seen the like, then or since; never seen such a wound heal so quickly.

However Robert remained feverish and ill, so Johannes began a different regime. For days Robert was fed a boiled water into which a type of mould gathered from sources which Johannes would not reveal, had been dissolved. It was, he said, a remedy known only to a few and he would be accused of malpractice if it became known what he had advocated. We were sworn to secrecy.

How did Johannes of Salerno know to use these methods on Robert? For every evil substance in the world, he said, there was a beneficial one to counteract it. It was a matter of working out what the poison was. If this could be deduced, then by applying the correcting substance, the evil could be defeated. The body itself would do the rest. Robert was young and fit and strong. Indeed, said Johannes, Robert had never been in any grave danger, once Johannes had been called.

We had shown him the needle which we had extracted carefully from the glove. He had sniffed it, immersed it in a tiny amount of boiled water to take off the sub-stance used to poison and then, to our utmost horror, tasted it on his tongue. He had nodded then and had gone off to the place we'd given him to stay and work from, in what we laughingly called our 'guest rooms', newly extended by our builders, to return with his mouldy smelling liquid. Robert returned to us within the week.

Happy though I was to see my brother restored to health, I was naturally very worried about the manner of his wounding. For there had been no doubt the hawking glove had been intended as a present for me. No, it had not come from John. Why ever should I think that John knew my name day or which birthday I celebrated, or that he had the time to think about me and choose such an expensive present for me, whilst engaged in the heavy business of helping to keep the country together. Foolish, foolish thoughts.

There was no doubt though: someone had tried to murder me.

Then the news came that Richard was dead. A man from the castle at Marlborough rode in on the first day of May to tell us that the king had been slain by a rogue archer on March 25th 1199 at the puny little castle of Chalus Chabrol in the Limousin and had taken till April 6th to die of a gangrenous wound to the neck. Foolhardy Richard had gone for a stroll around the walls without his armour and had paid the price for his hubris.

The King was dead. Long live the King. There was a collective intake of breath...you could feel it in the countryside.

John was crowned at Westminster Abbey in London on May 27th, despite some antipathy to his accession.

"What's that, boy? Was I there? Well, naturally I was there. Tut! Now pay attention."

Norman tradition favoured John, it seems as the only surviving son of Henry 2nd While the Angevins favoured Arthur, as the heir of Henry's elder son Geoffrey: the matter rapidly became an open conflict but John's mother Eleanor backed her son (at last), and so did the majority of the English and Norman lords.

So there was great rejoicing amongst those of us loyal to John from the beginning ,and much handing out of purses, honours and gifts; much back slapping and commiserating and a great deal of elbowing for position. Many of the old guard lost their places. I had the opportunity to become the under-castellan of Marlborough castle, to learn the role as it were, for the day when I might, should the King wish it, and I accept it, become constable. I did not really want the job but one does not say no to a King.

John needed a loyal man at Marlborough, for it was one of the gateways to the rich west of England. Set out from London to almost any city in the west of England and you will find that you either pass through Savernake, or reasonably near it.

The days came and went, blurred into each other as I juggled the manor, the forest and my new role at the castle. There were times when I felt as if I was throwing them all in the air, like a conjuror's balls and that I was bound to drop one, but it never happened. Indeed a government perambulation of Savernake performed in the summer of 1199, found that the forest was managed properly; that we had achieved, as we had been instructed to do, a spectacular increase in the size and that all was well.

***

Master Quimper had, for some years now, been retired from tutoring Robert. We had given him a place in our household because in truth, I liked the man and he was extremely knowledgeable, with a busy brain and a willing heart. When my son Geoffrey was a little older, we would need a tutor, and I had half an eye on this ready-made opportunity. Master Quimper had proved himself an able and kind teacher. We lodged the man in a room in the south row of buildings, which had been made as lean-tos against the outer wall of the courtyard, in the new building works. He told me he was comfortable there and needed very little: a bed, a table and stool, a shelf for his books, a chest for his property, a few pegs for his clothes and I gave him a prie dieu at which to pray. He was very grateful for his bed and board he said, and proved useful, as I have written before, in the still room, helping Cecily with the household remedies and concoctions. He was probably now over forty, nearer fifty and no longer young, but on some days of the week he would walk with his sturdy staff in hand, (sometimes if a cart were going to town, he would ride), the three miles or so to Marlborough and back, to tutor a handful of the younger lads of the town whose fathers had the wherewithal to pay for such an education for their sons. He was not short of money.

On one delightful summer's day, when my daughter Hawise was a few weeks old and her insistent cries for feeding could be heard though the solar window, I looked up to see him coming towards me with a frown of concentration between his brows.

He caught sight of me and bowed as he walked, rather a comical exercise I thought.

"Well met lord" he said "I was hoping to have a word with you."

"Good morrow, dear sir," I returned "How are you this fine morning? Are you off to the town to drum some Latin into the empty-headed young stallions you tutor?"

He nodded "I am in good health, thank you sir, a little stiff but...." He shrugged his shoulders, "Who is not, that is over forty summers old?" He smiled showing me a rather gap-toothed mouth.

I remember thinking, I can't recall him losing so many teeth, but...there you are. When we are familiar with something or someone, gradual changes go unnoticed, don't they? It takes a fresh eye to notice these things.

"Might I call on you when I return this evening my lord? I have"...he looked away, "a delicate matter to discuss with you, one I can no longer keep to myself. It has been exercising my brain for a while now."

"Good Lord, Quimper, you're not going to leave us to get married are you?" I laughed.

He looked shocked at that and made backing movements with his free hand.

"Oh no...certainly not that....the fair sex...is...ho no....no, no my lord." He smiled then.

"It's two things really. I simply cannot fathom what's going on. Some of my things are missing." He looked really perplexed. "And I have mislaid some of my money," he said.

He looked so serious then and so I said gently,

"Come to me before supper tonight and we'll talk. I'll be in my office."

My office was in truth since the building works, the old buttery off the screens passage and there I waited for Master Quimper from about six till supper at seven that evening. He did not arrive.

I went in to supper and afterwards went back to the office to work and to wait. I called to one of the army of small boys who fetched and carried about the manor, as he passed the open door.

"Did Master Quimper appear at supper tonight, even after I left, Bill?"

He frowned. "No m'lord, I don't think so."

"When you have stored that napery where it should be, can you run to his sleeping place and find him please and remind him that we two had a meeting planned, before supper?"

The boy bobbed an acknowledgement.

Five minutes later he was back.

I didn't look up from my figures. "Did you find him?"

There was silence. I looked up. The boy was as white as milk.

He swallowed and stammered. "Y..y..yes sir. I did. I think he's dead sir."

***

I jumped up, calling for whoever was in the hall to follow me. (Why did I do that? Perhaps because, in the light of all that had gone before, I needed a witness or two, to be further eyes and ears) and made at an easy trot down the outer hall steps and across the courtyard.

Only Hal of Potterne and the blacksmith's lad James were in hall, both eating a late supper. The two followed me at a distance.

Master Quimper lay on his back; Hhs eyes closed. Both hands were laid across his stomach and he looked so peaceful and restful, one might think he was sleep-ing. Leaving James at the door, Hal pushed past me without a word. He felt for a heartbeat, lifted the eye lids, laid his ear to the nose and listened, searching for a warm breath on his cheek, however thin.

There was no sound save one of the laundry maids laughing, far off some-where. It had been a washing day, I recalled. Finally Hal laid his ear to Quimper's chest.

He turned to me and shook his head. " 'E's gone sir, " he said.

After calling yet again for Father Benedict and his holy waters, I returned to my office and sat for a few minutes, dazed and saddened. I had really liked Master Quimper; we had had not a great deal to do with each other on a manor level or a professional one but as friends and wine cup companions of an evening round the fire, he was a good man; an interesting man, with a general knowledge of the world to rival...well...actually, no one else I knew.

I began to think about what he had said. He had a problem. Things and money were missing. He had wanted to thrash about the facts of it all with me, I suspect-ed. And now, now he could not.

I found myself staring at the wall.

"God...no...not another?" I jumped up and went into the hall. Hal had returned to his supper.

"Sorry, Hal, can you call for Johannes, if he's still here and ask him to meet me at Master Quimper's room please?"

***

Father Benedict was just finishing his ministrations as I entered. I crossed myself.

"I was not able to give him the full forgiveness of God, Aumary, for he died so suddenly," said Benedict." But if it's any consolation, I prayed to our merciful Lord that he will forgive the sins of this..." He sat down heavily on the stool next to the table, which was littered with parchments, "Well...this less than average sinner. He was a good man. He will not fail to enter heaven I'm sure."

I nodded.

"Can we keep a vigil for the dead for him in the chapel, Benedict?" I asked. "I know he wasn't one of us but....he had become so."

Father Benedict took both hands to his face and scrubbed and scrubbed, as if to scrub away the fact that he had officiated at too many vigils lately at Durley Manor alone.

"Aye" he said "I don't see why not. I have got too used to this, Aumary; too used," and he sighed deeply.

Johannes of Salerno came silently a moment later, clutching his robe to him for ease of running along the yard.

He took one look through the open door.

"Have you touched anything?"

We all shook our heads and I told him quickly what I knew and what I suspected. His eyes raked the small, relatively bare room.

"It may be as it seems, Johannes; a man over forty, dead of exhaustion after a long day on the heat of the road and a four mile walk. Maybe his heart gave out... maybe his brain became overheated." I gabbled. "But first, do make sure he is dead. I trust Hal. He has seen more corpses than any of us, on the battlefield, but...."

Johannes smiled. "We will examine him then and together we shall see what we can see."

Father Benedict gathered up his things, nodded to me and then to the doctor (I thought with a little reserve in the gesture) and padded off.

I watched Johannes as, with his usual lack of haste and customary gentleness, he began to examine the body of my friend, whom I suddenly realised, had no pronomen. I did not know his first name and had always referred to him as Quimper.

"No outward appearance of injury. No struggle." He looked once again around the room.

"He put up no fight if this is murder, Aumary," he said.

I folded my arms and leaned against the wall trying to make myself, I suppose, as small an extra item in the room as I could. I felt too large for the space and an encumbrance. I saw Hal in the doorway.

Johannes felt around the skull. "No blow to the head? No bones grating beneath my probing fingers. No. Help me, Aumary "

We turned him this way and that between us, undressed him and dressed him again. No injuries. No blood spattering anywhere. There were a couple of bruises on the upper arms, smallish ones; though suspicious, these could have been inflicted at any time today or yesterday.

Johannes then went to the head and began his search for poison, though I was almost convinced that he did not believe it was present. He palpated the torso, moved the neck, opened the mouth and looked for anything coming up from the lungs. He sniffed the open mouth.

"Aha," he said suddenly when I had retired to my wall again and was once more trying to be invisible.

I straightened up. "You have found something?"

"A very small something but if we look at his eyes we - might - find - that.... Yes. Here, see," he pointed to Quimper's eyes. "The reddening around the eye socket, the little broken veins."

"He was a man over forty. Does that not simply tell us he was old and his body was aging?"

Johannes smiled "I will make a doctor of you yet, young man. No, in this case I think we might use the word the Latins used for it; petechia. A rupture of the blood lines caused this little lumpiness. The actual eyes too have burst blood vessels, giving them a red appearance in the whites. It was not so in life, I think. There is blood too in the nostrils. His nose had bled a little."

He lifted Quimper's upper lip. "See here too, how the teeth have bruised the flesh of the inner lip? He has few upper front teeth and those he had left have been pushed quite hard against the lip. The skin too around the nose and mouth, is very white."

"And that means?" I asked...but I had it already in my mouth.

"Suffocation," we both said together.

I swallowed down bile.

"Though not with the hand, surely there would be prints on the face, bruising - no?"

Johannes nodded "Well done" he smiled. " But with a pillow...? He left the sentence hanging.

He looked around. Save the straw filled pillow upon which Quimper lay his head, there was only one other in the room. A coarse red linen cushion, quite well stuffed with feathers, which I had given Quimper upon which to rest his weary knees, whilst praying on his prie dieu. It was on the stool upon which the Benedict had rested his backside moments ago.

I picked it up. "This?" I looked round."It fits the platform of the prie dieu but not this smaller stool. See how it hung over the edge."

He took the cushion from me then, turned it in his hand. "A small piece of evidence on here, a little blood perhaps from his nose; yes, it could be."

He stooped and replaced it on the stool. "As I said, too large. It did not belong there.

Our murderer did not replace it where he found it," I reiterated.

* * *

Later back in my office, over a pint of watered wine, we discussed our findings again.

"But how? Quimper was not a very old man, he would struggle, thrash about. He might even manage to scratch his opponent. Something to defend himself," I said.

"The bruises on the arms.... I think he was held down, but yes, to kill a man so takes a full two minutes or more."

There was a silence. "He knew his killer. Allowed him freedoms. Perhaps he was asleep...yes, that's it!"

Johannes coughed a strange little cough of recognition, as if the wine went down the wrong way. "I think I have it. Please, Aumary, might we try an experiment?"

"Surely" I said.

"Lie here on your daybed, as Quimper was lying but with your arms to the side. Now, do not be afraid and I will try not hurt you as I kneel. I shall not press hard."

Johannes climbed on top of me, parted the robes of his cotte and knelt, as gently as he was able for he was not a small man, on my upper arms, pinning them to my body and to the bed. He mimed the action of pushing the pillow onto my nose. I thrashed about as Quimper must have done. I was a strong, young, fit man, one who exercised every day with sword and buckler, so I just might have been able to extricate myself and do some damage to my attacker. Quimper was a scholar, thin and small with little physical strength and a man over forty.

Just as Johannes was seriously getting into his play acting, my wife opened the door.

I was told afterwards, for I could not see, that her face went white but I did hear her scream "NO!"

Chapter Six

I was told later that my doughty wife was looking for something with which to hit the doctor on the head. As it is, in the scramble of us getting from the day bed in a tangle of limbs and long tunics, she began to belabour him over the head with her fists.

"Wife!... Stop that," I remember crying. "He isn't killing me!"

I fell on the floor.

Later, when we were all three in the solar and sitting comfortably, we told Cecily the tale of finding Quimper and of how we were trying to ascertain how he had been killed by acting it out.

Now we had to turn our minds to when he had last been seen and by whom. Had anyone gone to his room after his return from Marlborough? Had anyone seen him? He was, as I've said before, the sort of man who goes unnoticed. His clothes were good but not especially recognisable. Browns, murky old greens, dark greys. He would blend in anywhere. He wore a cap always, a Phrygian cap of dark brown, (that is with a small knop which hangs over and two ear flaps tied under the chin) and his greying brown hair was allowed to flow over his shoulders from the rear of it. He wore no distinguishing jewellery and had no particular habits which would be noticed, save his quiet, self-deprecating vanishing into the background.

"I saw him return at, it must have been some time after nones, so about the tenth hour of the day" said Cecily. "I was looking from the window when suckling Hawise and there he was, coming through the gate."

"He put down his staff and scrip, it was there in the room with him," I said. "Laid tidily. Do we think then, that he went directly to his room?"

"It was his custom to find ale and take it with him to drink and to rest after walk-ing home," said Cecily. "The kitchen staff will say if he was seen there and when. Before I was churched I used to sit long and often at the window just looking out. Many times he went to the kitchen first then took a pot to his room."

She meant that for a while after the birth of her child, a woman was confined to her room. The ceremony of churching then allowed her to move freely again. In Cecily's case the ritual had only been performed a few days ago and she had been beginning to be very bored, not being allowed to do much except stare out of the casement.

"I found him three hours later at about vespers, so we have a small hole of time through which our murderer could creep to do the deed," I said

"The state of the body will help tell us when he begins to stiffen," added Johan-nes, "for a corpse stiffens at two to six hours after death and it begins with the neck and jaw. I'll take a look in another moment. He wasn't stiffening when we examined him."

We needed to find out who had been in his room or who had been seen near his sleeping place, if anyone. How would we go about ascertaining that?

I groaned. "Oh no, I have to send yet again for the coroner,"

I groaned again. "And damn it, inform the sheriff!"

***

Johannes and I decided that there was daylight enough to return to Quimper's room and have one last look, for we might have missed something vital. It would be as well for Johannes to look at the body again too.

This time we took a small scrap of paper and a piece of charcoal to scribble down anything which might seem important.

I lit the only candle in Quimper's room and fished another from my pocket, lighting it and fixing it with wax to the deal table top, so that we might have more light by which to examine things.

It was then that my eye strayed to the parchment scattered on the table. I picked one up. A letter. There too was his ale pot, drained dry.

Cecily's eyes had moved to the body on the bed, now decently covered with a blanket. She crossed herself.

"The poor wretch. He was such a pleasant man. Never any trouble. Nothing was too bothersome to him, always so kind. Why would anyone want to do this to him?"

"I have a feeling that this death is about money and theft and keeping the identity of our pilferer a secret," I said. "I wonder if Quimper knew who had stolen from him? Perhaps if he knew, he was going to tell me. It was bad luck for him that the killer overheard him this morning."

A thought flitted across my mind and I almost lost it, just managing to grab it as Cecily answered me and I rode over her voice with,

"Who could have heard the two of us in the courtyard this morning early? There was no one else actually in the yard."

I walked outside and looked at my newly rebuilt south range of buildings.

I pointed. "Here, Hal and his men at arms, Stephen and Peter, when they are here. Next a store room, then Quimper's, then a spare room for guests, then on the end Robert's room." I rubbed my chin, "Not a lot to work with there."

"No, no one in the yard" said Johannes following us out. "But in these rooms? And have you never noticed how echoing the place is, all stone and hard surfaces, few trees and places to absorb the sound? Even the birds seem louder here than elsewhere."

I thought of the little sparrows in my tree and how noisy they had been the day Hawise had been born.

"Easy to hear us then," I said, sighing in frustration.

We walked back into the little room of death.

Again I took up a parchment from Quimper's table.

It was the strangest thing I have ever seen written down.

I stared at the writing. It can be very difficult to know whose hand writes what, for unless, like me, you have been taught to write as an individual, all write in the same way and most people get a clerk to write for them, because they cannot read or write at all themselves.

There is a format; a pattern to a clerk's hand and it's hard to know what had been written by whom.

On this page was a series of squiggles and letters which were no words at all. Johannes came up behind me and peered at the parchment in my hand.

"What have you there?" He picked up another. His brow furrowed. "A foreign language?"

"No" said a voice from the doorway, "I think you'll find it's a code. He was very fond of codes."

Robert stepped from the evening brightness of the sunny yard into our dim interior.

***

We took all the parchments back to the hall, laid out one of the trestles and sat round it with the papers in some sort of order on top. There were quite a few.

"So, let us take out the true letters from these codes of yours, Robert and each read one, so that we know what we are dealing with."

Robert hesitated. "Isn't that prying into the affairs of a good man? Should we be poking into his life like this? It doesn't seem right to read a man's private papers when he can't gainsay you."

Cecily's eyebrow went up at that.

"Robert" she said gently, "that good man has been unlawfully killed. If we can find anything, anything at all which helps us find his killer, we should read it and make it public."

I smiled. I told you my wife was very clever.

"Oh...oh..oh! Hand me...hand me the little vial there, the one with the wax stopper.

"Good. I'll take a sip. It's for my pounding heart you know. Sometimes when I think of things, how things turned out, what happened, I get upset and my heart pounds. It'll be back to normal in a breath. Maybe I'll take a little rest....yes..rest... that's enough for now. I'll just close my eyes for a few heartbeats. You go and...um... whatever it is you clerks do...go and pumice some parchment or something."

***

"Oh you're back. I've been waiting. Where did you go to? I only said a short while. What's that? TWO HOURS...don't be ridiculous boy, I can't have been sleeping for two hours. Really? Humph.

"Now get your pen out again."

We set to in the fading evening light and sorted all the parchments, those that were dated into date order. There were letters from other clerks, presumably friends he had known before he came to Durley, telling of their lives in various parts of the country. From Oxford, there were a few. There were some drafts of letters which Master Quimper himself had penned. These were mostly chit-chat which he had been asked to write down for those on the manor who could not write themselves. Amongst them there was the beginnings of a letter to Agnes' sister in Hungerford and one short missive from my head groom to a tradesman in Marlborough, a Master Saddler detailing the needs for various leather works for the manor. None was very revealing. Our Master Quimper had been an industrious and enterprising man, writing letters for our lesser manor folk and being paid pence each time. These bits no doubt ,he had kept in order to scrape the words clean and re-use. Enterprising, industrious and frugal, was our Quimper.

Once we had dispensed with these, we turned our minds to the codes which Robert had identified. One indeed was in Robert's own hand.

He laughed. "He used to get me to play with these when I was younger. He'd give me the code and set me a text and I would have to render it secret in such a timespan as he gave me." He shook his head sadly. "He'd never berate me if I got it wrong or if I was too tardy."

Then apparently, Master Quimper would make him do it the other way round. Give him a coded piece to decipher. He had said it was good for a developing brain to play about so. To manipulate facts which were no facts at all, inside the head.

Robert looked up from his parchment.

"I did enjoy it."

I remember pulling my mouth into a sort of grimace. "How will we know what is written here if we don't have the coded piece? Do we have the cipher here on the table?"

Robert rummaged. No, we did not.

"But there are other papers I think, in Master Quimper's chest." He ran towards the door and stopped before opening it.

He walked back.

"Do we have the key? He always locked it."

I had removed that small item from the room; it had been in the scrip Quimper had set on the side and had locked it behind me. I threw him both the key to the chest and to the room.

He was soon back with an armful of more parchments and another larger scrip made of very hard leather.

These papers all proved to be Latin texts of various kinds. Some on medicine and herb lore, some recipes,(I had not thought our Quimper a gourmand). Some histo-ries, some fables, a few on nature (I remember seeing Pliny) and a couple of old poems, all in his own hand.

In the scrip we found more of the strangely ciphered letters, except these were tiny and filled with a crabbed writing, if I can call it that and were so closely spaced that it was difficult to see where one part ended and another began.

Cecily picked up one of the tiny letters. It rolled up in her fingers. She picked up another.

This too rolled.

The whole bunch that had been in the scrip had been flattened to fill the pouch but as soon as they were freed from the scrip and each other, every one curled up again.

"They have been rolled and inserted into something" she said. "Why would that be?"

"Messages," said Johannes. "Secret messages."

Chapter Seven

We all stared at him. "Master Quimper? Sending secret messages? It's not to be believed." whispered Cecily.

We searched the scrip for the master cipher, the one which would tell us how to decode the letter. It wasn't there.

"Perhaps it was in his head" I grunted, "he had a prodigious memory."

Robert was shaking his head. "It will be there somewhere. But.....I just might be able to remember how to do it, well a little of it anyway. I can remember some of it. For example, in our language - sorry, in English, the most common letters are e and o so you look for repetitions of symbols which might represent those in a passage. Then you find the letters less common, say s or r and so on. You can fill in the gaps. I say English because the English used ciphering a lot. They were very fond of riddles."

"And you were doing this as a child?" I asked, rather amazed at my young brother.

"Oh yes, though of course, most of it was in our own Norman French or Latin."

I pushed a scraped piece of parchment towards him and the slip of charcoal I had taken into Quimper's room.

"You have a go. I'm going back into his room to look again."

I unlocked the door once more and looked round. I went to the small chest and unlocked it. Robert had emptied it of parchments but there were still things in it. Another cap, a tiny breviary, a vial of something sticky. I unstoppered and smelled it. It smelled like honey. There was a spare shirt folded tidily and a pair of indoor slippers.

There were two ink pots, several pieces of charcoal wrapped in a linen cloth and a pretty coloured stone, which, when I turned it over had the pattern of a sea shell in it. Nothing else.

I picked up the breviary. It was decorated but not too expensively so. Still, it must have cost him a mark or two. I dropped the book into the bottom of the chest. It sounded with a hollow thud.

I took everything out again and laid them by me on the flagged floor. I turned the chest on its side and stared at the bottom. It was quite heavy I noticed, and I swore something in the empty space moved but there was nothing to see.

However when I peered in again, I noticed that it was not as deep as it had seemed when looked at from the side. I put my arm into the chest, fingertips down and measured with my arm the depth of it. Then I used that same measure to gauge the outside. The inside fell short by almost half a hand's length. I prodded and I poked. I shook it. Most certainly there was something in it. I looked for a mechanism which might open it. I rose to my feet and in frustration, I kicked the rim which ran round the bottom.

The bottom of the inside sprang open. Inside were four bags of coarse brown linen.

I opened one. There were many coins in it but not a fortune; mostly small coins, parts of silver pennies. I opened another and another. The last one proved different. Here was quite a sum. There were also, at the very bottom, padding out the chest so as to keep the rest of the coins from chattering, a number of empty bags.

I replaced them all. This was Master Quimper's money, some of which he had said, was missing. The empty bags no doubt.

I ruffled my hair as I tried to make sense of it all. My hair was wiry and black and I did have a problem taming it. I kept it short for that reason and for fashion; a good Norman haircut was what my wife told me she gave me but not cut too short at the back. Now I pummeled and pulled it about in frustration. My brother Robert was lucky with his lustrous blond hair, falling in waves to his shoulder. So much more easy to manage.

"Yes....yes...I know...chuckle if you like. I am bald now..but then I had a good head of hair. You just wait my lad, till yer teeth fall out and the hair of your head comes out in clumps. I'll be laughing at you from heaven, then I will."

I picked up the little book again and thumbed through it. A piece of parchment fell out. Just a page marker. An idea came to me.

I strode to the bookshelf. Books are expensive but still, Master Quimper had five. I tried the pages of all five and the last book, a herbal, revealed what we sought. In the page between Buckthorn and Burdock, I found the cipher.

Brandishing it gleefully I strode up the steps and into the hall.

"Got it!"

They all looked up at me then. Their faces were blank, like they had all been thinking their own thoughts for the moment before I entered. No one spoke.

Then, "Good," said Johannes seriously. "Now we shall know for sure."

Sure of what I thought?

Cecily stood. "I must go and feed Hawise." I could hear my daughter bawling up-stairs in the back room.

"But I'll be back. I want to know." She made off up the stairs but turned with a sad expression at the very top, then disappeared though the door.

Robert, leaning back on the chair, turned a scrap of parchment to me.

I read the squiggles and letters. And underneath in Robert's hand what looked like,

A-t-ur -i-- -e -in-

"It says, I think," he whispered as he turned it and filled in the gaps with his charcoal and slid it back to me over the table top.

"Arthur will be King."

***

It was going to be a long job to decipher the little rolled letters so we felt that a rest from them was necessary. I asked Robert to do one more thing before we parted and went our ways, Johannes to his horse and the road home, Robert to his room and me to the solar with Cecily and my children.

The tiniest word, I assumed it to be a signature, filled the bottom of the little letters, almost falling off the end of the page. It was the same series of letters in each missive.

"Can you tell me what this says?"

Robert took the cipher from me and ran his finger down the columns of symbols.

"The first is E..but it has a dot over it so we know it's a capital letter. The sec-ond...yes, d, the last is also d. The middle letters are m and u and this one here must be an n..." He checked his guess against the main cipher. Indeed it was.

Edmund.

Robert looked up at me, "His brother was called Edmund, I recall."

"That is an English name" I said, not Norman."

"True, but names are so mixed up now. Piers was an Englishman but his name was French. Hal of Potterne is of Viking descent but his name is English..." he tailed off, then added

"His brother lives in Falaise, I remember, in Normandy, but both of them come from Brittany, from Quimper."

I thought hard.

"So his loyalties perhaps, are...were... not to John, as ours are, they are to Geoffrey's son Arthur. Light dawned.

***

I had arranged to go the next day to the castle at Marlborough and sort some ad-ministrative problems which had arisen in the sheriff's and the constable's absence. I persuaded Johannes to stay the night and ride with me the next morn-ing at dawn. He gratefully accepted.

I had also decided on a meeting in the town next day with the two people who might be able to throw some light onto the glove which had almost killed my brother or me.

We rode out in the slight chill of a summer morning, just as dawn was peek-ing over the trees towards Hungerford and gained the town before the church bell was ringing for Tierce. We didn't tarry. I for one had much to do. We parted on the road, this remarkable doctor and I and rode quickly down the main street; I would return to it soon, on my way home to Durley later that afternoon.

I broke my fast in the castle hall at Marlborough, called the King's Hall with its lovely rose window lighting up with the new day's sunshine. At the same time I peered at some documents and signed and sealed those I was able. Then not my favourite job: I oversaw the incarceration of two felons in the castle keep.

Once I had seen to my duties, I rode out again over the moat and through the eastern gate, with its tower, past the little bothies which were growing up around the nearer walls nowadays and into Marlborough town again.

My first port of call was the glover whose name, I had been told, was Wulf Hemmings. His was the first shop I came to, tucked in the yard opposite the town slaughter yard, for at that time there were only two glovemakers in the town. I showed him the hawking glove. Was it his work, or could he tell me who might have made it?"

"Bless me my lord" he laughed, "I don' make such fancy stuffs. My works are much more ordinary though I'll say, 'tis a nice piece. Wish I 'ad made it."

Before I could ask, he said "Try 'ol fancy pants, beggin' yer pardon m'lord, Master Glover, Henry," and he told me where I could find the man; a house on the London road, just as the hill started to rise.

It was a fine house and I scratched on the door with a little more confidence in my scratch than that with which I had approached the last glover. Surely here was our maker.

Master Henry Glover was a portly man who was obviously doing well for himself, for he dressed himself and his wife at the pinnacle of fashion and naturally kept a good table. His belly and her chins attested to it.

He was fussy and welcoming and offered me a good wine, which he said was imported from France, through his cousin.

I took out the glove.

His eyes lit up.

"Oh aye....I remember this one, perhaps a month back, sir." He handled it like it was a baby in his care, stroking the leather and fingering the beads carefully.

"Yes, I sold it. Though a course, I don't make 'em like that."

I was a little bemused and said so.

He spoke to me then as though I was suddenly an inattentive child.

"I make gloves and I make' em to fit hands. I make fine gloves, very fine with decorations and the like but this - this I bought to sell on, ready made, in London when I was there last year."

"So you bought this and sold it on. To whom, if I might ask?"

He drew a big book to him and ran a finger down the columns of writing. To me upside down, they all looked as complicated as Quimper's codes.

"A lady. She called herself Avice of Bristol, just passing through on her way home. She wanted it, she said, for her husband's name day."

A woman?

"What did she look, like this woman - how old was she?"

A beatific smile came over the little glover.

"Oh she was fair. About er, eighteen perhaps, skin like peaches, eyes as brown as conkers. There was a wisp of gold hair peeking from her veil though, in truth she went quite decently covered as a married woman should. Lucky's the man who gets the...."

Mistress Glover had coughed, just once and was frowning.

"Ah well...she was, from what I could see, quite beautiful, I'd say. Small, dainty and well made."

Mistress Glover coughed again.

"Where did she go after she bought it? Did you see?"

"Not, for sure; she paid cash and ran off clutching the bag to her very fine bosom saying her husband would be so pleased; he'd die of surprise when he opened it."

He chuckled. "Lucky b......"

Mistress Glover cleared her throat noisily.

Indeed he would, I thought, as I mounted my horse and turned him towards the main road again. Die of surprise. Pah!

And the woman had paid cash. Well, well.

Who was our mystery woman? I could think of no one who met that description on the manor. My mind ranged over my neighbours as I rode home. I came home by the Newbury Road this time and approached the manor from the northwest, down the little track which wiggled around the trees of the forest.

I sat in my little office, drew a sharpened charcoal stick and a scrap of birch bark paper to me and began to write down the names of local women of some standing and with money to spend.

Rosamund, the wife of Peter Faith. Fat and over forty and not all that wealthy.

My mother in law Evisa...No, no don't be ridiculous.

Mabel, the castle victualler's wife. Nah, she's auburn haired.

Maud the goldsmith's wife. Nah, she's tall and willowy and walks with a stick.

Felicity Puthall, the only daughter of one of the wealthiest wool merchants in the town. A possibility. Pretty but not beautiful. Nah. She'd never be allowed to go out without company, another female member of the household. Our lady was alone.

Nick's wife...the town miller. No that was just plain silly.

Matilda of Chisbury, wealthy widow. Oh no..she died last year.

And so it went on. Eventually after considering dozens of names, I drew a blank.

There were plenty of personable young ladies in the area and even some who might be deemed beautiful, but none had the money or they weren't blond with brown eyes.

I knuckled my tired eyes. Passing through she may have been, on her way to Bristol, but she stopped off here, calmly walked into my hall, laid the parcel on the table and rode off again.

And no one saw her? Never!

***

That season I was very busy. For one thing, in early summer we had an invitation. We were called to the wedding on the 24th August of John and his new paramour Isabelle, the daughter of Count Aymer of Angoulême. England would have a new queen.

I thought long and hard about refusing the invitation, citing pressure of work and the distance. Bordeaux was a very long way. However, Robert and I had managed to decipher quite a few of the little letters which we had found in Quimper's possession and what we discovered made us think that I should take our news and evidence personally to the King.

***

One day in mid May, when the cow parsley was beginning to show in the fields and the pretty red campions were coming out on the banks of the leafy lanes of the forest, a pigeon landed in our barn. 'Twas a pretty creature with brown on the wings and an otherwise quite white body and head. To its leg was fastened a small tube.

Like many others, we kept birds on the manor, for eggs and meat and I'd had small stone cells built into the wall at the corner of the south and east walls for thje birds to roost and breed. This resembled a little turreted tower with a chequer-board of holes covered by a stone hood with a plinth, on which the birds could land and I must say, it was a most pleasing arrangement to look at. I loved the sound of the cooing (though not everyone did) and in quiet moments I could look up at the end of the wall and watch as the birds flew in and out and wheeled around the sky in circles. I love birds of all kinds, both to listen to and watch and on my plate.

That day, as I had instructed him to do, Hamon, the man who amongst other things, now looked after the birds since the death of Master Quimper, came to me with the tube and the message.

Robert and I deciphered it. It was a series of names. Important names.

My dear Cecily had never been out of her native England before and naturally approached the journey with not a little trepidation. It was a trip of some six hundred and fifty miles and then back again. There was so much to organise, not least to leave the manor in the capable hands of Robert and our staff and to ensure that the castle at Marlborough was ready for an absence of some weeks of its under-castellan.

I shan't bore you with the details of our trip. It was like any other. We made good time; we were held up. We found decent places to stay, some with friends on the way, who like us were going to the celebrations; others who were not. Some at welcoming abbeys and inns and we found some awful ones.

We had our fair share of fleas, bed bugs and poor food, rain, fog and thunder.

Our boat, when we eventually gained it, was a serviceable and roomy vessel, built to carry wine, for we were going as extras on a ship bound for Bordeaux where it would take on sweet whites and doughty reds for the English market.

The seas were more kind than evil and we hugged the coast along the western side of France, travelling South and then making our way slowly across country, to Bordeaux. We saw no sign of any unrest or conflict.

We were not the most elevated of John's guests and so had to find our own ac-commodations in the town. That proved more difficult than we had anticipated until a chance mention of the fact that my great uncle Hervis de Belvoir, the famous crusader, had stayed in the place a while back, gave us an entrance to a fairly good room and stabling for our servants. We learned later that an unpleasant clergy-man and his entourage had been evicted for us. I wondered if it was more to do with the winsome smile my wife gave the landlord than our money or connections.

One royal occasion is much like another. There were many fanfares of trumpets, waving of flags, cheering and singing. Food was plentiful at the feast (we were quite low down in the pecking order and so sat quite a way from the royal couple who looked splendid and very happy) John obviously adored his twelve year old bride....

"Yes, you heard me correctly, young man, TWELVE. Write it down."

There had been some opposition to the marriage. (John had had to dissolve his marriage to his previous wife because of consanguinity - closeness of blood; she was his cousin.)

The age of the bride was considered obscene by some, and it was thought by many that John had married purely for lust. If they thought that, they didn't know the King. He was smitten, it was true, but who could not be by that intelligent, elegant, beautiful and gracious lady...well...girl at first; she grew to that later, with her limpid blue eyes, her perfectly oval face and a waist you could span with two hands. John was a political creature and everything he did, he did for a purpose. It didn't always work to his advantage, it's true but he knew what he was doing, I think, at the moment he married Isabelle D'Angoulême. Of course, it's the way of gossips to prefer spicy conjecture over the complexities of politics but John realised that if he did not, he would be at the mercy of the King of France and his minions.

"Are you yawning? I can see this is rather boring for you, but it's actually important and I want people to know, that what is said about John is not all true. This is my history so I will have it written as I want it. Write on. What? It's late is it? Oh all right. I cannot always tell what time it is, stuck here in my bed. A bit more then we shall rest."

Isabelle had been betrothed to a rather repulsive man called Hugh le Brun. John could not afford for him to annex his own lands to those of Isabelle's father Aymer, for if he did, the lordship of Lusignan and the counties of La Marche, in France would be joined with Angoulême. A huge swathe of France would be taken up and a lordship almost as big as Normandy would be created. The whole balance of power in Aquitaine (John's mother's lands and by inheritance, his too), would be threatened. If John submitted to the French king for his holdings in France and put himself under his protection, Aquitaine would be cut in half and John's chances of keeping hold of it, would be negligible.

For John to take Isabelle to wife was perhaps the wiliest move at the time. Natu-rally this would make an enemy of Hugh le Brun, Count of Lusignan. So be it. In hindsight, it was not such a wise move. However at the time, he bound many good men to him by this marriage.

Isabelle was one of those women who seemed more than the sum of her years. She managed John, as a good nurse-maid does a recalcitrant child, for the rest of their life together and yes, I think they had a relatively happy marriage, as happy as a life lived within a public kingship and queenship could be. There is no doubt he was a volatile man but somehow she was a soothing power and had the knack of calming and placating him. However, he always kept her on a tight rein so that she might not meddle in his politics.

That's not to say it was always a smooth passage. She tolerated his infidelities. He turned a blind eye, so it's said, once an heir was secured, to her series of lovers. She had as much a temper as he at times but, in all they were well suited and they did grow to care about each other.

"I must say though Paul that once John was dead, not one word was said about him by that lady and off she went to marry...well can you guess...? Yes, Hugh of Lusignan."

The chroniclers have had a wonderful time inventing names for this unfortunate queen. They called her the modern Messalina; they dubbed her a siren. Not really fair. Chroniclers are all old men; celibate crusty old men; they are bound to get hot under the collar about a nubile young girl's marriage to a much older man.

It is said that John did not immediately begin to cohabit with his new queen but waited a few years until she was fully a woman. It was certainly the case that the queen never fell pregnant in those early years, so perhaps it's true.

It was not unusual for an older man to marry a much younger girl. The age of consent was after all, twelve for a girl. He only did what many before him had done and continued to do after his death but as I say, poor John had a raw deal from those who wrote the records.

Petit, John's valet, managed to get me in at last to see John. I had been turned away for three days by this person and that but Petit remembered me from John's visits to Marlborough and beckoned me forward late one day when I was about to retire for the night to my inn down in the town.

I had asked if we might be alone for I was worried that anything I had to say might be misinterpreted by anyone who didn't know me well.

As it was, William Longsword, (Longspee as he was known), Earl of Salisbury and John's half-brother, was with him. Longspee was the son of Ida de Tosny, Henry the Second's mistress. These two brothers were very close, perhaps closer than the full brothers Henry, Geoffrey and Richard had ever been to John. William was all a chivalrous knight should be; tall, blond, handsome, broad shouldered and a fearsome soldier. I liked him and knew him for he was a Wiltshire man.

I bowed low, "Sire."

John rose from his game of chess and came to give me the kiss of peace on both cheeks. We embraced.

"Aumary."

"You will remember Aumary, Will, from our Forest of Savernake. Damn fine hunting we have had there, eh?"

"We have indeed sire," and Longspee nodded to me. I reciprocated. "And will again no doubt."

I was not there to reminisce nor to ask favours so I launched straight away into my tale of the death of Quimper and the little notes, what we had found and how we had deciphered the messages. John listened patiently, taking the tiny missives in his well-manicured fingers and turning them to the light of a tenfold of candles burning in wall sconces and on elaborate candle sticks dotted around the small chamber.

He gestured for me to sit and I fished from my scrip the list of little letters and their dates. Then, from the breast of my cotte, I produced a lengthier document. This was the translation of each letter which Robert and I had made, using Quimper's cipher. Then I sat and waited.

John took it and read a little of it in silence.

He passed it to his brother and then stared at the floor.

I broke the silence with "Sire, was this known to you? Am I telling you something you already know?" Then I took a deep breath for what I was about to ask might well irk the king, "Did you perhaps have Quimper killed to curtail this to-ing and fro-ing of information? I think I need to know, for my own peace of mind."

John looked up then. "Is that what you think of your king, Aumary? That we would kill a man, a non-fighting man, for choosing the wrong side?"

I was quite taken aback by this. "Sire, this is treachery. Surely...."

"The man was a Breton, it seems. Naturally his allegiance is to Arthur."

"He lived many years in my demense, sire, in your land."

"He swore no oath to me."

"Then what I bring you is of no use to you?"

"On the contrary, Aumary, the names contained therein" and he pointed to the paper which now dangled from Longspee's fingers, "will prove very useful."

He stood and I stood also, as is customary. He waved me down, went to the buffet table at the side and poured three cups of wine. I noticed they were quite plain and without decoration. He gave one to Longspee, another to me and sipped his own.

"Let us see what we have." He put down his cup. A large ruby glinted on his finger in the torchlight and a glittering pendant shone on his breast.

"One half of this network is now dead. The other cannot use that route again to gather information. It seems we have had a traitor, with whom your man dallied. The man is English or Norman and is perhaps in Marlborough castle or town. Quimper, you say he was called. Do we remember him right, Aumary, a small pinched man with a nervous manner, we met, we think some time we visited you, in hall at meat?"

I nodded, amazed that John had noticed him, when so many did not but then John was ever one for the small man, the ordinary man.

"Ah yes. A good listener we think." He smiled "Well the poor man is dead. No, not by our order, to answer you. We did not know of this. We know that we have a problem with that little corner of this country. Brittany is a thorn in our side, certainly. My nephew Arthur is yet a boy but there are," and he pointed to my document which Longspee had now laid on the table, "disaffected men who would use him against us, who would hand our lands piecemeal to Philip of France and then blink not at removing Arthur if it suited them." He steepled his hands before his lips. The ruby glinted again.

"Philip of France wants to remove us; there is no doubt. And now, we know for certain that he wishes to replace us with our nephew, if we didn't know it before. Philip hates me and wants my head." He sighed.

"We shall think on it. We have the names of those disaffected men for which we thank you greatly. Some are already known to us as enemies, Fitzwalter, Eustace de Vesci, Hugh de Lusignan," John passed his hand over his eyes.

"Some of the men mentioned in your letters, it hurts me to say it, we counted as friends and others we...shall we say, we would not turn our backs to them, were we alone in a room." I saw Longspee smile at that.

There was another little silence. Then John, jovial John, wine warmed John, slapped his knees and stood. "Now if my memory serves me rightly, you sir, are a very good player of backgammon. What say you we play a game or two before we retire?"

We played well beyond midnight. I lost only once and John did not scowl and took it well. However I won no money from him. He had none.

"*Off you go now and get your beauty sleep Paul. That is your name isn't it? Paul? I'll lie here and wait for them to come and give me my supper. Be here tomor-row after the Prime bell is rung and before Terce.*"

***

"*Ah yes, you're back. Did you sleep well? Good. I did not, so I may be a bit tetchy today. Just to warn you. I may not be my usual sweet self. And I have something to dictate today which I would rather not write about...but it has to be. I hope I do not weep. So.*"

Before we returned home, just as we were leaving, in fact I had all but turned my horse's head to move out of the inn courtyard, a servant in royal livery came run-ning in through the gateway.

He touched my stirrup.

Sir, my Lord Belvoir?"

I looked down. The man was handing me a purse. I took it, puzzled. "From our lord the King sir," he said and bowed. I opened the little bag and peered in, fearful to show too many eyes what was in it. One cannot be too careful. We were about to enter the open road; folk will ambush you for your horse or your cloak, let alone a purse full of jewels. At the bottom I spied some coins. I fished them out. Exactly the amount John owed me from our backgammon games.

I laughed out loud then. He must have borrowed the sum from Longspee.

The journey home was much the same as the journey out. Some good places, some not so good. When we were at last alone and in the safety of the cabin of our wine merchant's ship, I shook the contents of the bag out onto the table and Cecily and I examined our reward.

It was well known that John loved beautiful jewels. He wore many of them himself as many of the great lords did. Some he had sewn to his clothing and he wore rings, which were almost compulsory in a great man. It was said he was rarely seen without his favourite ruby pendant on his breast. He had, it is said, a fascinating collection of gems and jewellery of all kinds. Some had now found their way into our possession.

Cecily picked up an emerald which was as big as the nail on her little finger and grass green.

"I will have it set for you," I beamed. "It will be just right for your colouring."

She laughed then. "And when shall I wear it? I am the wife of a minor lord living in a small forest by a tiny town. I have no need of great adornments like these. I don't go to court. No, we must sell them and use the money for something."

How many other women would say such a thing, Hmmm?

***

We had been at home a matter of eight months when a mud bespattered royal messenger came clattering through our gatehouse and into the cobbles of the yard.

I received him, as was right and proper, in the hall and asked him to sit and rest and take food and drink.

"I am expected at the castle before nightfall, sir," said the poor man, "I must be away." And he vaulted up on his tired horse and was off again, leaving behind him a large woven fabric pannier, with the royal cipher embroidered on the side.

I was almost afraid to open it but I told myself that I had proved my fealty to my king, and had provided him with the names of several potential traitors. John and I had parted friends and there could be nothing sinister in the document contained therein.

Nevertheless my hand trembled as I removed it. It was large and it bore John's Great seal.

I read it out loud.

"Know Ye that we have granted and by this our Charter do confirm, to Aumary Belvoir such seisin of all the land and bailiwick of the Forest of Savernake as Geoffrey Belvoir his father had therein on the day that he died, with all its appurtenances to have and to hold to him and to his heirs, of Us and of our heirs by the service which the aforesaid Geoffrey and his ancestors were wont and bound to perform to our ancestors therefore."

There was more of the same - these charters are so wordy. I read on.

"Wherefore it is our will and we firmly enjoin, that the aforesaid Aumary and his heirs after him shall have and hold all the aforesaid land and bailiwick, well and peacably, freely and quietly, wholly and honourably; in wood and in plain, in roads and in paths, in meadows and pastures and in all places and things with all liberties and free customs pertaining to the said land as before stated."

It was dated April 28th 1200 and given at Porchester. I sat down heavily.

I realised that rather than be confirmed in the wardenship of the forest, as I had been the case when my father died (though truthfully it was almost a certainty), the succession would now go from father to son as a matter of absolute right. It was now written down for all time. My son Geoffrey's future was secured.

Cecily threw her head cloth over her face and wept with joy.

***

The days were drawing in but the weather remained fair right into October. The forest was a joy to ride through in that season, the bracken turning from its early yellow to rusty red, the docks a pink-brown and all around the leaves falling in a myriad of yellows and pinks and oranges.

The butterflies feasted late on the rotting blackberries and raspberries which grew wild along the rides and paths of the woods and as you rode along those orange and brown creatures would rise up in clouds above your head, to settle to feeding behind you again, once you were past.

On one such lovely day, Robert's horse came home alone, running into the gate, fully saddled. The grooms gathered round and checked him. It appeared that there was no fault with the horse but we had to assume that Robert had been thrown. My senior groom, Richard Marshall, said that he had been told by Robert that he was to ride over towards Easton, and he would be back before nightfall.

Four of us hastily saddled up and, taking a spare horse, rode out along the Pewsey road to search all the paths to and from Easton. Riding back, passing Big Belly Oak, we heard a distant yelling and followed the voice.

Luckily, we found him fairly soon, sitting by one of the many little natural ponds which littered the forest floor. Savernake was not a wet place being mostly on chalk with flint and thus free draining and with so many trees to drink the moisture but here and there small pools had developed where there was a clay capping. Robert's forehead was grazed and he was very disorientated having pitched from his horse and banged his head on a log, he said. He had zigzagged across the road several times and had not realised where he was. Finally he had stopped in his wanderings to bathe his wounds and to drink. He'd heard us approaching and yelled for all he was worth.

We picked Robert up and he groaned at the bruises and hurts. He told us he had rather aimlessly walked away from where he had been tossed from his horse and before we could heave him onto another mount to set out for home, he began to rail and curse as he tried to explain that the fall from his saddle had not been an accident. He'd been pitched from his horse, he said, by a rope strung between two trees.

"Chest height Aumary, across the short track, you know, the road that is the quickest one to get to Easton."

"Aye I know the one you mean. Shall we take a look? Do you feel up to showing us where?"

With one man leading Robert's remount should he begin to feel unwell as a result of his fall, the five of us slowly made our way back to the road and down for a while towards Burbage. Then we veered off at a track which left the main road at an angle and which eventually led to Wootton. A little way along we veered off again in a space between two ash trees, which was just a green track made by some badger or fox and which had been enlarged by men on horseback. This eventually widened out and became better for our horses to navigate. The width of the road encouraged faster riding here.

About four hundred paces in Robert shouted at our first rider, Richard.

"Here, be careful, do not do as I did and ride straight for it. God's Truth, had I been riding harder, I would no doubt have broken my neck."

We dismounted, my three companions and I and there, sure enough, was a sturdy rope stretched taut across the path between two trees. Sturdy, but hidden by the autumnal undergrowth around it and blending into the background.

There was no doubt it had been tied there for one purpose only.

"Who knew you were coming this way today?"

"It is no secret, brother," he cried throwing up his hands in exasperation. "I come this way often. I have been seeing Eunice, Fulke the verderers widow for some weeks now. It began when you went to France. Many know I ride here once or twice of a weekday, later in the day."

I looked at the men I had brought with me from Durley and raised my eyebrow in silent questioning.

"Aye m'lord" said Richard " 'Tis known by us all."

"Let us look at the rope."

It was a plain twisted hempen rope the sort one might use to drag logs, or to hang a man, or kill him swiftly, by sweeping him backwards from his speeding horse to break his neck.

We returned home speculating about the rope. It was the sort anyone might have purchased, made locally in Marlborough at the ropeworks and bought by dozens of people for their daily use. It would tell us nothing, except if any were missing from the stores of rope we had at the manor. We would look.

Later that evening, Robert's hurts tended carefully by Cecily, we sat over a pot of ale and turned the facts over again and again.

Why would anyone want to hurt Robert in particular? Was this meant for some other traveller on the green road? If he were injured, was the culprit lurking in the undergrowth ready to spring and finish the job but then realised it was the wrong man? Why had they not removed the rope? Was this a lawless man taking the op-portunity to rob a traveller? No rope was missing from our own store.

"I was out cold for a while," said my brother. "He could have just come and slit my throat and that would have been the end of it."

"Ah, but then it would have been an obvious felony and would not have looked like an accident."

"Yes, I suppose it had to look like an unfortunate mishap. It was meant as so, was it not?"

Robert fingered the lump on his forehead.

"Jesus, Aumary, what is going on? Are we being picked off one by one like some crows following the plough, by some enemy we know not of?"

"Are you sure that you have not angered anyone recently with your amours, Robert?" I quizzed lightly. "Is there an irate father or brother out for your blood, for deflowering their young daughter or sister? Perhaps you have a rival for Eunice's favours you are not aware of. She is a comely woman."

He smiled then, that disingenuous smile, which made all the women simper and coo.

"I listened to you, Aumary, my lovers are now all widows or married women with husbands away. I'm very careful."

"But still, there may be one who does not approve of your visits."

"If that is so, I cannot guess who. Besides, as I say, Eunice and I have been to-gether some weeks now. All other liaisons are old news. They know I have moved on. I let them down in a gentlemanly fashion, I hope."

I scratched my head, "Well, perhaps one of them has become jealous and has organised for you to be taught a lesson?"

He felt his head again. "Aye...a lesson indeed. Maybe. A final one perhaps?"

Chapter Eight

Geoffrey was now a sturdy lad of five, inquisitive, well made, plucky and talkative. Though he was still young we did allow him some freedoms on the manor, for he was not always to be tied to his mother's skirts. I had been teaching him his letters as had Father Benedict, along with his catechism and other important lessons which Geoffrey had to learn by rote. Soon we had to be thinking about his wider education and his squireship. I had begun sifting through those who might foster him and take him on as a page in their household; the first rung on the ladder to a knighthood, as I had been taught. His mother naturally did not want him to travel too far from her. Was there somewhere and someone fairly local who might serve our purpose? She didn't want him to have to go to the other end of the country, as some pages did. Finally we settled on Sir John Touchet of Ramsbury, a wealthy man with several sons and a large household.

Summer blew itself out in a series of winds which moved on into a mild autumn and the forest was a patchwork of reds and yellows, greens and browns.

We were given instructions to plant, replace and extend the boundaries of the Savernake.

Durley lay in the baily known as La Verme, a roughly triangular area which stretched from Marlborough in the north, Hungerford in the East and Burbage in the south. The King's Way ran along the northern edge of it from Bristol and car-ried on towards Newbury. We had instructions then to extend it beyond that road, further north towards Ramsbury. From the King's Road we would plant and plant until we reached the River Kennet. There we would stop. The forest was now bigger than at any time in its history and thirteen habitations lay on its perimeter.

Twenty or so small villages lay within its compass. It was a task to manage it all but I was ably aided by my right hand man, the capable John Brenthall as lieuten-ant; foresters and under foresters who were effectively the deer keepers; wood-wards who patrolled the forest, verderers, the judicial officers and the forester of the fee, who looked after the outlying bailiwicks.

We could not dig the ground beyond early November, so when the weather was too bad for outside work, we began threshing the grain we had taken in during August.

Walter the Reeve, the man responsible for the activities in the village of Durley and its occupants, had marked on his tally stick the exact amounts of sheaves each man had grown on his allotted strip of land in the autumn and to those set aside, the tithe for the priest Benedict.

Every man got what he had grown and carried home the sacks of grain accord-ingly. Ours were stored in our granary. Everyone was busy, even the manor cats. They stalked the barn floor or leapt up on the rafters chasing the mice that had thought the barn a good place for winter. Every man and woman had dried husks clinging to their clothing and there was much sneezing and coughing as the motes flew around in the wind from the open doors.

That day is engraved on my mind. November fourteenth 1200. The pictures of it are so vivid; the scenes so lifelike; as if they have been preserved in amber. I wish to God I could totally erase them. I have, I suppose, suppressed them to an extent. I have mentally wrapped the events as if in wool. Covered them like an oyster gradually covers with pearl, a piece of irritating grit in its shell, but I can with ease call them back, lying in my bed in the black of the night. We are talk-ing of events which happened over forty years ago but the memories can come unbidden into the mind, upon a sound, a smell, a sight.

"Oh it pains me so to speak of this but I must. No, Paul...don't write that down."

Everyone, as I have said was busy on the threshing floor, or they had other tasks to attend to. Cecily had been, I recollect, bottling in the still room with some of the girls, as there was a further amount of pickling to do. Robert was in the stable saddling his horse for he was about to go out to the town to meet with one of the wool merchants with whom we dealt. All others were about their work indoors for it was bitter out with a very cold wind. I think the courtyard must have been fairly deserted most of the time. Geoffrey had been in and out all morning with little jobs for his mother. Fetch more salt from the undercroft, get a pot of lard for the sealing of the necks of the flasks. Fold this, fill that, go tell your father his hot ale is ready, that sort of thing. He came in with a wide grin, with that last message.

"Uncle Rob's going now. He says I can have a new toy boat to sail on the stream. He has made me one he said, as a Twelfth Night gift. What about that Da?" he said. "We can have races up to the ford. You can use my old one and I can sail my new one."

"Aye, when the thaw comes, Geoff," I said. I laid down my pen and blew on my frozen fingers. It was cold in my office despite the heat of a brazier laid out with good charcoal from our own forest.

"And my old little boat...what was it you called her?"

"Poitou."

"Yes, Poitou shall thrash your new little boat...what shall you call her?"

He thought a moment, then jumping up and down called out "Galliard!"

"I see that you have been talking to old Hal again. Been telling you his castle stories has he?"

"He tells a very good story, Da, with lots of fighting and riding on horses and doing of sieges and stuff."

"You put under siege and then raise a siege, you do not do it, Geoffrey. Anyway Hal has never ridden into battle in his life. He was always a foot soldier. And he has never been to King Richard's Chateau Galliard."

However Geoffrey wasn't listening. He was fighting an imaginary Saracen in and out of my office door.

"Go on...off you go. Go back to Mam, I'll be along shortly."

He went then, with the same grin his mother had when she was being mischievous.

I carried on for a moment, then put down my pen, sanded my letter, folded it, lit the wax taper and dribbled the hot wax onto the join and stamped my seal ring into it. I waved it about a little for it to cool then gathered a few things, put them with the letter carefully into a pannier, laid it down and locked my chest. I left the office and locked the door.

I crossed the screens passage. I stopped. Noises came up from the threshing barn, through the open door. Laughter, voices, the sound of the folk in the barn beating the wheat with their sticks, the bark of a dog. I heard Robert's horse, out on the roadway (I knew it was he for he had slipped in just a moment ago to say he was off to Marlborough in a trice and was there anything I needed?) The hooves were striking the hard ground with a metallic clop. I heard a thud.

See how I remember the detail. The air was cold and thin. Sounds carried. Whenever I hear hooves now with that sort of frozen sound, in the thin winter air, I think of that day and what came after and I shudder.

Cecily smiled at me. "Here," she said. " You must be perished. There is nothing worse than sitting still on a cold day."

"I think I shall take a rug with me when I go back." I said. I wrapped my frozen fingers around the pewter cup. I made for our new fireplace which had a healthy log burning in it.

I had taken two sips when one of the stable lads came screaming up the outer stairs. Still screaming, he came first into the hall, somehow failed to see us and then went to the door of my study and battered on it. Then when he realised it was locked, he came back into the hall again, still screaming.

I met him half way down.

He was shivering and with more than just the cold.

He was crying, really crying, his eyes red and his nose running. He babbled and although I was his lord and master, he buried his head into my midriff and wailed.

I took hold of both his arms.

"Cedric. Compose yourself. Whatever is the matter?"

Before he could utter a word, Cecily (I still to this day don't know how she knew this was a tragedy meant for us; some mother's premonition perhaps), dashed to the door, slithered down the steps, for they were icy and dangerous and ran to-wards the gatehouse.

I was slower that Cecily, towing Cedric as I was. I had hardly got to the first step when I heard the most agonised scream I have ever heard in my life, then or since.

I looked down. There, almost at the opening of the gate, was a crumpled bundle in a blue tunic and over it what looked like a huge block of stone. I remember, then I let go of Cedric and slipped down the steps myself and across the icy paving slabs of the courtyard at a foolhardy run. I fell once and banged my knee but was up in a trice, unaware of the pain. I reached the gateway just as my wife slid down in a faint and I managed to catch her before she hit the cobbles. Then all was confusion and people and voices, screaming and shouting and someone, I don't know who, calling for Father Benedict. I remember looking out of the gateway. I was planted in the middle of the opening, holding my wife in my arms, searching the road for the just departed Robert, but there was no sign of him or his horse. Why I did this, I have no idea. Perhaps because I could not bear to look down. Down at the crumpled form of my only son. Five years of age. Geoffrey, under a huge block of stone, as long as my forearm and a hand's depth.

His head had been crushed beyond recognition. Nay, his head was not there for it was wholly under the stone. Blood and brain matter had splattered the roadway, the wall of the gateway, the side of the stone. The noise in my head was so loud, all other noise began to fade around me. All I could hear was a massive roar, deep and long.

They told me later that it was me who had bellowed like a wounded ox.

***

There could be no doubt that Geoffrey was dead. Benedict pushed past me. I handed my wife to Walter the reeve who had come up from the barn with several others. I leaned in to help move the stone but some were there before me and they gently pushed me away.

I cannot blame them. They knew how awful it was. They wanted to help. They did not want me to suffer any more than I had to. They were good people. One kind woman lifted the sacking she had put around her shoulders for warmth and laid it gently over Geoffrey's head. What passed for his head.

It was then that I noticed, partly under his body, partly poking out, a few bits of wood, painted yellow, with a little string attached and a crimped piece of fabric. I leaned to pull it out but another of my workers saw me and was there first. He handed it to me.

I am too lax, some would say, with my servants and workers, the men on my es-tate and sometimes, it allows them to take liberties they would not oth-erwise con-sider, in the way they address or treat me. Let it be known though, that I have never had any trouble with any of my staff or dependents, nor indeed my tied villeins. I don't see why I should be cruel or unkind, intolerant or heavy handed with them, if it is not necessary. I have no understanding of why they cannot be regarded as friends, more distant than good friends, true, but deserving of friendship none the less. Thus it was they treated me that day, with such kindness, such care, and Cecily too, for I think they valued me, do still, as a man, even though I am by God's will, it is said, far above them in station. Thus they felt no compunction manhandling me away and taking over the situation, leaving me feeling empty and foolish, but glad that I did not have to take my dead son, my little lad, my hope for the future, away to the mortuary.

I don't really recall much after that. I do remember I was shivering. Walter Reeve and Hal of Potterne took me to the hall and fed me brandywine. They took Cecily to her bed and for all I know did the same with her. I sat in the hall, staring and staring at the rushes, with the little ravaged boat in my hands, for so the yellow painted wood and string and material proved to be. Someone fetched my good winter cloak and put it round me. Someone else banked up the fire.

I heard a voice say that it might be a good idea to fetch the grandparents from Bedwyn. Had I been more in control, I might have said, "Oh God - not yet. Do not let them see their bright little lad so destroyed," for they loved Geoffrey greatly and would be so distraught.

Children die all the time. The priests tell us 'media vita in morte sumus - in the midst of life we are in death.' It does not help to know that God has taken them to him. That the innocents, for innocents they are (I cannot subscribe, no matter how I try, to the doctrine that they are full of the sin of Adam) will wait with God until the day of reckoning and that it is his will and we are not to try to fathom it. Heresy? Perhaps. It did not help me to be told my son, my lively, energetic, happy to be alive, affectionate, laughing little boy, was now beyond all earthly pain and human considerations. I was angry.

Tears would not come though I felt on the edge of it often. I was never alone that day. There was always someone with me and with Cecily, though we stayed for some reason apart until, in the afternoon Robert returned to the manor and riding in hot on his heels, Johannes of Salerno.

If I had no tears, Robert shed them copiously at the first airing of the news. He ran up to the chapel where Geoffrey had been taken after cleaning and was not seen for a good two hours, they tell me.

Johannes first saw to Cecily. The shock of finding her son battered by a falling stone, had sent her into one of her megrims and what we called her disappearing fits and she was for the moment, far from any help of normal mortals. Johannes prescribed a special brew and she took it automatically, drank, and then slept. In all this to-ing and fro-ing I had given no thought to my daughter Hawise but I was told later that she had been taken by one of the women up into the solar and out of harm's way. Later that evening Geoffrey's grandparents arrived. I had little to say to them. They went up to the chapel. They wept, aye both of them, as I knew they would and then went to be with their grieving daughter.

Johannes then came to me. The usual commiserations were given. He had, he said, looked in on our sweet Geoffrey, who lay in the chapel above my head and if it was any consolation, the boy had not suffered at all. The stone had done its work very quickly and cleanly. He would simply have blacked out and known no more.

I remember wondering if Johannes was saying these words to preserve us from a nastier truth but I discarded the thought as wicked, for I knew that the doctor was if nothing else an honest man and would not have lied to save us grief.

Robert came down, from the chapel a while after. White and pinched with cold he stood before the fire and railed at life, at God and at masons.

Then he saw the little boat which I had laid on the table. He came over, sat heavi-ly, picked it up and cried over it like a small child.

Once the tears were done, he sat back with a pint of wine and wiped his nose and eyes on his sleeve.

"I gave him the boat because I couldn't bear to see him so excited about it and not be able to have it. It was all made and ready. I was saving it for Christmas. He was just inside the gate with me and so happy about it. I turned once and he waved. Then I was out of sight."

"I looked for you," I said, "afterwards, but you'd gone."

"Aye."

Johannes poured himself a drink. "What happened, do we think?"

We thrashed it about then, for hours. The falling stone. Over and over without any real conclusion. Tomorrow we would go and look at the gatehouse from which it had fallen, we said.

Johannes stayed with us the night. All three of us wrapped in our cloaks dozed on chairs by the fire in the hall which we kept stoked with large logs. Occasionally one of us would wake and go out to piss in the freezing cold.

There was a moon, I recall and all I could see, when I went out nearer dawn, was the gate, now closed and barred, the frost riming everything and a darker patch in the middle of the gate space which was, I think, Geoffrey's blood. Someone had thought to move the stone to the side and out of the way but no one had thought to sluice away the blood.

I cried then, out there in the cold, in the light of the stars on frost, with the moon for company, leaning against the wall of the steps, until Johannes came to fetch me in.

The manor was so quiet that next day. The threshing continued but there was no singing, no laughter, no joking, and little talking.

I went up to see Cecily at last, early that morning.

She was asleep still and mercifully away from any grieving. I left her there, in our bed, with the little yellow boat and a kiss to her forehead.

***

A while into the day, I walked out of the gate, past the straggle of bothies outside the walls, past the poultry woman's home and out onto the track which led to the village centre. The forest crept up to the edge of the track here. I stood in the middle of the road and just stared about me. I don't know why I went out. Perhaps because the walls of the manor had become too much for me, too confining.

The forest beckoned. I ran into the scrub at the side of the road; just ran and ran.

Though called a forest, Savernake is not just a thing of trees. It is made up of small coppices, denser woods and small grassy meadows, scrub and small stream valleys. The trees are birch, oak, ash and some holly and it was one of these hollies which stopped my senseless running now by catching at my cloak. Were I not to tear it completely, I would have to cease. I was crying, I know I was and I am not ashamed to say it. I pulled my cloak free. I recall that I thought with a jolt that Cecily would have to mend the snag and how unkind I was to give her work like this at such a troubled time.

I turned back to the road. I know this forest as well as I know my own hand and I made my way back to the track by a slightly quicker route.

About one hundred paces out I came across trampled ground where a horse had rested and had nervously paddled the grasses and left a few droppings. The brush was broken and damaged as if the rider had turned the horse quickly in a circle. I leaned forward. I could see the gate from here. Had some felon hidden here and then leapt out on my unsuspecting son? I put it to the back of my mind and walked home.

Later, Johannes and I stood looking at the stone. It was one of the shaped coping stones which had been laid on the top of the gate parapet. Twice the size of my son's head.

There were at least fourteen or more along the inside edge of the gate house, newly rebuilt a couple of years ago. Fourteen more were fitted along the outside edge facing the road out.

It had landed flat onto Geoffrey from a height of about twenty feet. Why?

Johannes and I went through it yet again. As if we hadn't done enough examining of it last night, but here out in the open with the offending stone before us, it seemed the right thing to yet again go through the facts.

"It was very windy yesterday," I said

"It has been very blustery for a while now."

"Why then yesterday did it move?"

"Why this one and no other, why this one now, two years after it was laid and laid well by the masons?" asked Johannes.

He stooped and turned the stone over. I blanched at the underside of it for Geoffrey's hair and blood still clung to it. I looked away.

I saw the doctor's face crease.

"Let us go up and look where it came from."

We ascended by the steps which ran up between the stables and the gate-house. The first few stone steps were not covered, then we entered a dark passage of five or six steps, where the wall walk passed over our heads and then came again into the open of the heavens.

We climbed to the centre of the gatehouse and looked down. There was no doubt it had come from here.

Johannes rubbed his hand along the stone top, where the missing coping had been laid.

"It's hard to believe that the wind dislodged this stone. It's so heavy and..."

He broke off and leaned forward. The wind whipped his cloak away and he made a grab for it and wrapped it round him with two hands, stumbling a little into the wall. He frowned. Once the gust had passed, he let go again and moved his hand once more over the top stone of the wall. He moved to the side and pushed the coping stone to the left of the gap with all his might. It moved slightly. He went to the right and pushed. This too moved a little.

He looked up at me. Our eyes met and I, with two free hands for I had no cloak, put them around the stone next to the gap left by the one which had fallen and I lifted it.

It came away with a grating sound. I laid the stone on the walkway of the gate-house. I repeated the exercise with another and another. There were three further loose coping stones.

"The bloody masons have failed to secure the stones" I said angrily. "Damn them. I will ride west and will find them and...."

"Think carefully my friend, before you make a judgement" said Johannes. "Yes, it may be that a careless mason has used a poor mix in the mortar but I think it more likely the mortar has been disturbed. I think....."

He shook his head, "No it can't be. No mason would do such a thing. It would be overseen by the master. The mason would be fined. His work mates would notice.

This was one of the last pieces to be finished, I remember" I offered. "Perhaps in haste they became sloppy."

"Do you think they were the sort to do that?"

I recalled the seven masons who had worked diligently and with great professionalism on my works and Philip Carver the master who had become such a friend to us on the manor.

"No. Not negligent. Accidental, perhaps?"

"How?"

"I don't know."

I squatted on my haunches and looked at the wall which was, when one was standing, as high as my chest. I noticed some faint scratchings along the mortar joints. I ran my finger along one. Several of the blocks had these marks. Here were no mason's marks. No marks to denote where a particular man had begun and finished his work that day (I had seen this elsewhere on the castle and my own building works and so was familiar with them.) They were paid a piece rate, how much they could do in a day and a man would 'sign' his finished work each day.

"Johannes...what do you think of this?" He had turned to look out over the gate and was trying the coping stones on the other side. He strode over.

He too ran his finger along.

"The stone was loosened when the mortar was not quite set, I think. Taken up and put back again. If you do this, the bond is broken and the wall becomes weaker."

My head was pounding.

"NO!" I shouted to the sky and kicked the wall.

Johannes grabbed me by the shoulders.

I shuddered and with more than just the cold. I simply could not believe it but I had to say it aloud.

"Someone tampered with the stone. How could they do this TWO YEARS AGO...and wait until now to use the fruits of their labours? HOW?" I yelled into the wind. How would they know? How could they plan it so.....? AND WHY?"

Oh no. NO! How was I going to explain to his mother that Geoffrey had been murdered.

"You seem shocked, Paul? You will realise, the older you get, how wicked this world is. Aye, even from your cosseted place in the priory down in the town. You are young....you'll get used to it I suppose."

As it was I could not tell his mother for when she woke, she was as blank as she had been before Johannes had given her the medicine.

He promised me she would come back to me, back to life but he could not tell me how long that might take, nor what state she would be in when she did.

Robert had taken to his room too. We saw nothing of him and when he did sur-face, it was to get on with his chores and duties without a word. It was as if he felt that in giving the child the boat, he had precipitated the ghastly events of that day.

Johannes was with me as much as he could be, for he had his doctoring practice to serve and came and went as he was called to various parts of the forest or the town.

That evening he called in on his way home to see how Cecily was. No change. She ate, slept, and stared. No more.

The doctor and I shared a pot of ale in the hall.

"I have been thinking about this Aumary" he volunteered, as he sat back with a sigh on the backed bench Cecily had had made for my birthday. She had added her own work of padded cushions. "Thinking how it might have been done."

"The how is not the thing which exercises me, Johannes, it's the why?"

"If we know the how we might find out the why" he said somewhat glibly. So I nodded and let him speak.

"I want to look at Geoffrey again..." he put up his hand, "I will do nothing to upset you and I know I must seek your permission but I should like to look at the wounds, now they have been cleaned. You need not come with me. I can...."

"I will come" I said.

We two climbed the stairs at the end of the hall, opposite to the solar and to the side of the screens passage. I opened the door.

The little chapel lay over my office and pantry, (the room now used to store food and to serve the hall with bread and wine) and part of the screens passage.

It was in almost darkness save for candles on the altar and at the head and foot of the bier upon which my son lay; a tiny bundle on a larger plank over two trestles. Father Benedict knelt before the raised altar.

He turned as we entered and quietly closed the doors.

"How goes it with you, Father?" I asked. He shook his white head. When I had first known this man, his hair had been mousey fair.

"I never thought to see this day. I'm an old man. I thought he would be bury-ing me, not me praying for Geoffrey, asking for God to take him to his bosom."

There was lump in my throat. I swallowed. "We have come to look at him."

He got up clumsily from his knees and rubbed them hard, saying. "As is your right." Then with a nod to Johannes, was gone.

Johannes took one of the candles and asked me if I could hold it steady for him...could I do that and not be...not be what...? He did not finish. I nodded.

I watched as with the gentleness of a woman with a baby, he turned back the sheet which lay over the mortal remains of my son and began to examine him.

Geoffrey lay supine, his skull a strange shape but sunken into a snowy white pil-low, so that we might not see the major damage to the back. The nose was broken, the brow flattened and scraped. The chin too was flattened and the mouth (I suspected some teeth had been loosened, they were only baby teeth after all) was, well, not the mouth I recognised as that which gave me those mischievous grins in life.

Johannes, at the head of the bier, took the cranium in his hands and lifted. He leaned forward, almost bent double, and examined carefully. Then he stood and lifted the chin. The bones were loose and things seemed to shift. I caught a glimpse of a reddening of the pillow where fluids had leaked after Geoffrey had been cleansed, as Johannes laid the ravaged head back on the pillow. I looked away. I couldn't bear this.

Johannes then went to the shoulders and felt the bones there.

Finally, the tops of the arms. He laid all back as he had found it and covered the little body, took the candle from me and replaced it.

He reached for me, "Come, there is no more to see."

When we had regained the hall, Johannes stoked the fire and came to sit on the bench again.

"So can you, would it be possible for you, to explain to me how he lay, when under the stone? How it looked? They had moved it all when I arrived and I did not see the body as it lay after death."

I realised that yet again, the coroner might not be pleased. The law says we must leave a body in situ for him to look at, but my son could not be left in the gateway. Surely he would understand. I thought he would. He was a good man. He had sons of his own. If I had to pay a fine, so be it. My coping stone no doubt, would be taken as deodand.

I took a deep breath.

"The stone lay totally on his head. We could not see it, his head. His hands were out in front of him. No - wrong....one hand was out in front."

"Which?"

"The left."

"Geoffrey favoured his right hand?"

"Yes. The right hand was underneath him." Though it hurt me sorely, I pictured what I could remember of the scene.

"The left leg was slightly crooked, the right straight out behind him."

"Did the stone cover his shoulder, for I think it did, and part of the upper arms?"

"Yes, the stone was so big, bigger than..." I broke down and covered my eyes to weep.

Johannes waited. Then I said, "The back of his head had been cracked like an egg."

Johannes took this in quietly.

"And the little boat?"

"It was partly under his right side; a small part was sticking out. I bent to retrieve it but someone took it."

"Who?"

I looked blank. I couldn't remember.

Johannes said that it did not matter, he would ask around the manor.

"Now, think very carefully. Who was in the yard when you arrived at the top of the steps?"

"Cedric was behind me. Cecily was in the gateway. Two grooms were coming from the stables but they were at the farthest end by the wall of the blacksmith's workshop. They were frozen in shock when I saw them, stock still."

"Anyone else?"

"No. Everyone was indoors with their doors shut or at the threshing."

Johannes leaned forward and fixed me with his sad brown eyes, "No one was on the gateway walk, or coming down the steps, or in the gateway?"

I considered this carefully. "No, though if they were hiding in the dark of the steps under the wall walk, I would not have seen them till they stepped out. They might have done this when the furore broke."

He nodded. "Now, Cedric. We need to speak to him"

The twelve year old stable lad, Cedric, was fetched. He was twitchy and still in shock, even a day later but he answered the questions bravely.

Did he see anyone by the gate; did he see the stone drop, when did he find Geoffrey's body, where had he been before this and did he see Geoffrey before the event?

It was no to all these questions.

He did see, he said, Master Robert saddling his horse in the middle stable before he went into the end one to fork some hay.

Robert was fetched. Yes, he did saddle his horse there, yes he did see Cedric and the lad had, as he said, gone off to the end stable nearest the gate to do some jobs. The doors to that stable had been completely closed. He had left the boat on the bottom step of the stairs to the gate house, knowing that Geoffrey would find it easily. They were always playing games of this nature, I recalled. Robert had then ridden out of the gate, looking back just one moment later to see him and wave. Then he was riding at a gallop to the main track, he said.

"Why did you give him the boat there?" asked Johannes.

Robert cocked his head at the question, "I er... suppose I wanted him to have it before I left."

"When you came out of the stable, was the lad there in the courtyard?"

"No, he was at the top of the hall steps. I think I called to him," said Robert, "he came running."

Johannes frowned. "Tell me..." he looked at Robert under furrowed brows. "Why did you have the boat with you? If you had not seen Geoffrey, would you have tak-en it with you? Why did you not leave it at Durley if you were going out to Marlborough? A strange thing to do, take a child's boat with you."

Robert chuckled. "I have no idea. Except maybe I thought I might add some little wooden sailors and I could have had those made in Marlborough." His stare was steady.

"You made the boat, did you not?"

"Yes, Johannes, I made the boat." Robert's voice was hard and angry.

"Why? Could you not make the sailors?"

"I have no idea."

Cedric was fetched back.

Gently I asked the question Johannes and I had discussed when Robert had left us.

"Did you hear the Lord Robert call to Geoffrey, Cedric?"

"Aye, I did, m'lord."

I had been the last person to see my son alive, for he did not go back to the hall to report to his mother that he had delivered his message and that I was on my way but went out to the courtyard, the deserted courtyard to his death.

Chapter Nine

"Oh I am glad that is over. I think I will have a sip of my medicine, Paul, if you wouldn't mind? Thank you.

"And a wee sip of ale to chase it down? Help yourself to some too.

"Right. We shall continue. What? You haven't drunk your ale. Well, save it till later then."

***

Johannes and I were alone in the hall again, save for a few women to-ing and fro-ing around us, tidying before night draws in, as women are wont to do.

I stopped one of them and asked after Cecily. She just shook her head and walked on. I poured us some wine this time. I think we were in need of something substantial.

Johannes would soon be off into the fading light back to Marlborough, one for his journey would do him no harm.

The doctor sat with me for some time in silence. Then, just when I thought he dozed, he said "I think I know what happened."

I sat up straight. "I too have my ideas; let us see if they have anything in common."

Johannes began. "The stone was dislodged some time ago and failed to bond to its neighbours. Are we agreed on this?

We were.

"Why, we do not know, but we do know that someone planned to use these stones, all or any one of them as a weapon, not necessarily to kill. Perhaps not to kill Geoffrey but to do harm in some way to someone"

"Yes. The someone who dislodged these plans ahead, certainly," I said

"Now we come to the day." Johannes took my wine cup and placed it before him, then he took his own and placed it with a slight gap between, by my own. He reached for a dish of wizened apples which lay on the table for the lesser folk to eat after our earlier meal and dragged it to a position he favoured.

"This is the hall, (the apple dish). These are the gate (our cups)." He took out an apple. "This is Geoffrey. Here he is at the top of the steps. Perhaps he hears a voice calling him. He runs down the steps to the gate." The apple was now in the gateway, between the ale pots.

Johannes reached for his scrip and took out a coin. He balanced this on top of the apple. "This is the stone."

I frowned. "If the stone were dropped in this manner, Geoffrey would look up, he would hear the grating of the stone being removed and move...quickly. He was no fool, my son."

"But if the stone were already in the hand of the murderer?"

I thought a second "Nah. Why would he just stand there? Besides, the main damage is to the back of his head. The rest happened when he fell and was crushed."

"Exactly, my friend, you have it," said Johannes. He took out another coin and placed it on the table before the apple.

"This is our distraction. Let us assume it was the wee boat." I looked up quickly at that.

Then suddenly I saw what he was driving at.

"Geoffrey was bending when he was hit wasn't he? He was knocked forward. His hand was trapped under him, the hand either reaching for the boat or holding it?

"I think so yes."

He called for the reeve then and asked for him to find out who it was had fetched the boat from under Geoffrey and to ask him an especial question. The next day the news came in. Yes, when he had tugged the boat from underneath Geoffrey's lifeless body, there had been some resistance as if Geoffrey had had hold of it and even in death would not relinquish it.

This could mean but two things. Geoffrey had dropped the boat and the murderer had taken advantage of the moment, or the boat was on the floor already and Geoffrey was bending to reach for it, when the stone was dropped.

Whichever was true, they were the most horrible conclusions.

***

It is difficult for people to understand how, looking back, we did not see what had truly been happening over the years that I had been master at Durley.

Why did you not investigate more thoroughly, they ask? As if we could have stopped our daily lives and gone about looking for this clue or that piece of evidence? It simply was not possible at that time, to piece it all together. We did what we could, when we could. We had so little to go on. Who could we have relied on, to help us?

The coroner's job was not one of investigation. His was a role which had been resurrected by King Richard from an old pre-Norman office. The English had had coroners long before we came to these shores. He simply pulled this out of his governmental bag to provide a check to the power invested in the office of the sheriff and to make money. The sheriff, one to each county, was often an unscrupulous man who used his power to make himself as rich as Croesus. Coroners, however, were not paid; they had to be wealthy gentlemen who were able to keep themselves comfortably and so were (it was hoped) beyond corruption. Richard envisaged them almost as tax collectors and used them to screw whatever fine, fee or free gift he could from his people. It worked quite well. Sheriffs came and went, depending on their loyalty and the king's whim. It was their job, amongst other things, to glean as much information as they could about a crime and try to apprehend the felon. In truth, this happened rarely, for unless the culprit could be caught with the knife in his hand, the sheriff seldom managed to unearth the real perpetrator of the crime. He simply did not have the resources or the time. The best ones did their utmost to adhere to the letter of the law. The worst simply took the first man they felt would fit the felony and hanged him. Task complete.

"In some ways Paul...they still do you know."

After Geoffrey's death, though, Johannes and I began to be a little more wary, more careful, more thoughtful about matters. Somehow the doctor, Johannes of Salerno, had become enmeshed in the affairs of Durley and I was glad to have him at my elbow when I needed a keen mind and a fresh thought. He was a good and sincere friend as well as being a very fine surgeon and learned man and I did not feel as alone as I perhaps would have done, had I never met him. Geoffrey's death drew us closer together, it's true.

***

Slowly, Cecily came back to the world, though she was never the same again. To lose one's only son in childhood is, perhaps, a mother's greatest fear. As I have noted before, children were often those the Grim Reaper took first, in famine, in pestilence, in fevers, childhood diseases and in unavoidable accidents.

However, to have them taken from you by murder was ten times the horror that a mother was normally prey to. We tried to keep it from her but it proved impossible. She was a clever woman. She could work on the facts in her own mind and come to a conclusion no matter how we tried to lead her astray or deny the workings of her mind. The rumours too flying about the manor could not be denied. She could not be kept from it and so one day, when we felt that she had recovered sufficiently to be told the awful truth, we sat her down and laid it bare before her, Johannes and I.

Naturally she was, as we were, angry but she took that anger into herself so that she became depressed and yes, puzzled. Why was her son taken from her in this manner? What had he done? He was a child? He had hurt no one.

As time went on she became increasingly more desolate. She lost weight, her chubbiness giving way to gauntness. Her sense of humour, her interest in life waned, even though I pointed out to her that she had another child to care for who was just as deserving of her mother's love. She seemed distant to both our daughter and to me. I foolishly said one day that we should put effort into trying to have another child, not an onerous task, after all. Her look reduced me to jelly.

"We shall never replace him, Aumary," she said. I knew we could not. Geoffrey had been her firstborn. There could never be another firstborn son.

As it was she did become pregnant again in the summer but lost the child shortly after the third month and that did not help matters one speck.

Now I must come to things which were happening in the wider world beyond Durley. I need to recap a little and explain what had been going on for if you understand this, you will comprehend what follows.

"Do you hear that, Paul my scribe? Sharpen your ears and your pen nib."

The summer of 1201 was a good time for King John. Constance the mother of the Duke of Brittany, his nephew, died, fully restored to his favour. John saw to the execution of her will. She had been a stone in the hoof for a long time. Niggling, sniping, irritating and driving her young son Arthur against his uncle with claims to the kingdom of England. By the Treaty of Goulet signed in May 1200, John had been accepted by Philip as the rightful heir to his brother Richard's fiefs held on the continent, with a few minor modifications of the borders. John would then in his turn acknowledge Philip of France as overlord for his lands in Normandy and his Angevin possessions. Arthur, as heir to Brittany, had been acknowledged as John's vassal but, John promised not to diminish Arthur's prerogatives in any way.

John was given a nickname at home. Softsword, for giving in to Philip and making peace with him. In fact many of us felt that John was being prudent in preferring peace to war. It was an unjust jibe, for the King I knew was a determined man with a flintiness none of his predecessors could equal. The peace at Goulet had cost him 20,000 marks but even that was cheaper than war.

John's very elderly mother Eleanor had, at his accession, made over Aquitaine to him. It was an unquiet and fractious province and a pond in which Philip of France longed to fish. He had already cast his bait upon the waters before the Treaty of Goulet was thought of and he loved to poke and prod and set one head against another.

John had returned to England with his new bride in October 1200 and had left her in our capable care at Marlborough whilst he went on a tour. I saw quite a bit of our Queen then, though obviously, she had her own household to care for her at the castle.

Shortly after Easter the call went out for all John's vassals to come to him at Portsmouth at Whitsuntide ready for a campaign in John's lands in southern France. The Lusignans were causing problems again. I gathered together my contribution. Myself, my man at arms Hal and my two paid soldiers from the castle, some of my more able villagers and naturally, money. Other men in the locality did the same.

Perplexed as we were, for this, we began to think, was not the best army to take to fight in this situation, we answered the call of our King. Once there, he relieved us of our money and sent us home. This was certainly a way of raising funds to buy the mercenaries and the professional soldiers which John favoured above all and avoided the problems of resistance and delays which had beset his brother's requests, but it was shifty and underhand and many, including myself, I must say, did not like it.

John angered the Lusignans even further by charging them with treason. The King of France felt he had to intervene. He remonstrated with John. The wagging finger was just the thing to make King John dig in his heels. Philip asked for three castles as security, to ensure that John would treat the Lusignans fairly. John procrastinated as only John could. Philip could bear it no longer. His patience and diplomacy exhausted, he demanded that John appear before the court of French barons meeting in Paris, to answer for his actions.

John was a wily one. He sent back a message effectively saying that by ancient agreement the Duke of Normandy was obliged to attend the French court only when it met on the border between their territories.

This was, of course, true, but Philip was cleverer. The summons was addressed he, said, not to the Duke of Normandy but to John the Duke of Aquitaine, Count of Poitou and Count of Anjou.

John still did not appear.

Philip raged against his contumacious vassal. The moment had almost come for Philip to break the Angevin hold over France.

In May 1202 Philip 2nd attacked Normandy with great force and declared that John had forfeited his other fiefs in France. All fiefs he bestowed on, yes, you've guessed it, Arthur Duke of Brittany. All except Normandy which he was saving for himself, I think. At Gournai, in July 1202, the newly knighted Arthur did homage for these lands. An untried lad of fifteen in charge of all this: if it wasn't serious, we would have laughed.

John naturally, tried to persuade us all that Philip was the aggressor - and yes, in part this was true.

"You are no doubt aware how the King of France contrary to the peace between us, confirmed by oaths and charters, unjustly attacks us and strives by all means in his power to deprive us of our inheritance." John protested.

Many blamed John's marriage to Isabelle. The Lusignan, Hugh Le Brun's, anger over losing her as a wife, was swallowed up in the greater evil of John's problems with his continental lands and vassals. This in turn was wrapped around Philip's determination to maintain his hold over John and a personal hatred of the Angevins which would fester until they were all dead.

Thus the situation was like one of those fancy creations of clever cooks, where one bird is hidden in another and roasted and when you cut the meat you first eat swan, then goose, then duck, then pigeon and finally partridge.

Over our ale and wine at night, the men who slept in the hall and I and sometimes Johannes, if he were available for supper with us, would discuss this problem until our throats were sore. John, we thought, had brought this upon himself by bullying his vassals and playing games with his overlord, Philip. On the other hand, what else was he to do?

The thing that happened next was so amazing, it went down in legend, as the stories which are told by old soldiers round the fire of an evening.

It was 1202.

John did not at first bite at Philip's nipping at his heels. He stayed behind his protective screen of Norman castles. Then when he felt he had enough mercenaries (they were coming in to him daily) to give him a mobile army, he turned south to the vulnerable heart of his empire.

It is said that at Le Mans a courier nearly dead with fatigue managed to reach John with an urgent letter from his mother, old Queen Eleanor. She had been happily ensconced in Fontevrault, where she had hoped to live out her final years in peace and quiet. Arthur and the Poitevin lords had other ideas and they had sallied forth down the valley of the Loire intent on taking her, at the Angevin's spiritual home. She quickly set off for Poitiers but Arthur and the rebels were close on her heels. John showed his true Angevin mettle then, popping up like the devil of a miracle play through a trap door; for he took a detachment of his army and force marched eighty miles or more within forty-eight hours and caught up with his mother at Mirabeau.

Eleanor was trapped in the keep of the castle. The besiegers had gone to bed thinking themselves safe and had barricaded all the doors to the town; all but one. As dawn broke, William des Roches led the storming of that gate. Arthur had sought to keep out the enemy. But in effect, all he did was entomb himself in the town.

It was said that Geoffrey de Lusignan was at the breakfast table partaking of a dish of pigeon when John's men surrounded him.

No one escaped. They had them. Every one. John later wrote to all his loyal men in England.

They were safe, he said; two hundred knights had been captured but best of all William de Briouze had laid hold of Arthur Duke of Brittany and he was now John's prisoner.

How we all cheered and shouted at that! John's nephew he might be, but he was a pennant to which many disaffected men would rally and now he was to be locked up in honourable captivity in Falaise castle.

If we had known then what was going to happen, perhaps we might not have shouted so loudly.

I will leave the politics of the empire now, for a short while, to return to my tale of Durley.

***

We are now at roughly the beginning of August 1201. The whole cycle of the agricultural year was grinding on and yet again, we harvested our grain. A month later, the swallows left the barns and buildings and disappeared, we know not where. Some said that it was to hide in the mud at the bottom of ponds, others, including Johannes of Salerno, said that they had seen them en masse flying south to warmer climes. Wherever they went, they went all together and all of a suddenness. One day we could hear them twittering together, the next day was silence. In October the starlings too, began to mass in the evening, hundreds of them, and wheel in the sky with a loud chirruping as if all speaking at once. Then they would fall, as if by a single signal, into the bushes and small trees of the surrounding forest and were hushed without warning, like one lone bird. A little later the bats were to be seen in the less frequented barns and buildings, resting upside down, sleeping now till next spring.

I wished that I too could sleep the winter out for I was dreading another year passing and the anniversary of Geoffrey's death. His mother too became more quiet, if that were possible and one day in late September, pleading a headache and feeling unwell, she took to her bed.

I had to go to the castle for there were many tasks to complete; not least the taking into custody of a few of John's lesser enemies, for some had been shipped out from Normandy to England. At first we had about thirty (we could not have accommodated more for longer) and then we were left with just five, as twenty-five were shipped off to Corfe.

We heard later that many of them died there.

The fate of those twenty-five was held against John but he wasn't present at the time and I heard he did not sanction their demise.

We heard later from a reliable source, that they, to a man, had tried to break out of their none too unpleasant prison but had been foiled and had gained possession of the keep. They were surrounded and were begged to capitulate. Twenty-two of them starved, it is said, rather than give in.The fate of the other three I know not. This rumour or story, I don't really know what to believe, did John no good at all.

My own prisoners were much easier to manage. These were the men who could be ransomed. They were pleasant fellows who did as they were asked and caused no trouble. One by one, over time, the money for their release arrived and during the first few weeks of their captivity, I spent many days and nights at the castle. I simply could not go home.

Until a summons from Father Benedict made me drop everything and rush back to Durley.

Cecily had become very ill.

Chapter Ten

We come again to a part I have no wish to tell but must.

"Oh Paul...hand me again my drops, for I feel a pain in the heart coming on. Thank you. A moment, a moment please. Now we shall write on."

The message had simply said that Cecily had not risen from her bed for about three days and would I come and speak to her, for she was taking no food and little water and had developed a fever. They were obviously worried for her.

I dropped from my horse at about midday that day, having ridden through a drip-ping forest for the rain was coming down in sheets and I saw no likelihood of it stopping. Even then part of me was thinking about the damage done to the forest by the flashing flood.

I ran for cover, tossed the reins to a groom, I saw not who, pulling off my sodden cloak and tossing it to a lad at the top of the hall steps. Then I took the solar stairs at a run, two at a time and burst through the door like a besieger storming a castle wall. I stood there for a few seconds, dripping into the rushes, my heart rattling like an unfettered shutter in a gale, then walked forward.

Cecily lay on our bed. Her face was so pale and her eyes lids were fluttering like a moth's wings. Her brow was damp with sweat and her breath came in short gasps.

"The doctor?"

"Came and went," said one of her women. "He will return tonight."

"What does he say?"

"That much of it she has brought on herself with her grieving. That she is not eating and so has little strength to fight the fever which racks her. We must try to get her to eat and drink."

"We did it before with Tom the factor's tube. Can we do it again?"

"We can try. It's as if she has given up." The woman was Agnes Brenthall, I noticed and she was close to tears.

"We must send for her parents. They may be able to rally her."

"Yes, m'lord, I'll see it done." She backed off and disappeared into the gloom of the chamber.

The room was lit by a few candles but none placed too close to the bed, so I reached out and took one fixed in a chamberstick.

I looked at my wife carefully in the flickering light of the candle. I do not think she knew I was there.

I called her name.

I sat on the edge of the bed and chastised her gently for such foolishness. God forgive me, I told her that I needed her, that Little Hawise needed her and she was not to sink into the mire of self-pity at Geoffrey's death, for this was a sin and she must fight it with all the spirit left in her.

Her brow puckered at that.

I mentioned that her parents were coming to see her. I asked if she had seen Hawise today. She was a lively little lass and would have made her mother smile, surely. I was told that when Hawise was fetched earlier, the child simply screamed the roof down and had to be removed. Well, so much for my good idea.

I told Cecily that I would do as we'd done before and get some water and broth into her and that now I was home, I would take over the nursing of her.

I slept that night piled with blankets on a chair by the bed. Johannes came at last, just as the rain stopped and when Tom's little feeding tube was brought, helped me feed her some water. It took us two hours for her to take just a few sips.

We spoke in whispers. I asked him if this illness was likely to be mortal.

He could not tell, he said. The mind was a strange beast. She had been failing for some time and had now gone into a decline from which she might not recover. He was puzzled he said, because she seemed lately to be a little better, recovering well from the miscarriage of another child, but, after a while, perhaps a week ago (dear God, when I went to Marlborough to deal with my work there) she had taken an abrupt turn for the worse.

Her weakened state, he said, had not helped her fight off any illness. Doctors had little idea why it was the human body became ill. Many followed the ancients and stuck to the doctrine of the humours, those hidden elements which when unbalanced could cause mayhem in a body. Johannes was skeptical. He had studied many illnesses. Many of them he thought were carried from person to person somehow. If a father had a bad heart, it was likely the son would have too. (Oh dear I thought....and remembered my father's last days.) As a man may look like his sire or his dam, the body was probably made of the same stuff with the same problems inherent in it. He believed there were unknown vapours perhaps or small creatures which could invade a body, like a maggot does a dead animal, and it was this which was responsible for the illness. These were quite apart from bad food or water which could also cause the body to fail.

Cecily had been unable to keep down food, became listless, had voided her bowels often. Her water, he said, was a strange colour, black. He had never seen the like of it. She had fevers and was by turns cold and complained of a tingling in her feet and hands. Her heart jumped around, she said, as if it were unfettered in her breast.

Then, suddenly she would come round and rally and be much better, without any delirium.

Johannes prescribed a tonic which was one, he said, that cleansed the body and the blood. It was made from many different plants and had some charcoal in it, for he found that charcoal was very good for the stomach. A few drops were given every canonical hour or so, when they could get them into her.

We could only wait and pray.

Just after dawn, her parents came to stand by her bed.

I left them. I could not watch the grief on their faces. First their grandson and now, his mother.

Johannes had to go home, he said but he would be back in three or four hours. I thanked him for his care of Cecily. He had many patients and draws on his time, but he still found moments to be here with us and to support us whenever we needed it.

I answered the questions of Evisa and Toruld Congrye, my parents-in-law, as best I could. We knew so little. I do think hearing her parents' voices rallied Cecily a little towards the middle of the day and she did open her eyes for a moment and smile. That was worth the whole world to me. I grasped her hand then, told her that she would make a full recovery and that I loved her very much.

Robert came that afternoon and helped me give her the drops which

Johannes prescribed. We held her carefully, tilted her head and managed to get them through her lips. She swallowed. Robert shook his head.

"There is something wrong, I know it, but it is almost as if she does not care. She doesn't want to fight it, she's given up." And he went away with tears in his eyes.

That night, whilst I was sleeping again in the chair in the solar, piled with blankets and a fur against the chill, Cecily thrashed about on the bed and retched and retched though nothing came up, for there was nothing in her to do so.

I held her then, close to me and waited the fit out.

Tired at last she lay down and so did I. Exhausted by it all, I fell asleep.

I woke to a predawn chill. The blankets had fallen off me and I stood up to bank up the mean little fire which had all but gone out and blow on the flames.

I shivered and quickly used the pot behind the screen for I had a very full bladder. It's little things like this one remembers at times like this, isn't it?

At last I stood before the bed and I knew.

I knew that Cecily was dead.

She was dead.

My little bird, the light of my life, my angel, my bright flower, was dead.

I threw myself onto my knees and I howled.

***

True men are not supposed to howl like children when they bark their shins. I count myself a true man but I am not ashamed to say that for the second time in a year, I cried uncontrollably. I could not stop. The pain I felt was worse than any real hurt or injury I had known or imagined but eventually my sobbing ceased and I sat back on my chair and covered myself with a rug. I was shaking uncontrollably and I found it hard to catch my breath. Gradually, I recovered and made my way to the little room at the back of the solar where the children had slept with their nurse.

After rousing them (I was surprised they did not wake at my sobbing), I calmly asked them to fetch the priest. They were up in a trice. I picked up my sleeping daughter and holding her close, I returned to my chair in the solar, where the two of us dozed for a minute.

Benedict came quickly, rubbing his eyes. He took in the scene at a glance and hobbled off (a pain in his right side had been plaguing him of late) to the chapel to fetch his things.

A moment later I heard a horse arriving in the yard. I passed the still sleeping Hawise to the nurse who had returned and made my way down into the hall. Johannes came in brandishing a piece of parchment.

"I have it...I have it!" He was exultant.

"What do you have my friend?" I said, wiping my nose on my sleeve. I smiled to myself; oh, how Cecily would have been cross at that.

"It was plaguing me. So I went to the library at the Gilbertine canons in town. They have some good books there." He was smoothing down the parchment on the table and finding things to weigh down the edges. "And I found it at last. I've been up all night looking." He searched for a candle stub and lit it from the last one burning in a sconce. All around us men who slept in the hall each night, were waking to a new day, stretching and groaning, rolling up their mattresses and palliasses. Most were making for the door and the privy or the nearer forest.

"Looking for what?"

Benedict passed us clutching his robes and paraphernalia and slowly made his way up the solar stairs. Johannes stared.

"I fear my friend," I said, "you are too late."

Johannes sat down on the bench with a bump.

"Too late?"

I inclined my head.

He said no more but put his head on his folded arms and collapsed on to the table. For moments he lay there still and then I realised he was crying quietly. I left him with a pat to his shoulder and went to throw another log on the fire. After a short while, the exhausted man slept. I wrapped my blanket around him.

Whilst he slept I looked at the parchment which he had pinned down to the table with various bits of discarded crockery. He had copied a few paragraphs from some book and had drawn a few crude diagrams in the margins.

The name Dioscorides featured there and Nicander and a man, who by his name must have been an infidel; Ibn Wahshiyya who, Johannes had scribbled, had written the first real book on poisons.

My heart jumped into my mouth. I read on.

The words, black water leapt, off the page.

Johannes' scribbles swam before my eyes. Not only was I very tired but I couldn't focus, my mind was in such turmoil. I read on carefully.

He had not written whole sentences, merely a word or phrases here and there, to aid his memory, I suppose.

'Headaches, confusion, severe voiding of the bowels, and drowsiness. Poisoning develops, convulsions..Poisoning becomes acute, symptoms - voiding of the bowels, vomiting, blood in the urine, cramping muscles, stomach pain, more convulsions. Small doses, feigns food poisoning. Large dose? Tasteless, odourless, lethal. Final result of this - death.'

Johannes had then written a few names of plants or rare substances I suppose, for I did not know any of them. He wrote in a quick untidy scribble; if caught early enough, it was thought these could counteract the effect of the poison.

There was an unfamiliar word which he'd written three times at the bottom of the passage.

Sandaraca.

Sandaraca.

Sandaraca.

and then,

Arsenic.

Orpiment.

I stared at it. What on earth was that? At the very bottom of the page he had scribbled some names.

William

Cecily

Colmar

Quimper

Robert

Geoffrey

Cecily

I frowned. Then I took a step to the fire, searched for a piece of charcoal and added shakily, Piers?

***

Johannes slept for four hours and hardly moved.

When he woke (I had kept the hall quiet and free of folk) he was stiff and cold. He asked for a bowl of warm water in which to wash his grimed face and one was brought.

He then broke his fast, though truthfully it was the middle of the day by then, with bread, cheese and ale but ate sparingly. Then he was prepared to talk to me.

I gestured to the parchment. "I have read it" I said.

"I could have saved her, I think" he answered; not the words I had been expecting.

"It was not to be."

"I could maybe have saved her, if I had known..."

I came back quickly with "If we had known but we did not. We still do not. We can prove nothing."

"Can we not?"

He pulled the parchment to him. He saw that I written Piers' name at the top.

"You think his too was a murder?"

I shrugged. "It is an unexplained death and in this wretched place an unexplained death has to be considered with the rest."

The more we delve, Aumary, the more we are in danger ourselves," he said blankly.

I looked up from the paper then.

"You think so? We must be very quiet about this then."

***

The hall was not the best place to discuss our thoughts and so I took my key from my scrip and we repaired to my office and locked the door. Even there we spoke quietly. I shuttered the window, though we were on the first floor; it might be possible for someone to listen under the opening.

"We need to go back over all the deaths. Even though they are, some of them, events of years ago, we must see what else we can uncover." I started. "Piers was the first..."

" 'Twas before we met."

"Aye."

I scratched my head. "He fell. But did he?"

"Then Cecily. She was not meant to recover from that wounding by the river. If you had not been able to come to us, I think she would have been lying dead all those years ago instead of just this night." I fought back tears.

"Then William. We know that it was a knife which dealt the death blow. Then Colmar."

"That really puzzles me," interrupted Johannes, "an easy poison that one, aconitum -

Easy to find, easy to make. Why use another totally different one on poor Cecily?"

"Perhaps our murderer like to experiment" I said.

"Then Quimper. Not poison. Our felon departed from his method there as he had done first with Cecily and the first attempt on her life."

"Then Robert. Another poison."

"But yet of a different kind. I think that one was not pure poison but something unclean introduced to the body. Something that, if not treated, might result in death."

"Then Geoffrey" I said.

"A well planned evil that one. Two years in the making. The devil was truly in our felon then." We were silent. We need not mention the last death.

"What is this orpiment?"

Johannes stood, ran his hands through his hair and stretched.

"It is a natural substance, a liquid obtained from a tree grown mostly in the Africas. The ancients knew it. It solidifies and is sold as small slivers of yellow crystals. Sometimes called arsenic. There is another yellow substance which is also natural though this is found in the ground near hot springs and other natural wonders. This too is arsenic and can be just as deadly. I believe that those seeking to find the way to make gold use it."

"Where would you get these things from? Here in Savernake we have no trees exuding resin or hot springs throwing out deadly yellow poisons" I said.

"Apothecaries may have some. They sell orpiment to limners, they make a yellow paint of it. It is costly but is used in painting."

"God Johannes, this is all too evil for me," I said.

"What's that Paul? Too evil for you too. Aye, it cannot be good for you to have to listen to tales like this. I am sorry. What? Well, yes, it does make a good tale. However, everything I tell you is the truth and I have lived through it. Believe me, it's not good to have to recount it all and rake over all the memories. I must do it though..."

We went over the details as best we could remember them, of all the deaths which we might consider to be murder, in the past years. We did not count the old and young of the village who died of diseases the old and young die of, only those on our list and others which we felt were unexpected.

We decided to investigate the apothecary of the town (there was only one). However, the next thing which happened rather threw us from our mission.

***

We buried my sweet Cecily in the little churchyard at Durley and said nothing for the moment. Life dragged on and about two weeks after her interment one of my woodwards came to me and asked if I might go with him deep into the forest to the charcoal burners for they had something to show me. Johannes was not available to travel with me so I took Hal, my man at arms with me as a trusted man at my back.

I rarely visited this deep for I had confidence in those whose job it was to patrol the forest, to manage it all and indeed they did with great efficiency.

The charcoal makers were a taciturn lot, perpetually black with the fruits of their labours but they knuckled their foreheads to me as their lord and master and explained what they had found in their heaped kilns, as they called them. They had been raking out the charcoal, they said. They use rags to light the fire, anything they can get their hands on, then they clamp down their flames and let it burn.

In one of their kilns they had found the remnants of something which they most certainly had not used to fire up the blaze. Partly destroyed but still recognisable, they would never have used such a valuable piece of cloth. It would have been more use to them sold on, for the embroidered silver wires to be unpicked and re-used. The material was a soft blue wool.

I had the thing in my hand. It was a piece about ten inches long and perhaps two feet wide, screwed up and black with soot and burning. Pale blue, soft with small appliqued blue flowers on it.

I was holding the dress that Cecily had been married in.

Chapter Eleven

Hal and I raced into town as fast as we could travel. The forest and the roads were sodden and everywhere you looked was evidence of the amount of rain which had fallen in the last two days or so. We crossed the wooden bridge over the Kennet, usually a gentle free flowing, many branching chalk stream no deeper than ten feet at the most with a pebbly bottom visible though the perfectly clear waters and with trout lazing amongst weed. Now it was a raging torrent, brown and with a yeasty froth threatening the banks on the London Road side.

On up onto that London Road we carried, up the slight hill and I threw myself from the saddle and banged on the door of Master Glover's fine house. A flustered maid answered and I rudely barged past her, leaving Hal to the horse holding.

Master Glover was sitting down to meat in his parlour and looked up with a slice of ham speared to the end of his eating knife, almost to his lips.

I apologised profusely and told him the reason for my untimely intrusion.

He begged me to sit, take wine with him. I didn't mind (I remembered how good it was last time) and then turned his attention to my questions.

What had the young lady who had bought the hawking glove been wearing the day she purchased it from him?

"My Lord, you are asking me to remember something which...."He caught my eye and went on.

"Well...were I a girl of course I could tell you every detail. They have minds for such things don't they?" Then he said, "Wait then!"

He threw his head out of the parlour door and bellowed, "Corlis!"

After a moment and some smiling from me, and pouring of wine on the part of the merchant, there came a pretty young lady to the parlour. She was introduced as his younger daughter. The question was asked of her.

"Oh yes. She was very pretty and I did so love the dress."

"You were there, in the shop?"

"Aye with father."

"Then let you tell me."

She ran her hands down the front of her own serviceable rust coloured bliaut.

"Well, it was under her cloak of course but I could see when she stretched her hand out, it was a lovely blue the colour of a harebell and then over it she had a bliaut of the palest wool which had the sweetest little flowers on it. Embroidered, I think they were. She had...."

"Is this, do you think, anything like it?" From my cotte I produced the blackened and creased piece of the overgarment." I held my breath.

She drew in a small breath herself then. "Oh, what ever has happened to it? It was so lovely. Yes, this is it. There cannot be another like it, can there?"

My breath came out in a rush, "Thank you mistress. You have been most helpful."

She smiled then; a coy smile, and fluttered her eyelashes at me. "Always pleased to help m'lord" she said.

We stopped at Johannes' house, a small dwelling on the market square near the church of St. Mary. I would leave no message about the dress for that was too dangerous. When he came in, if he had time and would like a good supper, could he come to us? I left the request with his housekeeper Enid.

I was just mounting up in the little yard to the side of his house when he strode in, looking thoughtful.

"I'm glad to see you. Do you have time to come to Durley or must I impart my latest knowledge here?"

Johannes chuckled. "And pass up your Matthew's good cooking? No, my friend. Lead on. Let me just saddle my horse for I've been in the town today and have walked everywhere."

In no time at all we were on the road to the manor and I told him of the day's findings and the conclusion I had reached. We dawdled, a far different journey than the one I had made earlier, all hustle and splashing through puddles and mud. I realised I must look a sight, my horse mired to his neck, my boots grimed with the chalky white mud of the road, my clothes splattered. A stab went through me. No longer would Cecily berate me for the state of my fine clothes. To have her back, I would have taken any tongue lashing.

In the privacy of my office, I took the ruined bliaut from the breast of my cotte once more and laid it before Johannes on my table.

He did not take it but looked carefully at it, then up at me.

"This was left to burn in the charcoal-makers fire, you say?"

"Yes. As I see it, someone has stolen Cecily's dress and bliaut. She kept it, it was no secret - in the bottom of a chest in the solar for she wore it rarely now." I laughed, since Geoffrey and Hawise, it did not fit her as well as it once did. "She always said, where would she go to wear such finery? That someone then went into the forest to change, rode into Marlborough, as this woman, bought the glove, came back to the forest again and undressed, became themselves once more and disposed of the clothing in the fire."

"And then bold as a blackbird, marched up to the hall and left the glove."

"Christ, Johannes, they have back bone, I'll give them that."

"This," said my friend "is progress."

The weather became inclement again the next day. I did not venture out for I had much to do on the manor. The skies were grey and loaded with rain. The place had become too quiet for me. Hawise had gone for a little while to her grandparents at Bedwyn. She would enjoy it there, for they spoiled her hugely. The women had returned to their own homes for the time being. They would return when Hawise did.

I had not been able to sleep in our marital bed either. It was too full of memories, both good and bad, so I had bedded down of a night on my perfectly good daybed in the office. I locked my door at night and I bolted the shutters of the little window tightly. I felt safe there. How everything looked so miserable. Candles were needed for almost every operation in daylight for it was so dark indoors.

Late that night, very late, I was still at my books at my little table, almost falling asleep where I sat, listening to the drip of the rain from the eaves. I had a small brazier with me to take off the chill and realised that I was about to run out of fuel for it. That was odd because I had a young lad keep it topped up for me and it was not like him to forget.

Not wanting to go out to the store in the pouring rain, I recalled that there was some unused fuel up in the solar. There were about eight men sleeping in hall that night, most of them nearer the fire. I could have called to any of them, the younger men or boys; but I did not. Let them sleep, I thought. The candles had all gone out, even those in the wall sconces and I do recall thinking that a little odd also, for we always left a couple burning.

I would pick my way silently across the rushes of the fire-lit floor and up to the bottom of the steps.

The light from the fire did not reach here. Here all was in darkness. The stairs reared up before me but I could make out nothing but a darker black within a grey black. Feeling my way and thinking myself foolish for not going back to fetch a candle, I carefully ascended keeping my hand on the wooden wall rail and holding the banister rail tightly.

The shutters had been partially closed in the solar and a strange brown light filtered through the cracks, through the horn stretched over the openings. There were only two windows here. I remember thinking that I had promised Cecily that the money we had tied up in John's gems should go to putting glass in all our windows. I would keep my promise to her, I vowed.

The bed was in darkness and the curtains were closed. I wandered into the room. A room full of memories. I touched one or two things as if they were unfamiliar. All the room's corners were as black as pitch but I could just see the bucket where the charcoal was kept, lying by the cold hearth. Slowly, my eyes becoming a little more adjusted to the dark and so as not to bump into things, I made my way to the fireplace and stooped to pick up the charcoal bucket. It was then I heard behind me a sort of squeaking noise which did not sound like any mouse to me.

I listened. There it was again. I had left the door open and in three strides was there, looking out. A dark shape in a darker gloom was hurrying down to the bottom of the steps, perhaps with one to go. Why I did not call out, I do not know. It would have been the sensible thing to do for the men in the hall would have roused and apprehended our intruder. Instead I plunged recklessly down the stairs after them and fell headlong down about twelve feet of stairway banging my head, my elbow, my shin, my knees and my shoulder, not to mention my ribs, as I went.

Thank goodness for my quick reactions. These steps were solid stone and I went bouncing down them like a child's ball.

My father, God rest him, had taught me how to fall. "If you are to be thrown from your horse in battle, you must learn how to land and how to curl up and avoid the flying hooves, which will do you just as much damage as an opponent with a lance." I could hear him saying, "You don't want to be killed by your own horse. You must go with the roll, turn yourself into a ball and bounce as well as you are able, away from the threat." All this, whilst wearing heavy chain armour.

Naturally he was not thinking of twelve feet of stone step when he gave me this advice, but the lesson my father beat into me took over once I was airborne and I landed at the bottom, dazed and bruised but in one piece but for a small gash to the bridge of my nose.

I must have cried out for all was then rushing men and lighting of candles. I could see nothing for the lights suddenly swimming round me blinded me. Hal, I noticed, was feeling me all over for broken bones. A couple of the men lifted me up under the arms then and sat me on the bottom step. I sat on charcoal.

"A man," I said breathlessly, "on the stairs, shouldn't be there. Intruder. Go and look outside." I pinched my nose, which was bleeding then winced for the wound to the bridge of it was swelling already.

Hubert Alder the farrier and another man peeled off and ran to the outer door. It was still locked. They looked back at me then as if I had addled my wits in the fall but unlocked it and disappeared into the night.

Hal helped me to a chair.

The hall was much lighter now and the corners, apart from that part behind the stairs and the space underneath it, were beginning to be lit.

I shook my head to clear it and bitterly regretted it.

I called for a cold cloth and someone went running out of the kitchen door.

"What on earth did you go creeping about without a candle for?" asked Hal of Potterne with a wry expression. "Bound to miss yer footing."

Hal had lately insisted on sleeping in the hall instead of in his room by the south wall.

I chuckled. "I am an idiot, I know," but something was niggling me, and after a couple of heartbeats as I reached for the proffered wet cloth, I looked back at the stairs.

Pieces of charcoal were scattered all along the treads. One of the young lads was going up on his knees, picking them up and grimacing at the blackening of his fingers. He wiped them on the back of his tunic. His mother would thank him for that, I thought.

One by one, they went back into the little bucket.

"You'll be as black and blue as a crow come morning." Hal said with a laugh. "Black as yer charcoal I bet."

One of the women came sleepily in from the kitchen with a pot of hot water (well luke warm really) and gently began to bathe my hurts and my nose ceased to bleed.

Robert came in after the two men who had gone into the courtyard to check for intruders.

The manor gate was closed. No one about they said. Wyot the gate keeper had let no one in.

Robert was wearing his shirt and had hastily shoved on his indoor shoes. The sight of his bare legs sticking out of the end of his shirt and his ankle length slippers, all covered with his cloak, struck me as comical.

"These idiots woke me, with their running about - what's up?" he asked.

"I fell down the stairs" I said, "but I swear we had an intruder in the hall."

He looked askance at this. "Doubt it," he said, and then, pushing past the young lad on the steps, took the bucket from him. Carefully he went up the steps to the solar. He poked his nose in, then closed the door. Then on his hand and knees coming down backwards, began to search the floor again for stray bits of charcoal.

I looked away as Hal said, "'Twas a ghost you saw I 'spect."

"Oh Hal, you always gave Geoffrey nightmares with your tales of..." I broke off suddenly aware of what I had said.

Hal looked down at his hands.

"Aye well..."

My eye strayed to Robert kneeling four steps from the top. I turned my head; how it ached.

"I'll take a candle with me into the office and sleep now" I said and rose unsteadily, but not before I had seen him stuff something into the top of his felted slipper.

I searched for the little pot of arnica salve made by my wonderful wife, which I kept in the office and rubbed some on the bridge of my nose, my knees and my elbows. I looked down at my bare legs. There across the front of my ankle on the right leg was a thin line almost a scratch but not a scratch, a sort of cut but not a cut. A red line certainly. Before I slept I remember what had gone through my mind as I tumbled down the stone steps.

I had tripped on something.

***

Later the same morning - oh how stiff I was - I rolled off my daybed onto my knees, swore for they were very bruised, stood, dressed as best I could, swore again at the state of my ribs, wrapped my cloak around me and unlocked my door.

It was late and many of the men had broken their fast and were gone to their jobs. Two men were in the hall, dear reliable Hal of Potterne and Hubert the blacksmith and farrier who had a workshop in our courtyard.

I nodded to them both and they stood, as is right, when I entered.

"No ceremony lads," I said and waved them down.

I bellowed through the kitchen door for food and drink and then exiting into the fine morning, for the rain had ceased overnight, made for the privy tucked into the corner of the northern wall.

By the time I returned, I had food and drink and warm water with which to wash, waiting on the hall table. All through the washing and subsequent meal, I was thinking about my fall of the early morning. I rolled down my chausses to my ankle. There was the mark across my lower leg, a scratch which was more a burn.

Not my imagination then, and not a nightmare.

I ascended the solar steps with a piece of bread and honey in my left hand. There, all along the stone, were the marks of the scattered charcoal, black smudges. One or two tiny bits were left, too small for anyone to pick up in the poor light of last night. I reached the top and opened the solar door. Light flooded over the top step and down onto the first three or four treads. Someone had been up there and opened the shutters. I turned and looked down the flight.

Pushing the rest of the bread into my mouth and chewing, I slowly descended the four foot wide stair, till I reached where I thought I had encountered the obstacle. I turned carefully and carried on my descent, backwards.

On the fourth step from the top, when I was standing on the fifth, I noticed a tiny knot of hairy string no bigger than my thumbnail wrapped around the upright post on the hall side of the stairs. I undid it and picked it up. It was the sort of hempen string we would use to bind up our stooks or secure a small item somewhere on the manor or farm. It had a freshly cut end. Everyone at Durley had some of this. We used to keep it and reuse it. Too good to throw away, even small pieces. This had not been there when I ascended the stairs last night, for I would have tripped going up.

On the other side, the wall side, was a hole gouged into the wood which made up the stair rails. The railings were about six inches apart on the hall side and sturdy, made of good oak. Those on the wall side were a softer wood. On the tread in the very corner, was a small nail. It fitted the hole perfectly. These were all that was left of the string which had been stretched taut over the stair for me to catch with my foot and fall and hopefully, break my neck.

Only I hadn't.

I sat down heavily on the bench.

Another thing bothered me. Had I really seen Robert my brother stuff something into the top of his boot last night? It was dark, I was shocked and tired. What had I really seen? I had seen him kneeling on the stone steps, picking up charcoal, the soles of his feet pointing towards me.

Why, if the men had woken him up and he had walked across the wet courtyard from his room, why were the felt slippers he wore not wet on the sole?

***

Father Benedict was dying, Johannes told me. I had to think about a replacement for him. I had known this man all my life. Replace him? I could not but I must apply to the Bishop of Salisbury for my people must have a priest to christen, confess, marry and bury them. Johannes patiently explained to me that there was something wrong with Benedict's liver and this was turning his skin a vile yellow colour. I hesitated to ask Johannes if this too was poison but he said no, it was just something that happened in old age. We must let him rest wherever possible, take his heavier duties from him and wait. I asked the priest of Bedwyn to help now and again. He was only too pleased. There are still some good men in the world.

I tackled Robert one day about that night of my falling down stairs. He laughed at that, told me that I was seeing things, that I must drink less wine before bed. After all whatever might he be stuffing into his felt boot? Charcoal? There was plenty of that in the manor, he said, he need not steal it from my bucket. He chastised me roundly for wandering about without a candle. The door to the hall had been locked from the inside, and no one could have got in. He almost succeeded in convincing me that my overwrought and tired mind had been playing tricks on me.

I did not tell him about the string nor did I question him about his boot soles. I had the evidence locked away in my chest in the study with the jewels John had given us.

"This pains me. Oh how it pains me but I must now tell the most distressing part of my tale of what came after. If I weep, or rail against God or blaspheme, Paul, please do not write it down, I shall come to my senses soon enough."

One day I went up to the priest's house as I was wont to do when I had time, to take him a little tit-bit from my own table. His was a fine timber built house of two storeys and a good thatch above, close by the church. The old widow Joan tended him as she had always done since I was a child. I knew she cared for him better than many wives did their husbands and that he ate well, as a man in his position might. But a chance kill, by one of my dogs, of a pigeon that had foolishly strayed into the hall, was too good a dish to pass up and I took him the breast covered in a fine sauce, made by my cook Matthew.

I was shocked by Benedict's appearance. He had always been a spry man, spilling over with energy. Here he was, lying in his cot sleepy and disorientated (at first he thought me my father). When last I had seen him, he had been primrose; now he was as yellow in the face and neck as the aconites which flowered in the orchard. The whites of his eyes stood yellow in his head and under the coverlet I could see that his belly was distended and sore. He told me he vomited often, (ah…perhaps my dish of pigeon was not the best idea) and was so, so tired that he found himself sleeping most of the day out.

We reminisced. He often thought he was talking to my father for he would call me my lord Geoffrey and talk about events which had happened before my birth.

He began to talk about my father's marriage to Matilda of Collingbourne; of how they had had to keep it a secret lest the old king find out, halve their income and bite off their heads.

I listened, now and again nodding or asking him to go on. I had hope of learning something more about these times but was concerned that Benedict, in his present vulnerable state, would perhaps reveal something he should not, a secret of the confessional perhaps, which was a thing most certainly best left unsaid.

He chuckled his way through a few fond memories and then for some reason came to the day that he and my father had decided to make sure that Robert would be cared for and taken into the family should my father come to grief when Robert was yet a minor.

It was but a short few months before my father's death. Apparently it was not a decision they came to lightly.

Suddenly, Benedict drew his hand from the coverlet and grasped my arm. I was Aumary again.

"He loved the boy for his angel looks, so different from his own and yours, I might add. He was so beautiful - like his mother."

"Still is," I chuckled. "I think when he comes to take a bride, we shall have the whole neighbourhood in civil war over who has the right to bed him."

Benedict smiled. "He is popular, I know. With the ladies. He has a certain - um - reputation though in the town, with the rougher sort. I hope that does not leak out and ruin his chances. He has been somewhat free with his amours."

I laughed then, "If every man who was bountiful with his seed were pilloried, we should have a whole row stretching from here to the river."

He smiled at that, then said "But, Aumary he is not a kind lover, I'm told. There have been one or two hushed up incidents."

"Oh?"

"No, I speak out of turn. It's his business, not the business of a celibate priest lying in his bed with a mortal illness is it?"

"You have been his confessor," I said. "You above all know the workings of his heart."

"Bless you, he confesses little to me. I always thought he went elsewhere with his indiscretions and petty sins."

"Another priest?"

"Mayhap."

"Ah."

There were other such diversions and then, "He was always a wayward child. You used to tell me how difficult Matilda found him when she was on her own." I was my father again. "The tempers, the little petty hurts and that was to his own mother. You remember, remember the goldfinch, Lord Geoffrey?"

I sat up. "No, I forget, tell me again. It's been a long time" I said, pretending.

"Yes, you do Geoffrey. You were very angry. It was your name day present to your beloved after all."

"Yeees - but the details are hazy. Remind me."

He went on to tell me that my father had bought a caged bird for Matilda. That Robert had, in a fit of jealousy, killed the small bird by hitting it repeatedly with a stone and driving out its brains.

"He was very young and did not quite know what it was he did of course, but it was very upsetting."

I cudgelled my own brains. Where had I seen such behaviour before in my little brother? The honey bee came to mind at last.

"We thought, did we not," went on Benedict, "that the best we could do was ensure that Aumary became responsible for him, once you were gone. Oh, oh, you are Aumary. Oh, dear me. I am rather tired."

"Sleep then old friend" I said. "I'll return tomorrow."

The story played on my mind that night and I watched my brother carefully all evening, at meat in hall and afterwards when he was playing dice with Hal of Potterne. He looked up, saw me staring and gave me that beautiful smile, which had so won me over when I had first known him. I smiled back.

Further visits to Benedict as the illness took away more and more of his present life, and threw him, with a worrying acceleration, back into the past, gave me a greater insight into the times before I knew I had a brother.

***

Finally one day, when the birds were chirruping in Benedict's thatch, he reminded me of the oath I had taken when I had been seventeen.

"I do remember it, Benedict. How can I forget?" I said. "It was one of the most solemn moments of my life."

"We meant it to be so."

"But something has puzzled me all these years. Why was it so vast a thing? Why holy relics? Surely the Bible was enough to ensure my cooperation? Why the secrecy. It was not well done I think."

Benedict sighed. "No, it was not well done and I have agonised over it for these many years, but it was your father's will. He would have it so and I could not gainsay a dying man." He chuckled deep in his throat, "As you could not now I think - with me."

"Oh Father," I said, feigning horror, my hand on my heart, "you are not going to tell me of yet another something which requires my complete obedience at the peril of my immortal soul, are you?" We both chuckled then.

He dozed for five minutes and I watched the sparrows playing with the straw thatch from the roof. Then,

"Of course, we never really knew if it was true."

"Hmmm?"

"The death of the boy. We never knew if he had really drowned the boy. He said not but then..."

"Which boy?"

"Oh I can't remember, some lad he used to play with. It was an accident, I'm sure. Things like that happen when you are nine. Accidents. Childhood accidents. He fell, and went into the water...hit his head. Accident."

"You are telling me that my brother was accused of killing a playmate?"

"No not accused. It never came to that. Your father paid them off."

I'm sure my face must have shown what I felt but Benedict saw nothing. All I could hear in my head as the old man wittered on, was the oath I had taken at seventeen.

"I, Aumary Belvoir, do solemnly swear before God and upon the word of

God that I will, to the last breath in my body, offer unconditional support to and protect and nourish Robert Belvoir my half brother, son of my father Geoffrey Belvoir, for the rest of his days. If I fail and am forsworn, let my immortal soul be damned for ever more, to burn in hell for all eternity. This is my oath, before witnesses and I shall not break my promise to God." It was ingrained in my memory.

"Oh God," I said as I scrubbed my face with my hand as if to scrub out the memory of it. "Oh God! I am trapped."

"Yes, Paul. I was afraid."

I almost ran the short distance into Durley Manor to the safety of my office. I banged the door shut and leaned on it heavily with my back to it. Then I turned and locked it. I was shaking.

No, it could not be. I was wrong. Robert had not drowned the young lad. My brother would not. 'Twas a far cry from a bee or a bird, to kill a fellow human being in cold blood. Kill a child. I calmed down. I needed to go to Collingbourne to learn more of this.

As it happened, I did not need to for Collingbourne came to me.

I'd just felt I had found the time in my busy life, about three days later, to saddle up my horse and ride the six miles to our works at Collingbourne, where we still employed many folk in the spinning trade, when the reeve from the village came clopping into the courtyard on his donkey. Robert had overseen this part of the business for some time now and, though he never needed to be there himself, was assiduous in making sure all ran smoothly, with the help of this fellow, Thomas Honeyman.

Thomas was a large jolly man with a bushy beard and twinkling blue eyes filled with mischief. I knew him to be a master with the quarterstaff. I know he had beaten most of the other fellows hereabouts on fair days and at the Mayday and Twelfth Night celebrations. I winced as he stepped off his donkey, for stepped he did, his long legs dangling. The beast seemed far too small for him. We exchanged pleasantries. I think I have told you before...

"Have I Paul? Have I?"

....that the reeve is the man who is elected each year (and good ones are re-elected naturally) to oversee the business of a village and all its occupants. This means the agricultural business and any other in which the inhabitants engage. Decisions are made by the lord and passed on by his reeve, to the folk of the village. It had come to the notice of the villagers that the church at Collingbourne was in great need of repair. The reeve had come to set before us a list of grievances. The village was not great, they said. He had come, he intoned, to beg some funds for the repair to the roof, to the hay barn and to the priest's house.

I offered to bring him into the office but he seemed reluctant to step inside the hall. He felt, I think that it was not his station to enter into so elevated a residence, used as he was to hovels and cottages and villeins dwellings. I prevailed upon him.

Here was to be my witness.

I gave him everything he asked for and in return I quizzed him about the priest who served them. Might he help out until we had a new priest on our own manor for our Father Benedict was failing.

He said he would ask. He knew our man to be a good priest and a man favoured by God, he said. I told him I had also written to the bishop.

***

Sitting in my office with a pot of ale in his huge hands, leaning and dangling it between his knees, I asked him about Collingbourne, about the business which had begun on such a modest scale, twenty years ago. Thomas hadn't been reeve then but just a plain freeman, who was noted for his beekeeping and with a wife who had begun to spin with her distaff, for Matilda, the fleeces which were farmed from the land round about. They prospered.

At last I was able to say. "Did you know the young lad who drowned, Thomas, I don't have his name? Would have been about...oh quite a few years ago?"

He was mid sip and the eyes became a little wary as he slowly put down his wooden mug on the floor.

"I did m'lord. The son of one of the carters, he was. Name of Johnathan.

Johnathan Carter. Son of Belle and Joseph."

"Do you know what happened?"

His eyes became much more guarded then. Of course he knew. He also knew who he was talking to. He wanted to choose his words carefully and he longed to please me for I had unequivocally given him what he asked for. He did not wish to tell an untruth, but I could see he was not disposed to give me hurt.

"I didn't arrive so soon after the event but soon enough," he said. "Several lads had been larking about at the water mill."

"This is the mill which still stands on the Bourne, is it?"

"Aye m'lord, been a mill there since the Saxons sharpened their swords." He looked up at me with an earnestness I almost flinched at. "Johnathan had been in an argument..." He put up a hand, "There were witnesses to this, with Robert Belvoir, Robert Matildason as he was known to us then."

He drew in breath through his teeth.

"It was said that Robert pushed the young lad into the millrace knowing that the turning wheel would catch him and...well..."

"So the wheel dragged him under?"

"I don't suppose Master Robert would think about that when he pushed, would he? He would just be angry and lash out."

"No" I said, but suddenly unconvinced.

"It was not that they fought and the lad slipped then?"

"Well, like I say, I just heard what folk said. Maybe that was how it happened and he wasn't pushed at all."

"What happened then?"

"Master Robert jumped in after him, some said to help, knowing what he'd done. Other folk...."

"Other folk?"

"Some others say he went in and held him under but I doubt that's true at all. There was much arguing about it. Most thought it an accident."

His face said otherwise.

"And our father paid some money to Johnathan's parents to er..." I sought for the right words, though really they were not the words I wanted to speak at all. "To ease them in their grief?"

"Aye. It wasn't that he didn't accept the word of those that saw it all. Nor did he accept the word of his son straightways. The Lord Belvoir was a fair man, an upright man, you know that m'lord. He listened to us all. 'Corse in those days we din't have a coroner and all that."

"Are these people, the Carters, still there?"

"Bless you m'lord, no. She died two winters after you had the wolves, you remember and Joseph went a year after. Rotting disease - Gangrene."

I thanked him and sent him on his way with a slice of cheese and a pot of ale for his pains.

As he left, and mounted his poor donkey, he turned,

"His brother is still with us though, Thomas Carter."

***

Thomas Carter's name rang in my head all that day.

Here was someone who might have a grievance against Robert. Might he nurture his feeling of revenge for this supposed wrong and then take retribution years later? Might he have planned to hurt Robert but had his plan misfire and hurt others instead? Was this aimed at another and Robert was the unfortunate to pass by that day of the unhorsing? I must find this man and make a judgement about him. First though, I felt I had to talk to Robert.

I rarely went to Robert's room on the south wall of the courtyard. I had little need.

If my brother and I socialised, it was in the hall or up in the solar. I had been reluctant to use the solar for a while now...too many memories and in the evening the hall was always busy with men eating, chatting, making and mending or playing their games. The solar was for the women who looked after Hawise and this was really the only time I went there, to see and play with my daughter. I tended to live in my small office, with my books and my work.

Robert was lounging with his feet on the table when I knocked on the open door.

He tilted his head to look round the door jamb. His lightly tanned face beamed at me, he flicked back his beautiful blond hair, still lustrous and worn long.

"To what do I owe this pleasure?" he asked jokingly.

"You may not think it such a pleasure when you hear what I've come to talk about" I said.

He lowered his feet to the floor. "What have I done now?"

"Why should you think you have done something wrong?"

"Your face is as long as a December night."

"Ah. That's because something I have heard about you has made me sad."

He sat up straight. "Oh?"

I walked into the room. It was larger than Quimper's with more comfort, as befitted a member of the family. The floor was covered with rush matting. A bed with canopy and curtains stood in the very middle. Behind it, out of the draughts, was a chair with cushions and a brazier to keep off the chill. A small side table was placed next to the wall upon which were various items of food and drink, a little of all sorts on red glazed dishes.

The main table at which Robert had been lounging was an ordinary deal one, rather like Quimper's and it was placed next to the partition wall of the next room (a store room) and a chair was drawn up to it. Chests and boxes were piled here and there, a couple of stools, perhaps as many as five shelves with some books and more were piled under the table. Pegs were driven into the walls and held his cloaks and spare clothes that did not reside in the chests. I noticed that there was a solid oak bar at the back of the door. That had been added after the room had been built, as I did not remember it in the plans. Neither did I remember paying for a lock for the door. I supposed Robert had had that added.

A large leather saddlebag was draped over the edge of the table.

I closed the door, moved to the table and perched on the edge.

"I hear things I don't like about you Robert. So I want to know the truth. You will not lie to me, you will tell me the absolute truth of it. Then I will see what I think of it."

He opened his mouth to speak but I ploughed on.

"Benedict tells me and I have also spoken to Thomas Honeyman the reeve of Collingbourne, that you may have the blood of Johnathan Carter on your hands. Did he meet his death at your hands? Did your temper get the better of you and you lashed out and sent him into the mill race, as folk say?"

I didn't give him a chance to think. I saw his eyes narrow but his look was calm and unruffled. "Ah...that. It was a very long time ago. He was an older boy, eleven to my eight and bigger, more muscle than me."

"Is that an excuse for...?"

"No, no excuse, but he was a bad lot. They all were, the Carters. Mouthy, pig headed, proud, bullies." I moved the spare stool and sat opposite him.

"What happened?"

He drew in breath, then let it out again and stared at the floor.

"We were down by the mill, about five of us. Carter was, as usual, boasting of his father's good position in the village. The family had the rights to carry the fleeces and the carded goods, plus latterly, the spun threads to businesses in Marlborough and further afield. They were relatively well off, naturally. He used to pick on me as the smallest and youngest boy. That day he called me bastard to my face. I know he had done it before but never to my face. He laughed. I had no proper father -I was a by blow, a child born out of wedlock. My mother was a village drab, he said, used by many, so who knew who my father really was? It might be Geoffrey Belvoir, it might be a beggar who had been passing through. It was before father and mother married and father owned me as a Belvoir. Haha, things changed then I can tell you."

"Did you push him as they say?"

He looked up then, shrugged, "I did. He had been circling round me, pushing, pinching, scratching, trying to trip me. The others were joining in by penning me in, tripping me also. I pushed him away. He fell. The wheel was turning and before anyone had the chance to catch a hand or haul him out, he was taken under the wooden paddles."

He smiled at me, "If it had been you, would you have taken the jibe and not defended yourself?"

I didn't answer for truly, I did not know what I might have done.

"I realised pretty quickly that it was serious and I jumped in to grab him, avoiding the current which sucked water under the wheel and I dived. I couldn't see him. You know I'm a good swimmer and I knew he couldn't swim. It was very dark and dingy. After a few dives, I noticed someone had stopped the wheel so I wasn't in much danger of being hit after that. I went down a few times at the limit of my lungs. I stayed down quite a long time but eventually I found him, stuck between the wheel and the mill wall. He had a good gash on his head where he'd struck the oak. I think that's what killed him. I pulled him out and pushed him towards the bank. He was fished out dead by a few of the bigger lads and some of the men."

"And this is the truth...what actually happened?"

"Yes. Oh some folk say I was down there a long time and that I drowned him. The water was green and turbulent, so how could they see? They couldn't. They just like an exciting tale. Not so exciting is it, when it's an accident?"

I leaned forward and put my arms on my knees. Our heads were quite close together and I could see his expression clearly. He is either telling the truth, I thought, or he is the finest liar I have ever known.

"And the goldfinch?"

He took himself backwards from my gaze then, straightened up and looked away.

"Have you never done anything of which you are ashamed?"

"No doubt I have, though nothing like that. I can't help it, I have a kindness for small defenceless things. I could not kill for the sake of it. Yes, I have to eat and I will kill to put meat on the table, but I hope that I would not prolong the death or kill in such a way as to give real suffering to any creature, if it can be helped."

"Not to a man who has done you wrong then, who comes at you with a knife to kill you?"

"In battle I would like to think I would defend myself and my own but again, I would not wish to cause suffering where..." I sought for the right word..."where a clean kill could be the outcome."

Robert thought on this then, "I do not know why I did it. I was young, foolish, feeling neglected, perhaps. There's not a day goes by when I don't think of the suffering I caused Mama by that act."

"So you are contrite."

"About that, yes."

I sniffed. "So....do we perhaps have a killer who wishes to cause us, as Belvoirs, maximum anguish? Are we looking at revenge here?"

Robert stood and walked a way round the room.

"You mean Thomas?"

"It was one name that has been mentioned."

"Thomas, taking vengeance for the death of his brother? I doubt it. He suffered badly as a child at the hands of his bullying older brother Johnathan. He isn't the brightest of the stars in the sky and I doubt he truly cared but if, I had held Johnathan Carter down under the mill wheel, I have a feeling that Thomas would have been there helping me."

So there we had it.

I quizzed his face a moment longer. He stood, arms to his side, still, no fight in him, no conflict. I remember saying, "I will think on what you have said."

I stood up and as my leg left the stool, I brushed the leather of the saddlebag perched on the table, sending the whole thing teetering off the edge. It was open and some contents spilled out.

Robert was there in an instant, on his knees clawing the contents back into the pockets and compartments.

Letters, pens, a couple of small bottles, some cut up rags amongst other things and a strange yellow rough stone, rather jewel-like, which had broken free of its wrapping, a piece of pale, thin deer skin. It had rolled a little further than the rest and landed at my feet.

I apologised and stooped to pick it up.

It was a thing of beauty, shining in the reflected candle light, sitting in the palm of my hand.

"What a beautiful thing," I said, "I had no idea you liked jewels."

He smiled as he took it from me, "No Aumary, he said, " 'Tis not a jewel, though ground down..." and he gestured to a pestle and mortar sitting on one of his higher shelves, "and combined with other materials, it can shine like a jewel. It makes a marvellous yellow paint."

"What is it?" I asked.

"Orpiment" he said with no trace of mendacity.

***

I turned quickly to the door so that he might not see my face.

"And where do you get such a thing, here in the forest?"

"The apothecary in Chute Alley. He has many useful things in his shop. In Marlborough." Then he added after a short moment, "though I didn't buy it; 'twas Master Quimper's."

I leaned on the door post and stared straight ahead of me. Two grooms were walking an injured horse around the yard. Hal of Potterne was taking the hall steps two at a time, Warren, Joan the laundress' boy was playing with a stick by the kitchen door. I noticed all these things. Time had slowed but my mind seemed far away.

I remember asking, "Did you know that orpiment is a deadly poison Robert?"

It seemed as though I waited a lifetime for his answer but no, he came back quick enough with, "No!... Jesus. I didn't know that," and there was real horror in his voice.

Chapter Twelve

I strode off without further answer and locked myself again in my study. I went to the window and just stared out.

I don't know how long I stood there but by the time I turned from it, the laundress had collected a pile of washing wrapped in a large sheet and was lugging it through the gate, her stick playing infant on her other hand. The horse had gone with the grooms back into the stable. Hal had come out of the hall again and was talking to the farrier close by one of the store rooms. Life went on at a normal pace. My mind had slowed like a man wading through water.

I had work to do. I couldn't loaf about like a lovesick girl.

How, though was, I going to concentrate?

I had the job of overseeing the working out of how much weaving of wattle fencing we must have to repair the deer fences damaged by wind and animals, and then I would talk to John Brenthall who would speak to the wattle makers who would make it all. The estate carpenter would need to know how much paling we needed for the winter. I had to look carefully at the documents allowing certain folk the right to pannage; the right of feeding their pigs in the woods. There had been a dispute between two of the villagers and my word was needed to prevent it deteriorating into open warfare.

And I had the ceremony of the autumn showing to consider.

Every year the warden of the forest held a feast; we held it as our harvest festival just a little later than harvest time. All who worked in the forest were invited and there was free food and drink, provided at the warden's expense. At this feast, held in October in our largest barn and in the yard in front of it, just outside the walls of Durley, we would have the ceremony of the showing of the Belvoir Regalia. These were items given to the first warden by William the First to add some weight to his office and consisted of a saddle, bridle, sword and belt, and a huge ivory, silver decorated hunting horn, which it is said should be blown when the sovereign was resident in Savernake.

These badges of office and symbols of power were already one hundred and thirty years old when I came to the wardenship. The horn in particular was a beautiful item with a silver mouthpiece and a small silver edge with engravings of the animals of the forest: deer, boar, wolf, in small roundels. The leather strap had silver roundels also, of the heads of men but we never could distinguish what these were, they had become so polished away. I kept these locked safely in a chest bolted to the floor in the office. This in turn was locked and I kept the key on a chain around my neck. When I died, these would pass to the next warden.

Ah yes.....that was something else to which I needed to give some thought. I needed a son and heir. Naturally before that, I needed a wife.

The next few days were devoted to the work of the manor and forest, though I have to say I delegated where I could for I was not at my best, having developed a head cold and a rheum. I sniffed and coughed my way through my duties and through the feast, at which I ate little. I was conspicuous about the festivities wearing my regalia but at the first opportunity I disappeared, divested myself and gave the items to my steward, Henry, who would store them away for next year and bring back the key. Then I climbed the solar steps to find some peace there, to sleep away the late afternoon.

As the afternoon passed to evening, people returned to their homes, gradually trickling away. The women tidied the rubbish and chided their menfolk for drinking too much. The dogs scrabbled and fought over the scraps they found on the floor. Children grew fractious, tired, bad tempered and screamed at their parents. Those who lived in the hall came in and started to sing. The skivvies of the kitchen, at their washing up, in huge barrels in the kitchen courtyard, clattered and banged.

Johannes of Salerno, who attended our feasting, though strictly not a forest man, came up the solar steps and scraped on the door quietly.

"How are you feeling now, my friend?"

"Like my head does not belong on my body," I answered, sitting up in bed. "Give me an honest wound any day. I can stand those far better than this constant earache and blocking of the nose." I coughed, "and my throat feels like I've swallowed a hedgehog."

Johannes chuckled, "I can give you something to ease those for you. Send a boy to my house tomorrow and he can fetch it back for you."

I threw back the coverlet and padded barefoot in my shirt, to the window, throwing open the shutter. I noticed that John had brought back my key and it lay on the table by the window. I didn't hear him come in, so fast asleep was I.

"Folk are gone home then?" I said. "One more year done and the next major celebration will be Christmas."

"Aye," Johannes sat himself on a cushioned chair and put his feet, boots and all, on a joint stool. It looked like he was settled in for the evening.

I poured wine for us both, then, feeling a little chilly pulled my gambeson over my head and sat on the edge of the bed to put on my felt slippers.

"I looked for you in your office first. I hadn't thought to find you here. Walt said you were sleeping up here. Have you begun to use the room again a little more now?"

"No just today, it was quieter here. I'll be back in my office tonight I expect."

Johannes looked at me with his level brown stare.

"I know, I know, it's a good room, too good for just the servant women and Hawise."

"You should think about taking another wife, Aumary."

I sipped my wine. "I have been thinking the same thing but cannot bring myself to consider it seriously."

"I know that you loved Cecily with all your heart but you know that she would not wish you to spend your life alone. There's Hawise to consider, she needs a mother."

"There's a truth is ever one was spoken," I cried and then coughed loudly. "She is becoming a proper little madam."

"Paul, you know what to do with that sentence."

We talked and drank until the sun was down and well beyond and I did not return to my study. Both of us slept side by side on my fine bed, stretched out, snoring with the drink. Dawn found us with two bad heads and Johannes with a runny nose and a sore throat. Johannes went home to Marlborough taking young Peter Brenthall with him to fetch back the remedy for my illness.

Early that afternoon the weather changed. The wind, which had been growing slowly and steadily over the past day, tossing the leaves which used to sweep into the corner of the courtyard, into little whirlwinds suddenly howled like an Irish banshee and began to gather strength. The geese, always good forecasters of storms, began to honk loudly and had to be penned early.

We carefully watched the great oaks along the manor path into the forest, for they were an indication of how the other large trees of Savernake might fare in the gale. I looked out of the solar window. I was still feeling poorly, adding pains in my joints and limbs and overheating and shivering to the rest of my ailments and had spent the day hunched up in blankets in front of the fire, by turns dozing and reading documents. The tall birches towards the road to Bedwyn were flailing around as if tossing their heads in pain. Broken branches streamed across the sky like so many skeins of wild geese flying south. The sky was a charcoal black and as the sun went down the rain began.

When it was almost fully dark, Agnes Brenthall brought in my supper on a tray but I had no appetite for it, and with it a message from John. Their son had not returned from Marlborough.

Agnes was wringing her hands in her apron. "He's a good lad, you know that sir," she said, "He wouldn't dawdle. He's a reliable messenger. He should have been back ages ago."

"Had he anything else to do in the town ,Agnes? Sometimes if folk know a lad is going, they give them other tasks to make it worth their while and a penny to boot. Might he have stopped to spend it, if so?"

"E'en so my lord, but I can't see as he would be so long anyway."

"Perhaps he's stayed in the town to wait out the weather?"

"No. I don't think he would."

I thought.

"No. Which way did they go, top road or bottom do you remember? Would Peter come back the same way?"

"He would always come the shortest way. He was born in the forest, sir, knows his way he does. Knows the best way and with the storm threatening...."

I threw off my blankets. "The bottom road then."

I stood and was instantly dizzy. "Then we had better go down."

I dressed myself in my warmest and most waterproof clothing. If one of mine was lost in a gale in the forest, then no matter how ill I felt, it was my duty to lead the search. John was in the hall with a few others. He said not a word but his eyes followed me as I descended the stairs and came to stand before him.

"We shall go out and look for him, John." I said, patting him on the shoulder. He nodded.

***

The wind was now screaming through the trees and the horses' manes streamed out, this way and that as we saddled up. I had asked for volunteers. John was a popular man and his son was a good lad and well liked too. Many came out to help that night, on foot or on horse. In the end we had thirty odd searchers from manor and village, who knew the forest well.

Out of the protection of the courtyard the wind seemed like a living enemy bent on lifting you up and hurling you away. To stand you had to plant your legs wide and duck your head. Leaves were everywhere and many plants, those we could see, were torn and beaten, broken and gone or lying flat along the ground. Dead and uprooted bushes tumbled in front of you, over you and snagged you as you walked forward.

Heads down we rode and jogged out into the forest and fanned out in the pattern we had agreed before we left the hall. The wind buffeted and pulled us here too, despite the protection of the trees.

We rode the main rides, some jogging, some balanced on the stirrups of others and then took off on the smaller ones, on foot moving out towards Marlborough. Flares were useless in this storm but we tried anyway, having to relight them many times.

Some folk were hit, none seriously, by falling branches which as they fell were, whirled away on the wind to land we know not where, for we could see little beyond our flares. Our voices too were lost in the screaming of the gale and the rushing noises of the trees. Still we shouted and called Peter's name. The rain fell in sheets, so heavy at times, that it was almost impossible to see your neighbour a few feet away for the rustling transparent torrent.

I saw Robert shouting for all he was worth into the gale, his hair plastered to his head and the length of it tied back with a piece of string.

Head down I plunged into the undergrowth, halting at times to lean up against the gusts and then struggling forward again when the gust passed.

Two extra men had been left with our five horses and they kept pace with us on the main road as we quartered the area from Durley to the King's Road and out towards the main road to Salisbury. If we found Peter and he was injured as we feared, he and I would ride quickly into Marlborough and the surgeon. The rest would make their way home doubled up on the mounts or running the main road.

At Bytham's pond we paused for breath and to exchange information and then we floundered on again, clothes flapping like bat wings, hair plastered to heads, boots slipping in the mud and leaf litter of the forest floor.

I drove the rain from my face with the edge of my sodden sleeve only to have it back again in a trice and blurring my vision furthermore. I was hot, very hot despite the wetting and then I was cold again and shivering.

The wind seemed higher than ever but we struggled on, calling, beating the brush around and parting the undergrowth. Suddenly there was a huge booming. The sound seemed to go on forever, and one great old oak tree was uprooted and crashed onto its neighbours with a long drawn out crunching and splintering.

Then another and another. In the dark with just a small circle of light, we could only guess where.

We should come out in daylight and see what damage had been done when the storm abated. This will have happened all over the forest, I thought.

At last and without success, hours later we reached the top of the hill at Furze Coppice. Here the gale ceased to blow in gusts; up here it was one continuous shrieking that took your breath and flattened the lungs into your body, for here there were no trees to act as a baffle. Behind us the forest continued to boil like a cauldron of water and the deafening noise sounded like shingle on a beach being sucked vigorously out to sea. We heard more trees falling. It was a very sad sound.

I ordered the men to fan out along the top of the hill and then to descend into the outskirts of the town, through the coarse grass.

We found Peter half way down the hill, huddled into the lee of a solitary furze bush, shivering and wet through.

I scooped him up in my arms, took off my sodden cloak, wrapped him in it and yelled for his father who had been searching with me.

Twelve year old Peter had been so tired with battling the wind and he'd been afraid that the falling trees further in the forest would land on him, he said. He had turned back towards the town and safety, bright boy, but had fallen foul of a rabbit hole in the half light and had tumbled down the hill a little. His ankle was swollen to twice its size and he could put no pressure on it. He had crawled so far he said and managed to find a stick to lean on but on one leg could not make any headway against the screaming wind. He'd found somewhere to lie up and wait out the storm.

My heart hammering in my chest, I hugged him to me and as best I could, slipped and slithered towards the road and eventually made the safety of the horses. I jumped up and held my hands out for the boy but his father was there first and he took him up before him on his own horse's pommel.

Then it was a wild ride for Marlborough town and Johannes' house.

The rest turned back to Durley on the Burbage Road and their warm dry homes. Those that were still standing and undamaged that is.

The lad was strapped up and comfortable and Johannes, John and I talking in whispers later that night, decided that John should stay and I should ride home quickly with news for his mother. She would know that he had been found, of course, but not the extent of the damage to her chick, so I would take the message that it was a bad sprain to his left ankle, a few cuts and bruises but nothing more serious.

I was dog tired, not really any more dry than I'd been before, despite the good fire at Johannes' but my horse, Bayard was fairly rested after hours of standing waiting on the road and then a good rub down and some oats in Johannes' stable, so I felt he would carry me home without my having to guide him.

Johannes tried to coax me to stay for he was aware that I was feverish and should be better cosseted in front of a roaring fire but I would have none of it.

I said my goodbyes and gave my thanks, gently steaming in the passageway, mounted Bayard and then was off past the church and up towards the hill.

At the bridge I stopped. Since we had clattered over it not a couple of hours ago, the river had risen and had taken much of the structure with it. Houses on the north side were partly swept away. I agonised over what to do. Should I try to ford the river here or go upstream a little and try where the river fanned out naturally before the town mill? Nicholas Barbflet owned this and I knew he and his staff kept the river under control there well, as much as he could with the flood boiling over the bank.

I decided to try the natural ford there at Culvermead where there were two smaller diverging streams to cross.

Back along the High I went, and although this meant that I was out of my way a little, having to snake back to the London Road past the tanner's yard.

There, I became aware that someone was following me but tired as I was, the thought flitted through my brain and out again.

Here the bridge, for so it was called, was made up of several large sarsen stones placed in the river bed and I managed to ford leading Bayard and coaxing him across, for even here the river had submerged the stones to the depth of two feet or more. My boots were already ruined, I laughed, what more could happen to them to ruin them further?

Once more in the saddle and perspiring even though I knew that I was cold and shivering, I set off up the hill. Now, I really felt that I was being followed. I looked back. Nothing, but the poor town looked sodden and unhappy and there were several thatches down and some houses by the river under water. I hoped that good neighbours would have taken the homeless inhabitants into their own safe, warm homes this night. The road was streaming with water and Bayard had to pick his way carefully to avoid pot holes. Mud, stones and twigs were coming down the lane in torrents and adding to the general debris clogging the river bank.

I leaned in the saddle, tried to ignore the wind and rain and let Bayard have his head.

We made good time and turning back over my left shoulder, could just see dawn peeping over the trees at Mildenhall, though truthfully it seemed more of a less dark blue patch in an inky dark sky. Eventually Bayard and I veered off into the complete darkness of the track which led past the three tumps, or burial mounds of our ancestors and thence on to Durley coming in by the northwest track. This was the quickest but not necessarily the easiest way for it was narrow and not much used.

A few paces in I was stopped by a huge fallen tree, ash I think, completely blocking the path. I stood for a few seconds thinking. Could I make my way round? No. Could I hack my way through? Certainly not. I had nothing with me except my knife and that would be useless against such an adversary.

I turned the horse and clopped back a quarter of a mile. Yes, here was another path. I remembered it. It passed by the little pond some called Oak Hill pond.

Off we went again at a slightly faster pace for the track here was better underfoot and in a small degree, raised from the ground around.

Of the next few moments I remember very little. It was so dark that it was not possible to see the chalk track (which is often visible when glistening wet and quite pale in the night), in front of my horse. Bayard could see or perhaps he could smell for he reared up once, as we began to pass the small pool. I was nearly unseated but made an ungainly grab for his mane and hung on. I woke up quickly from my doze.

Something whizzed past me at speed. I ducked. Then another. This hit my saddle with a dull thwack.

The wind whipped my cloak away and I gathered it in quickly and set my feet to Bayard urging him on.

Another few paces in I was swept backwards from that saddle by a taut rope at chest height, and landed with a heavy thump and splash at the edge of the pool. Luck was with me that night, for I landed on moss and plants and in water which broke my fall.

I looked up, blinking at the lightening sky, and a huge branch came into my vision and down onto my forehead and then all was blackness.

Luck most certainly was with me that day for I know that had I remained unconscious I most certainly would be dead now.

I did not know it but my assailant was then dragging me further to the edge of the pool, turning me over and was about to hit me again on the back of the head, I think, and drown me, when Bayard, that clever horse whom I had trusted more than once to save my life, came to my rescue.

My father had seen much more battle than I. In fact, I had seen no battle at all but I did practice my sword work every day and was fairly confident on horseback in my mail, with shield and lance. One's horse for battle is a bigger horse than Bayard, for smaller mounts cannot support the weight of mail and they are specially trained to be calm in the face of an attack. I kept one solely for that purpose and would take him from the stables at the castle should I need such a beast. I had my favourite there and would train him when I was able but Bayard was a wily horse good for most journeys and for one more thing. I had taught him to protect me as one trains a destrier. The hooves of such horses are sharpened for battle and they are taught to rear up and trample earthbound adversaries, to push them over, to bunt them like a ram does with his horns. Bayard had no sharpened hooves but I had taught him to rear and trample, push and bunt.

As I was turned over, my face hit the water reviving me a little and I was aware of a much larger splash.

I heard Bayard trampling the ground, his head above my body and nickering.

I looked up and slowly drew my knees under me to rise. I shook the water from my eyes.

A darker shape was floundering in the deeper water of the pool.

Bayard stayed above me blowing through his nostrils and pawing the ground.

I lifted my hand to my head. Yes, I had been hit. It was not my imagination.

There, struggling out of the water, was my brother Robert.

"God's teeth, Aumary" he said, " Your bloody horse damn near drowned me!"

Chapter Thirteen

I was very dazed and extremely fatigued, ill and wandering in my wits a little but I knew then that I was in extreme danger. I felt for my knife, the one I kept strapped to my side. Yes, there it was.

I stood shakily.

"Did you not know he could do that?"

I would not let Robert know what I suspected.

"I was bending over you - I saw your attacker make off in the woods and I was just checking you to pull you out of the water when your bloody horse got his head under me and tipped me in the pool!"

He laughed. "Handy horse to have, that."

"He is indeed, and he will protect me with his life, should he need to. I can't tell you the damage his hooves can do if you get too close," I warned.

Robert stood wringing out his wet clothes.

"How is your head? Let me look. He gave you quite a clout, the attacker." He reached for me.

I pulled away. "Fine, really, I should get on."

"Are you sure you can ride?"

"Bayard is a home bird. He can get me safely back to Durley. Why don't you go after the man you say attacked me? He went that way I think." I pointed back towards the road.

"Anyway, what were you doing on this track? I asked. "The others must long ago have reached home."

He undid the string which kept back his hair. The light was better now and I recognised it before he stuffed it into his cotte. He shook the long blond locks and water cascaded everywhere.

"I was worried about you when you didn't return. It's been hours. I came back by the lower track as it's the quickest. Then I found that I couldn't get through because of a fallen tree so came this way instead. I saw someone lurking here and then heard a noise. Then I found you. Good job I did."

I so wanted to confront him but I knew if I did, he would prove even wilier and I would be in mortal danger, weak as I was. I mounted Bayard again. I felt safer on horseback. My face was grim.

"Perhaps we shall go home together then. Find your horse. Things will look different in the morning." He laughed then, "It is morning now see," and he pointed to the eastern sky.

I had been on my guard until then but something in me, tired and as unwell as I was, relaxed its grip and I took my eyes from him for a moment to look eastward at the lightening sky. Quick as a flash he pushed my foot up out of the stirrup and tipped me off Bayard and onto the ground the other side of the horse's body.

With an 'oomph' I hit the ground and was winded, but I had the presence of mind still to roll (once again my father's training saved me) away from the danger.

Robert danced away from Bayard's now flashing hooves and picked up a large and wicked branch. He swung it at the horse's legs and Bayard backed out of reach.

Then he came for me.

"You knew it was me didn't you?"

I was watching him carefully this time; my hands on my knees trying to gasp in breath, all I could do was nod. The pain in my lungs and midriff was excruciating. 'Play for time, Aumary,' I thought, 'you are a warrior. You have been taught to fight. He is a pen man, a clerk, an administrator, he's had no training. You can beat him. And he is not your size, nor so powerful.' Robert was only five feet six and I was six feet with wide shoulders and strong arms.

And then, unbidden into my mind came my oath.

My breath was easier now and I circled him watchfully.

"Come, Robert," I said eventually. "We need not quarrel. Whatever it is I have done to you to make you so hateful of me, I will put right. Let's go home."

I feigned more hurt than I felt.

He laughed loudly then and his voice was taken away with the wind.

"Oh, you are such an innocent." He raised his head and laughed again, loud into the sky. I judged my moment and sprang. He did not expect it.

I hit him with quite a force and we fell to the ground, just to the edge of the pool again. Tangled in his cloak as he was, he couldn't move well, but slippery as a fish, he wriggled from my grasp, leaving the cloak under me. I rolled over. The branch came down again grazing my hairline. I grabbed his long locks and pulled.

Down he came and we rolled into the water. He dropped his branch.

He tried to push my head under the surface but I was too strong for him. I reared up and smacked him hard in the face.

'That' I thought, 'is my first dip into the fiery pit of hell.'

I grasped the back of his tunic and hauled him up.

"I have sworn an oath not to hurt you, Robert" I said, "But right now, I am not sure I can keep that oath."

He wriggled and bucked under my hand and tried to get an elbow to my ribs but again I was ready for him and I dipped him, by his long hair, head first into the pool. He struggled and spluttered and eventually I let him up, still holding onto him.

"If you are going to attack people face to face, brother, you should have done more wrestling practice. I can't be overcome as easily as a ten year old in a mill pond."

My anger was making me stronger than I felt.

I reached for the string he had shoved into the top of his cotte. He wriggled and cursed. I turned him and held him by the neck and pressed hard on his windpipe, with my forearm. 'That is my second dip into the fiery wastes, I suppose, I thought'

He reached up and grasped my arm saying, "You are strangling me" or at least I think that is what he was saying. However, I did not let go but relaxed a little.

My head was swimming but I managed to get the string. I did not doubt it was the piece he had salvaged from the hall steps.

He had tripled it to wrap his hair and I undid it with my teeth and pulled his hands to his back and tried to bind him. Really the string was not strong enough.

Suddenly he kicked out and his boot met my thigh. I let go.

He backed off a way and then reached into his shirt. There in his right hand was a slingshot and in his left a pebble. He smiled. Oh such a sweet smile. "Yes brother," he said, "you know how deadly I can be with this."

He circled me. I moved. Bayard was watching carefully from a distance, waiting his chance. He knew this man, he had known him for years. Why should he harm him? On the other hand he knew danger when he smelled it.

Robert looked at the horse and quick as a flash, threw his pebble. Bayard neighed and reared and backed off further into the trees.

"No, Aumary," said Robert, "no help there."

He reloaded. I backed away. He swung. I dived. He missed. He danced away. I stood once more and felt for my knife.

"Ooooh ho" said Robert. "This is serious." He grinned, tutted and slightly shook his head. "Are you going to kill me? I think not."

Once more he aimed the sling-shot, once more he failed to hit me.

I circled some more and with my knife out before me, closed in on him. Sling-shots do not work at close range. He fiddled for another pebble. Loaded it swiftly. I walked closer. To give himself time to load, he backed away a little and then he was swinging.

Too close to the trees. He cursed as the sling-shot caught in a tree branch and he threw it away in disgust.

I closed in further. The only thing I could think to do was to render him unconscious. Perhaps a strike with my knife hilt to his head?

I was almost on him when he too pulled a knife from the back of his tunic. It was a two inch wide double-edged weapon and as sharp as a scold's tongue. I knew it. I had seen it before.

He slashed at me and missed.

I darted forward and despite every ache in my body, my head pounding like a blacksmith's hammer tried to wound him on the head so that perhaps I could get him to the ground. There he would be much more vulnerable.

I missed him, probably because I was so tired and so ill. I slipped on rain sodden, fallen leaves and fell to one knee.

He came in for the kill.

I reached up and grasped his wrist and twisted. He yelled. The knife he held spun from his hand and on the way down grazed his right forearm which was partially exposed and which poked from his muddied shirt sleeve.

I let go and stood. Robert screamed as if the fiends of hell were after him and ran away a pace or two.

Somehow I chuckled. "Aw come on Rob," I said, "if you are going to fight, you must learn to take petty little wounds like that one, like a man."

He was shaking his head like a man demented. Then he bit his arm and spat and bit again and spat.

Puzzled, I picked up his knife and going to Bayard who had moved a little closer, threw up the flap of my saddle pannier and dropped it in.

Robert was almost sobbing and in one last effort and with a yell loud enough to cause some birds coming to from their nightly roost, to rise up in alarm, he ran at me. God knows what he thought he would do.

Before he reached me, Bayard turned and bit him on the shoulder.

Robert screamed then.

"Ah yes," I said "You haven't seen him do that one either have you?"

He fell to his knees before me, totally submissive.

"You don't understand," he said blubbering, "if I don't get help soon I will die. The knife, my knife, it was poisoned."

I turned to him, aghast.

"Get me home," he said. "Quickly."

***

We made good time, as we were not far from Durley. He nursed his arm the whole way in silence. Once in the courtyard he staggered to his room and rummaged in the panniers in which I'd seen the orpiment. A small vial of green pottery came out and was drunk greedily and the rest he tipped on his wound. He seemed to know what he was doing.

I stayed watching quietly in the doorway. A couple of manor folk passed us both with furrowed brows but few people were about that early, especially after the searching of the night before so no one asked any awkward questions.

I would, though, when I had seen to myself and slept a little.

I asked him for the key to his room. He snivelled but he gave it and I locked him in, saying, "Rest a while now. If you want me to send for Johannes, I will do it forthwith."

He shook those sopping blond locks, "I will not know for a while if the stuff works, though according to the book, it should. If I begin to fade in a couple of hours or so, I will bang on the door."

"Be sure you do, I do not want your death on my conscience."

I found Wyot, the nightwatchman, in the kennels with the dogs and asked him to send a message to Peter's mother in the village and to look to brave Bayard and Robert's mount. Weary and drained, I slowly mounted the steps to the hall and those of the solar and fell on my bed fully clothed, caked in white mud and sopping wet through. I had left the door open and one of the women came in shortly after. I think it was Old Joan. I remember her tutting at the state of me. She called for help. Hal of Potterne came running up the stairs and together I think, they pulled off my boots, undressed me, dried me off and put me to bed with hot stones to warm me. I only vaguely remember it all.

I slept till nearly midday. I luxuriated in the warmth for a moment, then realising what had happened in the hours before I reached home, I sprang out of bed.

No, I did not spring. I tried to spring! I was yet a young man and in the full vigour of life but that day, every part of me ached, not only with the pain of being unseated from my horse, bruises gained in the fighting with Robert and the small nicks and scratches sustained when searching the woods for Peter, but with a pounding head and sore limbs and fiercely stabbing joints of my illness. I also realised I had a raging thirst. The solar door was still open and I called down to the hall, but no sound came out. I croaked again, this time a little more effectively but not loud enough for anyone to hear.

I grabbed a blanket and tried to rise again. The movement knocked over a small wooden box which lay on the night table by the bed. Hal heard it and came, yet again bounding up the steps.

"Drink" I squeaked. The effort cost me much and I fell back on the bed.

He lifted a cup to my lips and I have never tasted better nor sweeter water than I did that day.

Whispering I said, "Hal, will you go to Robert's room. Here is the key. No, do not ask why I have it. Can you perform the same duty for him please?" I did not add, 'if he lives.'

He nodded. Then I said, "Lock him in again and bring back the key. Do not talk to him and be wary."

He did look askance at that but Hal was used to obeying me and so he clattered down the steps and was gone.

How long he was gone I cannot tell for I dozed again where I lay.

Robert's key was on the small table when I awoke at last and Hal was sitting on the joint stool by the bed. I turned my head to look at him. I did not speak. I did not ask if my brother was still alive, nor if he had spoken, indeed if he had asked for me at all.

" 'E slept," said Hal "I din't wake him. He had drained the jug of water by 'is bed an' 'ad changed 'is clothes to dry uns. By the fullness of the pot by the door 'e's pissed a good deal too."

I sighed. "Good."

Then I slept again.

***

Johannes came in with Peter over his father's saddlebow a few hours later. He fussed and petted me and gave me some medicines which he said would take down my fever and help with the pain. I asked him to look in on Robert. I said nothing of the fight we'd had, nor of the wound which Robert had sustained. Let my brother tell him what he wished. I had no doubt he would spin a fine tale. Doubtless, I would hear of it anon.

Of only one thing was I certain. Until I had mulled it all over and I felt I could better contend with my new found knowledge, Robert must stay locked up in his room.

Then for a short while I took pen to parchment and wrote. I wrote with a fury which cramped my hand and shoulder and which made me blurry-eyed and hot. Then I slept again.

I awoke to a fierce shouting and yelling. I did indeed feel better and was able to put my legs over the edge of the bed and stand unaided.

Creeping like an old man and with another cloak wrapped around me, for decency, I descended the solar steps, went to the outer hall door and looked down into the courtyard. Several people were listening to Robert yelling through his locked and bolted door, one of them Johannes.

Hal was remonstrating with him through the wood. "You stay there young master till the lord tells us you can come out." I heard him say. "An no amount o' blasphemin an cursin is goin to 'elp you get out quicker."

I listened to the short conversation, which went as follows.

"He's mad I tell you. I went out to help him last night in the wood and he turned on me. He turned on me, his own brother, with a knife. Christ's Blood I have never seen him in such a fury. Never have...."

"No neither 'ave I, so perhaps we'll just wait....."

"Hal, let me out so I can speak to him, I don't think he understands..."

"No, none of us understands, Master Robert, but my orders is to keep you there for a while and keep you I shall."

Johannes took a step nearer the door.

"Peace now Robert, this isn't doing you any good."

"Johannes, c'mon, you know I have the wound to prove it. And bruises. He grazed me. Why would he take a knife to his own loving brother, Johannes? He's run mad I tell you. It must be the grief....."

"Madness don't run in the family, young sir," said Hal, "so I reckin in good time we'll see what's 'appenin an' then all will be made clear."

Robert banged on the door with his fists.

"He's ill, his wits are gone. He attacked me, ME, Hal....who only ever loved him as a loving brother should..."

" 'Ush now young sir, you'z makin a bit of a fool of yerself. Let's have peace and quiet about it until the lord is feeling better and then we shall get a story I'm sure. Then you'll 'ave a chance to say what you want."

So, that was the way Robert was going to play it.

***

Johannes turned then and saw me. Our eyes met. Nothing was said and then I moved back into the doorway and on into the hall. Once more in the solar, Johannes caught up with me.

I had been sitting for a short while at the table, my head on my arms. I felt numb. Looking up at last I saw Johannes loitering in the doorway as if afraid to approach.

"Have no worry Johannes, I shall not attack you with a knife. I'm not mad in my wits. God! I wish I was."

He came in then. "Can you tell me what happened?"

I lowered my head again. "No. I cannot. I shall never be able to."

He sat opposite me and laid a friendly hand on my arm.

"He has a wound, it's true, it's just a graze and he seems to have treated it himself. How did he get it?"

"I cannot tell you."

"Cannot, or will not?"

I remember shaking my head.

"Did you fight?"

"Yes."

"Why in God's name? You are good friends. There has never been a cross word between you that I know of."

"You cannot know, Johannes."

I lifted my head again. "What you do not know cannot harm you. Let me think - I need to think. One thing you can be sure of though. I meant him no hurt, in that fight. Make of that what you will. No harm. No harm at all."

***

Another dose of medicine and one more short sleep later and I was ready to face my brother. I ate and drank a little, washed, dressed and slowly, weak as a day old kitten, I descended the solar steps again.

I had agonised about the decision of where to meet him. I needed somewhere quiet, away from prying ears, somewhere safe, a place from where Robert (for I did not trust him one iota) might not be able to escape easily, should escape be in his mind.

I sent a message to Father Benedict in his sickbed, in his house by the church. I called for Hal of Potterne. I sent to the village for Walter and John. They came running within a few heartbeats.

I gave them their instructions. There was no doubt they were puzzled, but when your lord and master tells you to keep guard and not let someone pass, no matter what they might say to you, it is a thing you do without question.

I asked Hal to go into Robert's room with me and search him for weapons. Hal lifted an eyebrow at that and was about to say something which I forestalled with, "I would not ask it if it were not important, Hal." He nodded then.

Outside Robert's room in the twilight of yet another day, I called to him that it was Aumary and that Hal and I were coming in to see him. He was lounging on his bed and did not move as we entered. Hal stood in the doorway with his arms folded.

"Get up please" I said and nodded that Hal should search him. That completed, I asked Robert to fetch his cloak and to come with the four of us.

"What? Am I to be strung up with no trial on the say so of a madman? Jesus, Aumary, I had thought better of you."

Walter answered for me, "Madman he may be Master Robert, but he is lord here and is justice in his part of the world, so keep a respectful tongue in your head."

Robert saw his face and was silent. He stood and put on his boots.

We surrounded him and though a few folk stared and nudged and questioned each other, we marched him silently through the gate of Durley Manor. The wind, though much abated, was still skirling around the open spaces and lifting leaves and debris. At the wall we turned left and into the churchyard. In the left hand corner close by the edge of the village wall, we entered the garden of Benedict's house. Here we stopped and I told my men to take, one each, the front doorway, back doorway and the window on the roadside on the back of the building and that they were to stay far enough away from the wall so that they could not listen. Robert and I ascended the steps to the first floor.

Benedict was looking a little better and was sitting up in bed, propped on pillows. There was evidence of food and drink taken, with pots and mugs on a small table at his elbow. He was still the vile yellow colour and his face had become so puffy, he almost looked like another man but his eyes twinkled as usual. Joan was with him, fussing like an old hen, when we dipped our heads under the beams for we both Robert and I were too tall to enter the loft without banging our foreheads. I thanked her for her care of the old man and she bobbed a curtsy and left.

"Well, this is a pleasure. I hope you have come to tell me all the news about the storm. I wondered if my thatch would last at one point."

Benedict saw our faces and stopped. "Ah, this is more serious than storms I think."

I sat. Robert continued to stand.

You got my message?" I said.

"Ah...yes...well....though I haven't quite..."

"You are the only person I can trust with the thing I am about to do, Benedict," I said.

He put down the parchment he had been reading and folded his hands.

"Am I to take a confession?"

"Pah!" Robert snorted and tossed his head "Confession? Of what?" He took a step towards me and I stiffened my pose, ready to spring should I need to.

"Confess that I had to defend myself from this madman, this murdering liar who went for me when I was trying to help him...?"

"Robert," I was trying to stay calm. "We three in this room know the truth of the matter. Let us have no more pretences."

I saw Benedict flinch then, "The truth? Well, only Robert knows that."

I turned to the old man, "I have evidence, Father, that Robert is responsible for at least two attempted murders and probably the death of my wife Cecily and others as well.

Johannes and I have been gathering information for a while now and as we speak, I have two men searching Robert's room for further proof. Naturally Johannes does not fully understand and my men have no idea what they are looking for, but they will know when they find it"

Robert sucked in breath then and called me 'Bastard.'

Benedict shook his head. "You have kept faith, Aumary."

To Robert he said, "Your father was worried that you were not, when you were a child, shall we say, a whole person, but he could not believe that you, being so beautiful a child, could not mend as you grew. He loved you well. I am sad to say his trust was betrayed."

"Lies."

Benedict shrugged his shoulders.

Robert looked round for somewhere to sit and as cocky as a sparrow, dragged a stool forward with his foot and perched on it with his boots on the bottom of the bed.

"You want me to confess?" he chuckled, "to a madman and a priest who will be dead within the month? Not much of a confession is it?"

"Benedict has had his suspicions for a while now, Robert. When I brought him my thoughts, he admitted that for some time, he had been as worried as I."

Robert laughed. "I could tell you this and that and then when he," he gestured to Benedict, "when he is gone it will be your word against mine. Not enough to hang me, brother."

"I have no desire to hang you. No, correction. I have a burning desire to string you up, then string you up again and see you suffer but I am unable."

Robert laughed again. He clapped his hands, then stood. "Well, then, if you have not the slightest bit of evidence for anything, I shall be going."

I was up and at the door and pushed him back onto the stool.

"I saw you last night with your slingshot. You tried to murder me with it. You used it to make my horse bolt. You were so busy sniveling into your chin about your grazed arm that you didn't see me pick it up. I have it."

He shook his head "Many folk hereabouts have a slingshot. Lots of the younger boys do."

"Yes, they do. You used it all those years ago to try to kill Cecily and failed. Then no doubt when we go out into the forest we shall find the rope you slung between two trees to sweep me from my horse, a trick you have used before, I might add. Men are bringing it in now."

He came back as I knew he would with, "Yes it happened to me remember? Why should I do that to myself? It wasn't a pleasant experience, I can tell you."

"Ha! Except that you strung it up and were never truly felled by it. You made the same mistake there as you did with me last night. You struck yourself on the forehead, perhaps with a branch. Not too hard, enough to bruise and break the skin. When you fall off backwards, it's naturally the back of the head which is hurt." I fingered the egg on the back of my head and I could feel the bruise on my rear and on my elbows. "Not the front, I know to my cost. You had no bruises, not where they mattered."

He snorted and again, cheekily and slowly, raised his feet to the end of the bed and folded his arms.

"Then, there is your knife. I have that too. Perhaps Johannes can tell me what sort of poison there was on it. He can probably also tell me what it was you drank last night to bring yourself round again, after you were scratched with it."

"You will not ask him."

"Don't be too sure."

He stared at me.

Father Benedict coughed "Poison? Oh dear me."

"He is not going to die of his wound, Father."

Benedict scratched his bald pate, "Then shall we start at the beginning?"

I took a shuddering breath.

"Johnathan Carter. You did kill him, didn't you, as people said? You did hold him under and drown him?"

"No."

Robert's face became ugly for the first time.

"You did."

"No, I had no need to, I held him so that the paddle of the water mill hit him, then I left him to drown."

Benedict groaned at that. "You must confess properly, Robert, or your soul will be damned forever."

Robert shifted on his stool and cocked his head. "Damned? Who says so?"

"Holy Mother Church teaches...."

Robert raised his voice and chuckling said, "I do not recognise Holy bloody Mother Church, Father. Never have, never will. It's all a complete nonsense. There is no such thing as God. People like you set up gullible folk, like him" and he pointed to me "to use them and control them. I don't think I know a real churchman who believes in God. I don't believe in anything, so getting me to confess and to ask for absolution because I am terrified of hell is not going to do you any good." His chin came up and he was staring us out.

Poor Benedict, this was almost too much for him. He shivered and whispered the word "heresy" to me and crossed himself fervently.

Robert leaned forward. "All that is going to do you no good either, Father. I'm impervious to silly threats and nonsense."

"So now we know you killed Carter. Is there anyone else we don't know about?"

Robert merely smiled and chuckled.

"Why, Robert? That is the thing that puzzles me most of all. Why do you feel the need to kill?" I pulled from my cotte the piece of parchment which I had scribbled on earlier that evening.

"These are my thoughts. I wrote them earlier today when my mind was clouded and in turmoil. I hope to God I'm wrong because here we have six deaths and I hope against hope I cannot lay them at your door." I dropped the parchment on the table.

Robert shrugged and looked away. "I shall say nothing."

"Let us first consider Piers. He was a good man, Robert. Did you kill him?"

"Why would I? What was he to me?"

"It was as you said. He fell, missed his footing?"

"Aye, and he had been drinking a little, was none too steady on his feet that day."

I considered this carefully. "He did not reek of drink, that I could smell, when I reached him and I had not known him to be a toper before. Ever."

Robert shrugged again.

"What were you doing up on the wall walk at that time, to see him fall?"

Robert leaned forward once more and met my gaze, "Looking out to see where everyone had gone. Remember, I was not all that familiar with the place then. That was my first harvest, I'd only been here since that spring. I was looking out over the fields to see where everyone had collected. I was coming out to help the girls bring the food to everyone."

His answer did not satisfy me but it was just possible that it was somewhere near the truth.

"And now Cecily?"

He sat back again, "Ah yes, our sweet, simpering, roly-poly Cecily."

"Did you try to kill her by the river?"

"I may not have liked her much. She was bossy and when I was younger kept me on a tight rein, but kill her? Again, why would I? Absurd. I told you. I wasn't the only one with a slingshot. Didn't see you asking some of the others about their weapons?"

"Then why, last night in the forest, did you say to me, 'you know how deadly I can be with this?' "

He smiled. "I think you are mistaken brother. I don't think I said that. Remember, you were feverish and unwell. By the look of the sweat on your brow now, you are still. I don't think, when you attacked me that you realised who I was."

His gaze snaked quickly to Benedict to see what effect this utterance had had on him.

"But you have seen me bring down rabbits for the pot with it, so yes, you do know."

Benedict looked at me with such pity in his eyes that I swallowed. This was not the confession I thought I might get.

"And now we come to William, Uncle William."

"Not mine. Your family. Not my mother's brother, yours."

"Was it easier to kill him because he was not?"

He folded his arms. "I have told you what happened. Colmar was there too. He told you what he saw."

"I think he lied. Or he was uncertain and you convinced him. Maybe he thought about it and realised it could not be so and that is why he had to die next. He was about to tell the truth."

Robert guffawed and leaned backwards in his joy, tipping the stool on two legs. "That man wouldn't know the truth if it reared up and bit him on the arse. He was a greedy, grasping, greasy little toad."

"Ah, so he tried to blackmail you?"

Robert regained his calm demeanour. "I am saying nothing."

"How did you do it?"

There was silence.

"You made a mistake there Robert, with Colmar."

"Oh?" His chin jutted aggressively. He doesn't like to be told he's got something wrong, I thought.

"If Colmar had drunk himself to death just there between the blocks of stone, the jug or barrel or flask, whatever he had drunk from, should still be there. That alerted us to the fact that something was amiss."

"Us? You and bloody Johannes the genius?"

"We never did find it. I suppose it is lost in the forest somewhere, thrown when you went out sometime later, on your horse. Who is going to ask the lord's brother what he has in a sack over his saddle bow? Who will question?"

Robert snorted as he chuckled.

Benedict said quietly, "I can take no more Geoffrey. Such evil."

Robert cocked his head towards the bed with a questioning look.

"He thinks I am father sometimes" I said. "He has done now and again for some time. I think this business will finish him."

I ploughed on.

"Quimper? Did you suffocate the man?"

I thought that I saw Robert's pupils dilate with shock then. Johannes and I had told no one but Cecily about the fact that we believed Quimper smothered with a pillow. My brother recovered quickly.

"Is that how he died? I didn't know."

"With a cushion, we believe."

"Ah. He was an officious, silly man and of course we know now that he was passing on messages to Arthur of Brittany's party, so he was not whiter than white, was he? However, kill him for that? No."

"So why did you kill him?"

Robert moved his head sideways in disgust, tutted and sighed. "What does it take to convince you I had no reason to kill Quimper?"

"Did you know that he kept quite a large amount of money in his room?"

"He thought himself so clever, but yes, I knew it. So did others I think. You cannot say that I stole from him. If so, where is the money? You are searching my room. You'll not find it there."

"No, I suspect you have another safe place somewhere. Perhaps out in the forest, where you might hide things. Like a charcoal burners' heap, for example."

His head came up in alarm. Those beautiful brown eyes narrowed. There was anger and fear in the pinched white around the nose and lips, a frightened quality to his face.

I had him. He recovered well, I'll give him that. "We might find money there too"

"What would I be doing there? I'm sure I have no idea what you are talking about."

Benedict stirred in his bed. He too had seen the shock on Robert's face.

"A part of Cecily's dress was found in a charcoal burner's fire out in the forest. It was used as a disguise by someone who went into Marlborough to buy the hawking glove of which you fell foul. Only you didn't, did you? You were never really in much danger for you knew that Johannes would be summoned to help and that he would mend you fairly quickly. Johannes said that it was a different kind of poison, easily treated. Had you seen him do something like it before? I recall he healed John's leg when it went bad. I suspect you knew he had the skill to bring you round."

"Oh no....why would I do that? I could have died. I would not poison myself, would I? Someone set that glove out to catch us. That would be stupid. Too much to risk."

"Or very, very clever" I said slowly. "None of us would ever consider you a murderer after that, would we? After all, you had been a victim. Much like the rope between two trees. A second attempt on your life. Only we know now that it was a pretence. Perhaps a practice. Oh yes ,very clever. Robert the victim."

He stared at me under his eyebrows, then with his eyes never leaving my face turned his head to Benedict and said, "Do you believe this nonsense, Father?"

Benedict sighed. "Sadly I think I must. I have never known Aumary to be a liar, nor has he ever been given to, forgive me my boy, making up wild stories. He hasn't the imagination."

I smiled.

There was a little silence. I could hear Hal of Potterne at the front calling for flares to be lit around the cottage, for it was now fully dark and my guards could no longer see what they were guarding.

"Now we come to Geoffrey." I lit a candle and placed it on the night stand.

"I loved Geoffrey. You cannot...."

"I think," I rubbed my forehead; my headache was returning, "that Geoffrey was your -forgive me - if I might say it - finest murder. I have no doubt you killed him."

Father Benedict drew in a breath in shock.

"I think I know how you did it. The fact that it was planned when my son was a babe in arms still..."

Benedict groaned.

"...shows that you are possessed of a devilry of the utmost evil."

"Geoffrey's death was an accident. We all know that. It was a terrible accident," said Robert.

"Not so. I think I can prove it."

"I cried with the rest of the manor and village when he was killed."

As if that made it believable. I remember the day of my son's death and Robert coming in from Marlborough, recalled him racing up the steps to the chapel, the way he looked when he came down at last, the tears and protestations. Yes, that was grief, of a kind.

"Yes, you cried Robert. I have no doubt the tears were real that time. I don't think that his was a murder you enjoyed but you did plan it far in advance and waited your moment. I will think hard on it and see if I can work out how you did it. Then, I will let you know and you can tell me if I am correct." I smiled at him. "Tomorrow"

"Oh, I have a tomorrow then?" he sneered.

"Do you know, Robert, I think you should have been a player, a showman, acting in one of those roving mummers plays we sometimes get at Twelfth Night, you know the sort. You have such a gift for lies and that is all it is, acting. Lies. Pretending to be someone you are not, feigning this emotion or that." I shook my head. "I have never known anyone so clever at pretending or telling lies."

I heard Benedict whisper "Deus egerit dimitte illi " God forgive him.

He sighed and, with his finger ends worried the blankets covering his old bones. So, he was still awake and listening.

Robert clenched his teeth and I saw the muscles of his jaw working. I have rattled him, I thought.

"Yes, you are a very good actor. You had one or two people in Marlborough fooled, too. You stole Cecily's dress and a veil and changed, probably somewhere in the forest ,and became Mistress Avice of Bristol, just passing through."

"Dress as a woman, you must be mad. Now I know your wits are touched. Don't listen to this rubbish, Benedict, it's the stuff of fables and children's stories.

I would no sooner dress as a woman than..."

"You were very convincing with your skin like peaches and your lustrous eyes. No doubt you batted those long, dark eyelashes of yours at Master Glover. He's very susceptible to a pretty face is Master Glover, Robert. You have little beard and that very light, you must have shaved very carefully that day. Though as Master Glover said, you were decently covered as a married woman should be. He remembered your lovely long blond hair peeking out. Oh yes, Avice of Bristol was you. You went back into the forest, became Robert Belvoir again and disposed of Cecily's dress in the charcoal burner's fire. You then strode in to the hall as large as life and laid down your deadly gift...after you had doctored it, of course. And no, we won't find much of the money you stole from Quimper because you paid it out in cash to Master Glover for the hawking glove. An expensive murder weapon. No, not a weapon...was it? A diversion. Pah!

Come to think of it, had I put my hand into that glove first, I might be dead now. Who would send for Johannes? My wife would. I have no doubt the messenger would not arrive. Time would pass. Another message would be sent. You could oversee it all, should you wish. Slowly I would slip away with no help to bring me back from the brink of death. You might even have tried to poison me further, when I lay on my sickbed. So yes, it might have been a weapon for murder."

Robert chuckled and shook his head.

"I do know that the orpiment which killed Cecily was in your possession. I myself found it in your room didn't I? You told me yourself that it was used to make paint. You used it to paint Geoffrey's little boat yellow, didn't you? You have a perfectly good reason to have it in your possession but, I have no doubt, you also used it on my wife and poisoned her slowly with arsenic. She was low at the death of her son, she was fragile and vulnerable. Over time, you edged her towards her maker and then with one final fatal dose, perhaps, nudged her into death."

He smiled then, as he saw my grief.

"I probably helped you." Benedict's head whipped round to look at me at that. "For I think that the drops which had been prescribed by Johannes were not the drops we were giving her to ease her pain. Unwittingly, whilst you held her head and murmured words of support to me, I was dropping death onto her lips. God forgive me."

I broke down and my voice quavered. "I think you had substituted them."

Robert took in a great breath. "You know, you have never once considered another for these crimes, if crimes they are."

"Who is that?"

"Johannes of Salerno."

"Again you slander a good man, Robert. No. Johannes has no motive."

"What motive do I have, for Christ's sake?"

Benedict braced himself and sat up in his bed,

"Do not let the Lord's name pass from your lips you foul unbeliever."

Robert just chuckled at that, "Why what will you do, throw the bible at me? It's a heavy book I'll admit, but the state you are in...."

"Apostate!" Benedict shook with anger and pointed an accusing finger.

Robert ignored him.

"I repeat. What motive do I have?"

"AH!...I was coming to that" I said.

"Am I going too fast for you, Paul? Is your hand cramping? Shall we stop awhile? Ha-ha...you want to know what happens. Write on then."

I stood and paced about the room, for I could contain my anger no longer. This would help dissipate it.

"I wrote down a list of people who I think you have dispatched since you first came to us years ago. I couldn't at first find a connection. I was thinking too far afield. I was thinking that no one here would wish me ill. Quimper had the right of it when he said to me, cui bono? Who benefits?"

I leaned on the window edge and looked out. Walter was visible by the light of the flares, sitting on the wall, eating what looked like a pasty. My own stomach began to grumble telling me that it was supper time. His wife must have brought some food out to my guards.

"There seemed at first, no connection, as I say, between the people killed. Piers, my steward; Cecily my wife; William, my uncle. Ah...yes...all folk connected to me. All my help and strength. Then we had the death of Colmar. This threw me off. Not particularly connected to me. Quimper, certainly not connected to me. It was the death of Geoffrey which made me sit up and think."

They were both listening to me assiduously now.

"Then there was an attempt on my own life."

"Oh my dear boy," said Benedict, scowling at Robert.

"Late at night, a string passed from one part of the solar stair to another gave me a tumble down the steps. By good luck and my ability to bounce, I survived. Had I not, who might have benefitted?"

Our eyes were on Robert.

"I have made a will. Naturally it names Geoffrey my heir. Hawise has a home here until she marries. Cecily too was safe at Durley until Geoffrey was old enough to take over, or the King decided to change things around. But of course Geoffrey is dead. Cui bono?"

I waited for a moment.

"Your name, Robert, might be passed to the King. He might think that, since you are a Belvoir and you know the manor and the forest, he would give it to you. In the light of the good deed we did John, passing him the names of the traitors here in England, he might even be grateful and allow you to take Durley and the wardenship of the forest. However, he also might take it away all together. He is that kind of monarch. He might bestow the whole lot on Hawise and marry her to a man he likes who will take the titles. Then you must do away with Hawise too, for she and her spouse would stand in your way."

Robert was breathing hard, like a buck who has been chased in the forest.

"That is a pack of lies."

"I have a fraction of the string, Robert, which you used, I have the knot and the nail which you fixed to the stairs. You used that broken piece of string to bind your hair last night when you attacked me in the forest. I also noticed that you had not crossed the courtyard as you said because your felt slippers were dry on the soles. I suspect you waited for me, oh not one night but several perhaps. You are very patient. I also think you removed the charcoal in my study, and put out the lights when all were asleep in the hall so it was very dark. How many nights you did this until I appeared, I do not know. You banked on me doing my own work. That was clever of you. You know what manner of man I am. If I can do my own work, I'll not inconvenience another. I did not call for help. Up the stair

I go. Out you come from the Stygian gloom, probably from under the stairs and quickly....you have already knocked the nail in place - fix your tight trip wire. You hide again and appear when all is over and I am lying dead at the bottom of the stairs. You retrieve the string, but the knot and the nail you could not see in the gloom. I found those. You have backbone, I'll say that, Robert. You take your chance, you are bold. You wait, you have daring.

"With me dead you have a chance to make a play for Durley and the forest. THIS is what it has all been about. All these years, all these deaths. You want to be me."

Chapter Fourteen

Benedict was staring from one to the other of us with his mouth open. "Well!" he exclaimed. Robert was completely calm.

"So what do you propose to do about this phantom story you have concocted?"

"I had hoped that you would admit your evil and I must say that I would feel better about what I have to do now if you had done so, but..."

Again Robert folded his arms and crossed his ankles as if he were digging in his position.

"You cannot hang me. I am your brother."

Benedict growled like a dog then, "He ought to, with what he knows. He is justice in the forest, he could have you locked up until the Justices in Eyre arrive and that could be years. They are notoriously slow but I know he will not."

I felt like a deflated pig's bladder which had been kicked around in a game of football.

"No, I will not. I am angry. I am so angry that I would personally like to take a club to you, Robert Belvoir, now, and beat you till you are no more than a bloody blot on the floor. I shall not, however."

Robert sneered. "You cannot give me to the justices. I have committed no crime in the forest. That's their job. The forest. You could take me to the castle and have me tried there but you won't. You think I don't know. You think I have no idea? Well, I do know. You talk in your sleep, do you know that, brother? Oh yes. Your secret is out. I've heard you. I s'pose this canting apology for a man knows it too. I expect it was he administered your oath all that time ago...."

My heart sank. Oh how badly I wanted to kill him.

"I , Aumary Belvoir, do solemnly swear..." and he repeated my oath to me.

I closed my eyes and I am sure I swayed with anger and tiredness and the sup-pressed desire to do murder myself.

I did not answer him.

"You can do me no harm, Aumary Belvoir...not a hair of my head. Neither can you tell anyone what you know, for that would be a betrayal of me and count as a breaking of your oath."

I stepped towards him.

"Aumary!" Benedict had leaned from his bed, with one hand outstretched and was looking pained. I stopped.

"You are a fool, Aumary Belvoir" yelled Robert. "That oath is worth nothing. If the tables were turned I would kill you out of hand and not even blink, but no, you are afraid. Afraid of a myth, a legend, a nonsense. Hell does not exist. Who has ever seen it? Who has spoken with God? Not these stupid priests. Your oath is as a whisper on the wind. Hell is what you are making for yourself, here and now!" Spittle was leaking from his mouth, from a grimace like a church gargoyle and he was red in the face. "You are a complete fool. A bloody dupe. I scoff at your stupid oath. I spit on it. What does it really mean? Words. Puffs of air. You are held in thrall by gibberish. A story to frighten children."

I heard a worried Hal clomping up the stairs. He could not fail to hear Robert roaring.

"No, Hal, all is well, thank you," I shouted and eventually the footsteps retreated.

When Robert's breath returned to normal I said, "I shall leave you locked up for tonight and then tomorrow, I will ask you to abjure the realm, to go away, away from these shores and never return on pain of death."

Robert jumped up at that.

"You cannot do that. I have not claimed sanctuary. I have not admitted a crime before the sheriff. I shall appeal to the King."

"No," said Benedict, "you have not claimed sanctuary but if it were to become known what you had done, I think you would consider it a fine thing to do, for there would be a hundred people baying for your blood in Savernake alone. They would tear you limb from limb and, do you know what, I would not grant sanctuary to you in my church. I would point out to them where you were hiding."

I was bone weary and was feeling the effects of the stress of recounting my tale, notwithstanding the illness which came and went, the symptoms of which were not quite departed. Robert was not looking his best either. He was pale and grey about the eyes like a man who wakes after a night of debauchery. The effect of the poison I supposed.

"I think the King would be very interested to hear what you might have to say Robert."

Part of me thought, he is very plausible, what can he do that will make difficulties between me and John my King? The other half of me thought, John is a canny old dog, he will see what is afoot straight away.

I turned to Benedict, "I had hoped you would give him a blessing Father. Something to send him on his way. He has not confessed, as I had hoped. His story is not subject to the strictures of the confessional but nevertheless please could you see it in you to bless him, to forgive him his sins. I would rest better with my decision if you could do that for me."

Benedict looked aghast. "He has denied the existence of God, Aumary. He has blasphemed. He is an apostate. I cannot bless or forgive him."

"I had hoped..."

"No, he will fall into the fiery pit and burn forever. And I for one will be glad, I will not save his miserable soul."

Robert just laughed out loud. "You two, you make me puke," he said.

I bellowed for my guards through the window. I was so angry. We marched Robert back to his room and there I told him, "Tomorrow, you will gather what you can carry. I will give you a little money and a horse, God knows why I am doing that. Probably to get you as far away from me as quickly as possible. You will then ride, under escort. I will send Hal and the two men at arms with you as far as the nearest port to make sure you get there. I think Bristol will be your best choice and you will go. Forever. If I ever see you again, I will forget my oath and kill you. Count on it."

I swept off. They locked him in and guards were posted by Hal.

I wearily ascended the steps, crossed the hall, despite the strange looks from the men gathered there at meat and pulled myself up the solar steps.

I threw off my cloak, sat at the table, put my head in my hands, and I cried.

I cried for my uncle, my wife, and my son and for a brother, whom once I had loved. Yes, I had loved him.

***

Later that night, a tearful Joan came and scratched on the solar door.

Father Benedict, she said, had died in his sleep, before he could eat his supper.

I had expected it. People often rally before they slip away. Another good man gone. Another part of my youth flown.

I wept some more.

"Paul, my lad, can you get me something with which to wipe my nose? I appear to have a dew drop on the end of it."

***

I lay awake almost all night, edgy and troubled, in the big bed in the solar, thinking. I heard the slight pattering of rain which came just before dawn. I heard the kitchen servants lighting the fires and calling to each other, for they were always the first up of a morning and I listened to the cackling as a boy let out the geese into the orchard. A picture of the orchard then came into my mind and after hovering over tree and grass, it came to rest ultimately, on Benedict of Cadley's bee skeps. I would have to go out there tomorrow and tell them that their master was gone. Peter Brenthall, John's son, had an interest, I know. Perhaps I would ask him to take the bees in hand for I was not sure we had another beekeeper in the village.

My mind ranged over Benedict's successor. Would he be as amiable and competent as Benedict had been? Would he have the same fellow feeling, one of fair play and common sense, for his frail, fellow men? This was one thing over which I had no control. A man would be appointed and we would all have to get on with him.

Finally, just after dawn, I slept a little and woke ravenous and thirsty. My head cold had now settled to a bunged up nose and ears which felt like they were full of stones. My mouth was a dry as the Bourne brook in summer, with having to breathe through it all night. My nose was red and sore.

Mischievously I wondered how Johannes' cold was progressing?

And I also realised that I could not share my new found knowledge with him. He was a very intelligent man and might come to his own conclusions, but if I were to stay faithful to my promise, I could not confirm nor deny what he might think.

I rose, broke my fast, and when the maids had heated enough water, I washed my whole body and hair in a half barrel, left up in the corner of the solar for just such a purpose. I felt I had to wash away this part of my life, and besides I was filthy with the mud of the forest and the sweat of my illness. Sitting in the water I thought about the times when Geoffrey had been washed by his mother in this very barrel and I laughed when I recalled his squealings and wrigglings. Let me always remember such good times, I thought.

I went down to my office and unlocked the door.

Then I called for Hal to fetch Robert and sat at my table. Best we keep that block of wood between us, I thought.

They came back in the time it takes a man to say three or four Paternosters. I had a feeling that Robert had not slept either, for he looked red eyed and tired but he was still cocksure and smug. He had changed his clothes again and was dressed this time for travel. I asked him to sit. He would not. Hal waited outside.

"I told you yesterday that I think I know how you murdered my son. No! Don't try to deny it. We are past such idiocies, Rob. I am convinced of the right of it and as my word is law hereabouts, I may pronounce as I see fit."

"I don't care what you think."

"That much is apparent."

I studied him.

"I am going to tell you how you did it, because I want you to know that you are not, as you think you are, matchless in cleverness, if I can call such a hideous act, clever. Remember, as you go into the unknown; for today that's where you go; you have met at least one who can surpass you in thinking. I have unravelled the workings of your horrible mind. I do not need to think as you do, with evil in my heart; to solve the mystery, merely logically go through the events and turn over the evidence and what I can deduce and come to a sensible conclusion. If I can do it, others will be gifted with the power to unmask you, if you should think to work your iniquitous way into another's life. Think on that. You are not as clever as you think you are. Another may trip you up."

"Oh spare me the lecture. Just get on with it."

"Very well. You made the boat for Geoffrey, of that there is no doubt, but I don't think it was ever designed to be a present for Twelfth Night as he said you had told him."

Robert shifted his feet.

"You always intended to lure him to the gate with it. You called him to you. Folk heard you."

"I never denied it, I admitted as such."

"Yes, you did, that's true, you just did not tell the whole truth about where you were when you called."

"About to ride out of the gate."

"No, you were up on the gate house, crouched, looking into the courtyard. You made sure it was empty."

Robert was very still.

"Many folk were in the threshing barn that day, some were by their fires, all were indoors for it was a raw day. No one saw you. However, one did see you lead your horse out of the gate and leave him for a second or two, hidden by the wall, on the other side."

His head came up, "Who?"

"I will not tell you for I value his life, Robert, as you would not." My brother looked away. "Lies. He speaks lies," he said.

"This person saw you but didn't really know what it was they had seen until much later. So, you have your horse, saddled and waiting outside the gate. You call to Geoffrey from the top of the gate. He comes running. That was his uncle's voice but where is he? He can't be seen. Perhaps it is some fun game? I have seen you play such games before. He approaches the gate. Am I right so far?"

No answer.

"And he sees, oh joy, the little boat which you have promised him. It is a game. He was meant to find it there on the ground. He bends over to pick it up, a happy little boy. An excited little boy. His hand closes around it and…"

"No!"

"Thud. The stone from the coping on the gatehouse, which you loosened a long time before this, in readiness for your plan, is at that moment in your hands.

You drop it on him as he bends. He is knocked forward. The boat is trapped beneath him. He is dead or dying. You know it. There is no need to check as you run down the steps, searching the courtyard for folk who can identify you and where you have come from. You keep to the shadows, you leave through the gate, stepping over Geoffrey's lifeless body as you pass. You mount your horse and ride as fast as you can for about one hundred paces, where you dive into the undergrowth and turn your horse about as quickly as you can so you can look back at the gate. I noticed the next day, when I walked abroad, the broken twigs, the trampled ground, the choice of evergreen, so that you would not be seen standing, waiting, watching, through the leafless trees and bushes. You stayed hidden so anyone coming to the gate would think you long gone and not just fled a couple of minutes."

"You were there then, that you can describe it so accurately?"

"I was there shortly after. I looked at the stones of the gate. I could not believe that the wind had lifted them. I looked well. They had been scored and left out for a while so that the bond on the cement was broken and then replaced, so that they were loose. It did not seem so to look at them, but if you leaned on or pushed them? You planned to use those stones long before you actually went up there and dropped one onto Geoffrey."

"Perhaps I designed it for you, brother?"

"Maybe you did. So, am I right? Give me that satisfaction Robert. He was my own son. Tell me I'm right."

There was a small silence in which was heard, the sound of someone beating a mat for dust with a paddle.

"God's truth, Aumary, you are the very devil, a witch, that you know exactly what I was doing. Yes, that's how I did it."

"How could you kill little Geoffrey, Rob? He loved you, you know that. He loved you well."

He shrugged. "That was hard...so hard, the hardest thing, but I made sure that he did not suffer."

"Yes, it was quick. I'll give you that, and his last thought was a happy one, before you drove it from his head onto the cobbles."

"But you must see that you could not have an heir. No boy child," he said, unimpressed by my graphic description.

"Yes, I see that. Now."

I sat back and took a deep breath.

"So then, you rode for Marlborough as quickly as you could. I don't think you rejoined the main road till much further up, when you would not be seen. I think you used the smaller tracks until it was safe to reappear. I looked through the gate moments after you left. I didn't see you riding. You had gone. Of course, we all thought you were long gone. No, you were watching and waiting."

"I saw you."

"I'm sure you did. I hope it gave you a great satisfaction to see me broken, tormented and inconsolable. I don't think you have it in you at all to be any of those things. You are inhuman Robert."

I called for Hal.

"Return Robert to his room. Collect his things, allow him to put whatever he wants to take on his horse and then ride with him to the castle please, Hal, as we discussed. Provision yourself there. Here is a letter which will allow you to do so freely. Here is a purse to get you to Bristol and a note for you to be able to call on the Belvoir monies at the port - you know where, to get you home and to provision yourselves. Collect Peter and Stephen and then make sure you ride with all speed to Bristol. I want him on a boat and away, anywhere he chooses. I never want to see him again."

"Right you are m'lord."

"Be sure not to enter into conversation with him, Hal. He is a plausible devil. Silence all the way but for instructions or unavoidable words."

Hal nodded. He did not ask why.

"Oh and Hal." He turned, "Watch him carefully."

I did not want to see Robert ever again. I wanted to get on with what remained of the rags of my life; pass on, move away from the sorrow.

Sadly, it was not to be.

***

I had done little work that afternoon. I could not stop thinking about Robert on his way out of the country and out of my life. I began a note to Johannes asking him to look at the knife which I had taken from Robert. Naturally the owner's name remained unwritten.

I heard through the little window of my office, a fine voice singing, first high and then the sound would break and a pleasant light baritone would interrupt the alto. Ah, it was Peter Brenthall, hobbling on his bad ankle with a stick, in the orchard. His father had told me that he was to take over from Benedict as the keeper of the bees. Benedict had apparently been grooming him for such a role for a year or more. I realised I did not know everything there was to know about my own manor.

Peter was singing to the bees, telling them of the sad news and the change of ownership. He was twelve, nearly thirteen and his voice was beginning to break. I smiled at the absurdity of it. Then I heard Peter talking to an older man, his father I thought. The voices were quiet at first and then John's voice was agitated and after a while, raised in alarm.

Moments later I heard the sound of two horses running hard on the cobbles through the gate and what sounded like a third, lighter and being towed, perhaps by a lead rein, behind them. I dashed to the door.

Peter Devizes and Stephen Dunn, my two men at arms from the castle, were dismounting. Behind them was Hal's horse. There were no panniers, no luggage. No Hal.

I groaned and slowly made my way down the steps. Both men nodded.

"Hal?"

"Is in the abbey with a broken head. The abbey leech has looked at him and we left him - thought it best. He'll live but he has had a nasty crack on the skull and him with a head as hard as boiled leather. Something heavy, lucky to be alive, sir," said Peter Devizes, a tall skinny man with not a hair on his head.

"Aye, he is," I said. He had no idea.

I took a deep breath. "Could he say what happened?"

At that moment, John Brenthall, my forest warden and right hand man in the forest, appeared in the manor gateway. He scanned the horses, saw me and ran up. I put up my hand to forestall him a moment and he subsided into an uneasy silence.

"On the decline into Marlborough, where the road bends round the old trees there, the bit where it's straight ahead and you can't see the road behind, Master Robert asked that he be allowed to get some water from his pannier. He said he was feeling feverish and had a sore throat. Hal kept on walking his horse, slowly. They didn't stop but Master Robert was just behind him."

"He 'it him from behind with something very 'ard," said Stephen, who was the opposite of his friend Peter, dark haired and stocky.

"Hal is no fool and I did warn him." My brow furrowed. "Robert had no weapon. Nothing. So what did he use?"

"Sir," said John....

"Shh John, a moment. What happened then?"

"We suppose he took the provisions and bags from Hal's horse and was off down the hill."

"Which way?"

"Hal doesn't know, he was out by then. A kindly monk from the priory coming back from one of their granges, found him on the road a moment later and put him on his horse and led him into town. Hal sent a message to us to come to him and then you and then...."

"Did Robert take Hal's weapons?"

They looked at each other at that. "Yes," said Peter.

"But left the horse?"

"Too recognisable is that 'orse," said Stephen. "Funny lookin' beast. Can't ride through town with that, everyone would know it was 'Als'?"

"You think Robert went through town?"

"Yeah, we saw 'im"

I squeezed my nose and rubbed my face in a gesture of impatience.

"'E came into the castle bold as a bawd, waved at us. 'Corse, then, we din't know what had 'appened nor what we was supposed to do."

"No, you wouldn't."

John piped up "Can we go into your office sir, it's important?"

I put up my hand again. "This means, I suppose, that he has collected the provisions from the castle and has the letters and the money?"

Stephen and Peter looked at each other.

" 'Spose so."

I sighed. "Go to the kitchen and get yourselves kitted out for a ride. Three days. Then wait here. I'll follow shortly."

I clenched and ground my teeth, My brother was, as Stephen had said, as bold as a bawd. I turned to John but he was already running to the hall.

I found him in the office, staring at the chest in which I keep the Belvoir regalia.

"I think I can answer one of your questions sir," he said. "And I count myself responsible. If folk are hurt....." He looked so pained, I patted him on the shoulder.

"No John, it's not your fault."

"Yes, it is. I think if you open it sir, you'll find it empty."

"What are you babbling on about, man?"

"The chest sir."

I blinked.

"I think he hit him with the horn sir. Or the sword maybe."

John swayed and I led him to a stool.

I took the key from my neck and opened the hanglock.

As I lifted the lid I heard John say.

"I gave him the key you see. The night you were ill. He asked me. He said he would put everything away. How was I to know?"

The chest was empty but for the ceremonial saddle. All the other smaller, more portable items, were gone.

The story came out in dribs and drabs.

I had been asleep, ill in my bed and had asked John to put the regalia away as usual and fetch back the key to the hanglock. I remember waking later that day and seeing it lying on the table. I'd just assumed it was John who had placed it there.

John had met Robert in the hall. Robert said he would return the items to the chest in the office. Naturally, John trusted Robert to do as he said. Why should he not? Here was the lord's trusted brother. John had not replaced the key. Robert had. God! Robert had been alone with me asleep in the solar. Knowing what I know now, I would sooner have slept in a bed of vipers. Somehow, he had not been tempted to do me injury then. No, he was waiting a much better opportunity, a safer option. One where he could explain away my death.

John said that as Peter his son set off on his journey to fetch my remedy from Johannes, he saw Robert with a large leather pannier. Yes, we know he had one of those. I myself had seen it. It was very heavy, said Peter, and he could see what looked like the belt of the regalia sticking out. Master Robert had taken it into the stables.

He thought it odd at the time, but had a duty to perform and after all, how could a twelve year old trainee woodward, quiz the brother of the lord? He couldn't.

John had just heard the story from Peter when they met in the orchard, and he ran straight to me. Both Peter and John were late catching up with the news as they had been asleep at Johannes' house when the tale about Robert's detainment had become known around the manor.

I sat down heavily. Now, I would have to follow him.

"Which way?" I asked myself. "He won't go to Bristol now."

John drew a shaky breath.

"Why sir? Why has he gone and why has he taken the regalia? I take it he does not have your permission."

"No John, he most certainly does not. It's a long story and it may seem odd but I can't tell you anything." Winchester, or Salisbury Road, heading for Portsmouth? I thought. Nah. He'd have to double back through the forest.

I scratched my head.

Three ways only....inland to come out again at the coast, God knows where. No, I don't think so. The road over the common, thence to Beckhampton and west. Or the road to the southwest. Out by the castle, he's already been there, then Pewsey, Oare, Shaftesbury. To Dorset and that coastline.

"John, help me pack some things" I said. "You and Henry are in charge while I'm gone."

Chapter Fifteen

Robert was more than half a day ahead of us. We rode through the forest to the Shaftesbury Road. Why did we go that way? I don't know. Except that Robert's outburst, that he would appeal to the King kept ringing in my ears and I knew that John was in Normandy. If Robert thought to go to the King, this is the way he would travel to avoid us and any place where he was well known, and he would certainly circle the forest and its villages.

Eventually he would come to the Dorset coast and would try to take ship for Normandy from there.

We reached Oare before we knew we had made the right decision. A carter coming from Upavon remembered a well-made blond young man travelling alone with a laden horse, an unusual sight, for those of any birth rarely travelled without an escort and it was foolhardy to travel so. The news spurred us on.

As fast as we could ride we could not overtake him. He changed horses in Shaftesbury, for we found the mount he had ridden from Durley, sorely blown and misused at the first inn we came to, just inside the town wall. This news too was welcome, if not for the poor horse.

Two days later we reached the small town of Poole. Why did we go there? Kings had used this natural harbour many times for mustering their ships and it was a well-known place for embarkation to Normandy. I was trusting that I knew what was in my brother's mind. He would, I was sure, make good his threat of finding the King, wherever he was and appealing to him for justice, as he saw it. I had to follow. I had no choice.

It took us a further three days to find a ship to take us across the sea. Three infuriatingly long days filled with negotiation and disappointment, of waiting about staring at the grey choppy waters of the channel. It was late in the season for travel, the ship masters said. The weather was inclement, the wind still high. Our wait enabled us to search the town for if we were pinned here, so might Robert be. But he was not there. He had gone, or had never been there. No doubt his golden tongue and his pretty face had seen to that. That, and my good silver.

Eventually we settled for a small boat which was just big enough for our three horses and a sailor who seemed to know what he was doing. I had thought to leave them and hire new horses when we reached Normandy but felt we were better in unfamiliar territory with our own beasts, who knew us. Besides I had no wish to leave Bayard behind.

We landed at Cherbourg a dingy little place on the Cotentin with marshes and dunes either side, but one which would remained stubbornly for John almost throughout the troubles of his reign. Then taking the road south we travelled through dense woodland to Bayeux and hence to Caen and into the body of Normandy.

Here we learned that John was in Falaise. Good, only a mere twenty miles away. It was a sorry party who passed by the donjon at the castle of Falaise at the end of that day in early November. It had been raining steadily for hours and we three were soaked to the skin. We would not, I thought, try to find a billet at the castle and announce our presence to all; besides it would not be easy with the court in residence. We found good lodging far enough out of the main town, where we would be quietly hidden for as long as I deemed it necessary and we waited and recovered our wind.

I sent a note to the castle and we waited again.

I am a man of action. I am not one who can sit and wait without I have something to do. My life had been one of activity, both indoors and out and sitting staring into space did not suit me. I was irritable, I own it. I was even more irritable when a message came back a day later. John had not been in Falaise at all. He was in Alençon further south. Then he moved to Mans in Maine.

We packed our bags again, Stephen, Peter and I and rode in more pouring rain, deeper into Normandy. Less than a day into our ride, I became ill and passed out, falling from the saddle.

It was apparent that I had not recovered properly from my rheum and illness earlier in the autumn. I grew feverish again and this time the cold turned to my lungs.

Time passed very slowly and, laid up as I was, I worried about the damage Robert might be doing to my reputation, had he been able to get to John. Robert was a nobody to the King, so my thoughts were foolish really, because John would

never have given him an audience long enough for him to really make a differ-
ence to our own relationship. A moment here, a five minutes there. John was a
very busy man, a restless man and he had a country to defend but as Christmas
approached, I wondered if Robert might be able to insinuate himself into the court
and at leisure, over the festivities, poison the ear of our monarch.

We spent Christmas at Alençon but John had moved on again, to Chinon.
I cannot in truth remember much of it. I was, they tell me, very ill and they
despaired of my life.

We were stuck in Alençon for a month, whilst I recovered enough to take
charge again and to work out where John had gone. Shortly after New Year, we
had word that John was at Lisieux. Then Lire, then Bretueil. Would the man please
keep still a while so we could catch him? These Angevins were all the same, always
away here and there, on the move, so full of energy.

I was still very weak. It was the end of February before I felt we could again
pack our bags and head for Rouen where we knew the King would be staying
put for a while.

We arrived in Rouen on a glorious day, full of winter sunshine and snow-
drops.

Again we dug in, again we quartered the town. We found no trace of Robert
Belvoir. It was as if he had disappeared into the throng.

Perhaps I was wrong. Maybe Robert had not come to Normandy. This
journey had all been for nothing. However, I must report to the King, now I was
here. What exactly I would report was open to question.

Once, when we were walking along the river bank on the way back to our
lodging at St Quen, the sight of a man idling in front of me, green hood up, some
thirty feet away, struck me as familiar and I increased my pace, my hand on my
sword hilt, only to have him turn slightly and for me to see that the man was
dark haired, worn short. I did not recognise any of the clothes he was wearing.
However, it unnerved me.

Letters were sent to John. There was no answer. I appealed again to Petit,
John's valet whom I had known quite well, from John's sojourns at Marlborough,
these many years past.

At last on the last day of February, after a short stay in Molyneux and Pont-

Audemer where John had gone merely for two days, we watched as he swung through the gates of Rouen once more with his entourage; admittedly not many men; but John often travelled light of followers, leaving the baggage train behind, and clattered up the road to the castle.

Now we might have a chance.

***

A few days later, at the close of day, we were called to the castle. The hall of the building was teeming with folk bedding down for the night but once out of the main public area, all was quiet. Why was it always late in the day when I was able to see John?

No one gave us any particular glance as we threaded our way after Stephen of Thurnham, the usher and doorkeeper and an old retainer of John's. We were searched for weapons, a new departure and the beginning of John's paranoia about the threat of traitors and hurt to his person, which was to last to the end of his life. Petit was there and smiled at me.

I left Stephen and Peter outside and stepped inside the small room. The door closed silently after me.

It was some moments before I could see in the gloom.

John was sitting almost up to his neck in a bath of hot water. Steam curled up into the rafters and candles were positioned on the floor around the tub. The room was heated by charcoal braziers. Two walls were covered by large painted cloths showing 'Susannah and the Elders' and 'David greeting Bathsheba,' from what I could discern in the darkness. All shutters were fastened tight.

I bowed, fell to my knee and waited. John sloshed about a little in his bath and water cascaded over the edge on to towels placed on the floor. His hair was plastered to his head, his beard was dark with water.

"Greetings Belvoir," he said, "we hear you have been unwell."

"Yes sire." I coughed almost to illustrate the nature of my sickness, "They tell me I have had pneumonie."

"Then draw up a stool and sit, my friend. We cannot have you falling into our bath water."

So far, so good, though conversations with John, I'd been told, lately often began with such an innocuous levity and ended in something quite different.

I pulled to me a stool which had been placed by the wall and sat. It was hardly big enough to contain me, being more a rest for one's boots than one's backside.

"I have, sire," I said, "been chasing you around the countryside some time and then, to my shame, I fell ill. So I apologise for my lateness in approaching you."

John reached for a goblet of wine at his side, more water sloshed out of the tub. I got up and put it into his hands. I sat again. John said nothing, merely watched me.

"Nothing but a crisis, sire, would bring me to you here, would make me leave my duties at Savernake for so long. I come personally to put some news before you which...." I ran my hand over my sweating forehead. It was warm in the little room. "Which only you must know and only you can understand how to deal with."

There was more sloshing over the edge as John shifted the royal backside on the little stool placed in the water for him to sit on while he bathed. He dropped the empty cup over the edge and snapped his fingers.

A boy; I had not seen him in the darkness at the edge of the room, came into view and, as John rose from the water, he deftly wrapped a linen towel around the royal loins. Then he disappeared behind the painted cloth and I heard a door closing softly.

"You look most pained, my friend," said John as he pulled on a robe and began to towel his hair dry.

"Aye, it gives me no pleasure to tell my tale, sire. I must tell it from the beginning and forgive me, in advance, if I cannot tell the whole of it. Not even to you."

"Perhaps we shall compel you?"

"As much as I love, submit to and revere you my lord, and am your devoted servant and most earnest friend, I owe a deeper loyalty to a higher power."

"I see."

He stood, I sat and his eyes met mine over the few feet between us. Strictly because he was standing I should have risen, but he seemed not to care about this.

He sighed. "We hear this so many times and from so many who use this as an excuse not to obey us; who seek to hoodwink and obfuscate. From you, we shall accept it as genuine, for we have no doubt of your truthfulness and love for us." He threw the towel at the wall.

A part of the tension in me released then and I felt much lighter. He was going to listen. However I had not been resident in Normandy this month or two without hearing the tales of John's tempers and outbursts, his unprovoked angers and arbitrary punishments. True or not, I would tread carefully.

He moved to the bed, again in the dimness of the room I had not seen it; taking one of the candles with him and lit another and another. The red bed curtains came into view. Then he gestured for me to follow and sit on a chair whilst he sat on the edge of the bed.

Two goblets of white wine appeared and one was thrust into my shaking hand.

"Speak," he said.

Hesitantly, I told John of my oath. I told him how it was obtained. I told him that I had, until now, kept that oath. I told him that I would endeavour to do so to the end of my days. I told him that Robert had taken the regalia and the difficulty that posed.

I did not tell him of my suspicions that my only brother was a murderer many times over.

"Sire, I cannot relate to you for I should be forsworn should I do so, the events which have led up to this moment. They are painful and...." I almost wiped my hand across my eyes but held back at the last minute, "painful and abhorrent to me."John leaned forward. Many people have said that John Plantagenet was a monster. That he killed, maimed, stole and bullied his way through his realms and his reign, like a Roman tyrant of old. But at that moment, he was my friend and a feeling man like any other and I was grateful to lean on him. He grasped my forearm.

"You wrote that you had lost your wife and son Aumary. May God hold them to His bosom. I do remember your letter."

I noticed the change from the royal 'we' to the familiar 'I'.

"Aye sire. I am completely alone but for my brother Robert. Can I ask you sire, has he been to see you? Have you talked with him?"

He sat up. "He has made overtures but frankly, I am not inclined to see him. Now I have seen you, perhaps I shall grant him a moment or two. Moreover, I have been much concerned with matters of state. With matters of war. You know how they all hard press me Aumary. It's an arduous task to know whom to trust. I ask for advice. I get self interested babble. I make plans; they thwart me at every turn."

I ploughed on. "But surely sire, the Marshall and your brother...you have friends. There are many who will leap to your defence should it be necessary."

What did I know of high politics?

"Fewer than you think. I am being pushed and pushed, Aumary, into this little corner of Normandy. If I could rely on those who swore me loyalty, every one, I could reach out and crush Philip of France with one hand tomorrow but no. I am hedged in on all sides and I am betrayed. I must fall back on my wits as I must fall back, I am sure, on England soon."

"No sire!"

"Unpalatable but true I fear."

There was silence.

We heard the snoring of some man at arms outside the door. Probably Peter, I thought.

"Sire, the Belvoir regalia?"

John furrowed his brow. "Oh yes..... I remember it, aren't you supposed to blow the horn whenever I come to Savernake to hunt?"

"Yes.." I chuckled, the only laughter between us that night. "Though I don't think we have ever been able to get a good note out of the damnable horn."

John chortled at that. "No, I remember trying it myself when we were younger," he said wistfully.

"My brother Robert has it, here I suspect, in Rouen."

"Why?"

"I don't know, but I think he means to try to discredit me. It's hard to know what he thinks."

John leaned back then and contemplated the rafters, though truly they could only just be seen in the gloom.

"That treasure belongs to Savernake. It is the symbol of our power, vested in you, Aumary, as warden of my forest. It will be returned to you."

"Thank you, sire. That is all I want."

There was some further talk, none of it important. It was late. We were both tired.

We parted then with the kiss of peace and John told me that now I was here, I had to stay on for a while, for he was pleased that he had at last a worthy partner for backgammon. He would call on me again and we should talk further. I mentally counted my funds and wondered if I could afford to play with him.

As I walked to the door John said "Aumary, we shall have Robert Belvoir here and you shall be at our side and we shall see what he has to say."

I nodded my thanks.

As I left the room, I did not know that another was coming in through the back door behind the wall cloth. That fact was, at that moment unknown to me, and it transpired that it was of great importance to me and to my cause.

"Shall we break Paul? The girls want to come in and light the candles and bring me some food. Go to your supper now too. If you wish we can resume after we have eaten. You do? You youngsters. You do love a tale of murder and mishap. Very well. I'll see you soon but I warn you I'm very tired and I get tetchy when I'm tired."

***

"Ah you're back. Good Morning. 'Tis a new day Paul. A new day to hopefully finish my tale."

John stayed in Rouen until March the 7th, when he departed for Molyneux. I had no summons to play or to talk before then. He was back in Rouen on March the 17th and away to Chambray the next day. Peter, Stephen and I, along with others of John's friends, those who had stayed behind, idled the time away, talking, dicing and gaming and walking the town and in my case reading. (I never once saw my brother there, though I know he was in Rouen.) I sent back letters to Durley whenever I could, explaining that we were detained here with the King and would return soon. I organised funds from my accounts in Normandy, for our monies were all but depleted and sold

Some of the smaller gems John had given us all that time ago and which I had secreted in my shirt, and converted them into silver.

Day by day I grew physically stronger. I was able to take some exercise on Bayard and even practice some swordplay with the other knights, when the weather allowed, for it was a very rainy spring. Gradually my illness left me and I regained the strength I had had in the previous year. My lungs would always remind me of this time in Normandy, whenever a rheum reared its head, and they were never quite the same again but I felt whole now in body and as whole as I ever would, in mind.

I had almost despaired of ever talking to John about the regalia again, or managing to win a silver penny or two from him at a game at which he excelled, when after a to-ing and fro-ing of many weeks, John came back to Rouen with a large retinue, and put down roots for a while.

I had not requested that we be housed in the castle. I was happy at our inn. It served our purpose. Sometimes, though, I would go to the castle and eat with the assembly at dinner and keep my ears and eyes open. It was on one such occasion that I first saw Arthur, Duke of Brittany.

They treated him well. He was not bound or shackled though he was watched and had a guard at all times. He was not allowed out of the castle pale but could walk free in the fresh air at any time he wished, in the castle grounds. I was told that he had good lodgings within the building and had plenty to occupy him should he wish. He lived, in short, a life of captive, but luxurious leisure.

Not often did he dine in the hall, but when John was present, he seemed to be trotted out to be paraded and shown to the assembly. 'Here is Arthur. He is still alive. I am a merciful King. I have not blinded him as has been said, nor castrated him, nor cut off his hands, as I have been asked to do.' All these whispers went round the town but they were just that, whispers.

That day he was dressed well in a silver tunic with a cotte of blue over. It had been raining again steadily, almost the whole of March had been wet ,and I could see that he had been outside for the shoulders of his gown were spotted with shining droplets.

He wore a sullen expression; he seldom wore anything else. John favoured his mother Queen Eleanor in looks, with dark red hair and fine skin, Arthur favoured his father who in his turn was the image of Henry the second, his paternal grandfather, stocky, dark and brooding.

The surly expression was hardened further when John, in a flurry of fanfares, came into the hall to eat.

We all stood. John bade us be seated. Arthur did not rise with the rest of us but lounged in his seat playing with his eating knife, turning it hilt over blade over and over on the table top.

Food was served and John carved from his own dish, a partridge I think, a breast for Arthur, placed it carefully on a plate and passed it to his nephew with a smile.

Quick as a flash, the plate, with its sauce, was upended, and flung at John.

Just in time John reared back and the food passed him by, landing on the floor.

Ho, ho - here was the famous Angevin temper. Arthur had it too.

John smoothed down his gown. There were stray droplets of sauce down the front.

"You are the most infuriating fifteen year old it has ever been my misfortune to know," he said, rising. "But you are only fifteen. No, now you are sixteen are you not, only just, yes? I shall overlook your bad behaviour. You have been inadequately raised, young man. Your manners are impossible. When someone passes you the choicest cut, you accept with grace, thank them and eat with relish...."

"You!" Arthur spat "you would seek to poison me with such meats. Snake, viper!"

John sat, shaking his head. He took the remaining breast of fowl, picked it up in his fingers and bit into it, saying as he chewed, "Then I too will be poisoned in a moment."

The whole hall was holding its breath. I had the feeling this was not the first time these two had come to blows.

Then Arthur stood, flounced into the space behind the dais and was off, his guards close behind. The noise in the hall gradually returned.

I turned to my neighbour, with whom I too had been sharing a dish.

"I take it this sort of thing happens regularly?"

"Oh aye, nasty little shite is our Arthur. Last time, he threw his eating knife at the King. Bounced off his arm. I'm surprised John hasn't banned him from the hall. He's too soft on him."

I saw Arthur three times further and each time in some way, he insulted his uncle. The next time, he spat at him as John passed and the spittle struck John on the cheek. The night after, he launched himself across the table with a heavy goblet in hand but was hauled back by his body guards. The last time I saw him, at the dinner meal, he had succeeded in pinning John to the wall behind the chair - I did not see how; I was too far away and had his hands around his monarch's throat. John was much stronger and pushed him off easily and others wrestled him to his knees.

As he was dragged from the room, Arthur cursed and shouted, railed and blas-phemed. We heard him until the outer door banged shut.

John could be heard saying, whilst he rubbed his throat, "And he would rule my realm as King? He who cannot rule himself."

There was much tutting and nodding of heads.

Lord, I thought, Arthur makes Robert look like an innocent milk maid.

***

It was April the third when John sent a message to my inn calling me to him after supper. I fetched my purse and prepared for a lengthy battle of wits. The room I entered was the same one I had been in last time, though now there were three chairs, not just the one and stools. The bath was missing too. In the wall was a fireplace I had not seen last time, for it had been in darkness, unlit. It was a cool evening for early April and the flames licked the logs hungrily, hissing as the rain now and again came down the chimney. The cherry red curtains of the bed were closed this time. There were more lights too. A flare or two in sconces on the two outer walls and candles inserted into cups on a wheel pulled up almost into the rafters and suspended by a chain.

Once more the shutters were tight closed and the wind buffeted and drove the rain against them. The draughts made the lights flicker and dance. I waited.

I could see that tonight, there were three boys one on each wall. I smiled at them and they bowed.

John laughing to himself, bowled in through the door behind the painted cloth panels a moment later. I lowered myself onto one knee.

He was there in front of me almost instantly, raising me up.

"No...no need...no need at all. Harold, shall we have some wine?"

One page detached himself from the wall and fetched a jug and two cups. John waved him through the door. "Stay and wait."

"Have you eaten?" He asked. I had, so the second lad was sent back through the door and the food, placed on a side table, remained untouched.

The third boy stayed put and set out the backgammon table.

He was obviously used to staying whilst his master busied himself for he crouched on his heels in the corner and leaned against the wall, keeping silence. Two large wolfhounds I had not seen before had followed John into the room. One sat with the young page and cuddled up to him. The second went to John and nuzzled his hand.

John was talking to me and fondling the dog's head. "And so you see, no matter how I try to come to terms with the slippery French snake, it comes to nothing. Weeks of negotiation...nothing."

"No, sire." I had missed the first part of the sentence because of my wandering stares, and was hopelessly lost.

John was staring pensively at his dog.

"Ah, Aumary," said John "You cannot hope to understand. The Bretons are uneasy of the fate of Arthur and drive against my western border. Philip nibbles at the toes and flanks of Normandy...." John looked up suddenly and the atmosphere lightened.

"No...no... You have not come here to discuss the war. Let us forget it for a night. Let us play. White or black?

"Off, Gog." John gestured to the hound, "Go to the fire now." The dog padded off and flopped down before the hearth. The logs crackled.

We seated ourselves and began to play and to sip our wine.

As we played we talked.

John explained the precarious position of an English monarch whose barons will not obey him. For, he said, they cannot rise up against their overlord, Philip of France, to whom many of them pay tribute for their lands in France, and at the same time satisfy the need of their English overlord John, who required them to muster for him.

I told him that I had seen Arthur of Brittany in the hall and that he seemed a spoiled, troublesome and dangerous young man.

"You and I have a problem in common, Aumary. What to do with an errant relative. My choice is simple. I allow my nephew to live and I will have an aching tooth which I would dearly love to pull. I watch as his followers rally to his cause and harry me at every opportunity, for as long as I am King. Or I discreetly dispose of him, as my advisors would have me do. Yes, he is my brother's son and sixteen a few days ago, and whilst a man, a very young one. I am loath to do it. How can I do it? After this, I will watch the rush of blood which comes with the pulled tooth and wonder if I will ever staunch it. You on the other hand, have an errant brother, whom you cannot punish; you cannot allow another to punish without you must intervene and if necessary with your own body defend him to the end, be it with your own life. My punishment is to be forever branded the murderer of, they would have us believe, a harmless young man. Yours, to be roasted in hell if you seek justice or to fester as an inadequate, for the remainder of your life."

We played in silence then for a while, each with his own thoughts.

After a short time, John sat back and rolling the gaming cup between his hands said.

"Now is the time for our guest I think, Fulke"

The young page jumped up. He went to the door through which I had entered and whispered. A heartbeat later, Robert Belvoir ducked his head under the door frame.

***

I was so surprised I dropped the gaming piece I had been holding.

Robert it was but I hardly recognised him, for his hair was brown, dark brown and cut short over his ears.

He wore green hose with a brown tunic and a green cotte over. I recognised it. I had seen it in the street some months ago when we had reached Rouen.

When he saw me, he took in breath and I heard him whisper,

"Damn"

Then Robert was all sweetness and smiles and trying to embrace me and asking after my health. 'Where had I been and why had I not made myself known?' He had recovered his poise.

John just watched, rolling the gaming cup between his hands.

All at once Robert pretended to realise who else was in the room and fell down on his knees.

"Oh my lord King, I did not see you there. Forgive me for the unseemly display and my rudeness." He bowed his head.

John gestured it away as if it were nothing but a fly landing on his arm.

"Up Belvoir," he said "And take wine should you want it." He nodded to the young page, now back in the room.

The page, Fulke, brought the cup and seated Robert by my left hand a little way off from both the King and myself. Then he left the room leaving the dogs with us.

"Thank you, sire, for seeing me at this late hour."

"You did not expect your brother I think?"

Robert was thinking fast, I could smell it.

"No, my lord King. I had heard he was here in Rouen. I was not able to find and speak to him. I thought him here at your request. Perhaps a muster of loyal knights...?" He tailed off as he saw John's face.

No, John was not taken in.

I cleared my throat.

"What ever possessed you to cut and dye your hair, Robert?" I asked.

His eyes widened.

"But Aumary, my hair has always been this colour, like this. For years, it's been short. Do you not remember?"

"No," I said "You are blond and you wear your hair long. Always have."

Robert put down his cup. He shook his head sadly from side to side.

"This is what I came to talk to you about, sire," he said. "I fear my brother is not in his right mind. I worry that he has suffered some terrible brain failure. For a while now he has been distracted and I am very sorry to say that he has not been able to discharge his duties to you in regard of your Forest of Savernake.

There has been so much negligence, sire...."

I took in a breath at the audacity of his words.

Robert stumbled on as if the speech were distasteful to him. Yes, he was a good actor; the sadness at my incapacity as warden, the helplessness he felt as he watched me blundering about here and there making mistakes, allowing the regalia to almost be stolen by a band of roving men...Oh yes...did John know that there were such wolfsheads in Savernake again after years of freedom from such parasites? I had allowed them in.

John shook his head and tutted.

Robert took this as affirmation and ploughed on.

"Yes, sire...but the worst thing....oh I can scarcely believe it myself and it is awful to have to tell you. No, I cannot." He drew back. "He is my own brother and I cannot speak the words I must."

"Half brother." I said as I saw the face of my monarch and friend pulling itself into a semblance of incredulity. I knew John. He too was a good actor. He had to be. He also knew one when he saw one.

"See, even now, he quips and quibbles. His mind is gone. I think it is the hardships he has suffered," said Robert. "They have been considerable. I left Durley, bringing the regalia with me for I feared for its safety. I feared for my own safety too for the day before I left, Aumary attacked me in the forest and tried to kill me."

He pulled back his sleeve. "'Tis but a scratch and healed now, God be praised, but it is one he gave me, a blow he struck, meaning it to be mortal."

John leaned forward to look, all concern and disquiet.

I could see by his eyes he was finding this most amusing. Does he think it amusing because he does not believe it or because he does, I thought?

"And there have been such things happening at Durley, sire. You can hardly credit it. I know that you cannot be conversant with everything that happens in your realm, the little things, why should you?"

Robert did not know that I wrote to the King regularly, as the warden and as a friend.

"I throw myself at your feet and ask that you be merciful to my brother for I am sure he is not in his right mind. He cannot know what it is he has done. It pains me and breaks my heart to have to say this but I am sure, sire, that he has murdered his wife and child."

That was enough. I had heard enough.

"Robert!" I exclaimed as I jumped up, the wine spilling from my cup, the counters flying onto the floor. "DO not do this! You are not on safe ground."

Only I could see his expression as he turned to me. And it made my blood freeze.

Suddenly we could hear shouting in the stairwell and feet pounding on the steps. Petit, John's valet stumbled through the door.

"Sire, forgive me, you are needed in the hall, there is a riot. Bones are being broken. Please come quickly. Only you can calm the hot-heads."

John jumped up. To us he said, "Stay here."

"What do we have, Petit?" he asked as he strode to the bed and grabbed the sword hidden in the folds of the curtains.

He buckled it on quickly. All knew that if he drew it in anger and it was the only weapon in the hall for all others had been confiscated, and you defied the armed monarch, it would mean instant death. John was not a weak king who hid behind his soldiers. He had always been in the thick of the fighting, having many scars to prove his battle prowess. He flew off now to calm his followers.

"Oh, the usual, sire, partisan fighting. The mercenaries and Hubert's lot and.....come quick."

The dogs rose and loped off after them. The door closed on them all. We were left in silence.

I took the opportunity to remonstrate with my brother.

"Robert, how can you say such things? It will avail you nothing. The King will not believe you. You cannot hope to convince him. You will never be Lord of Durley. The forest will never be yours. Leave it all now, go away and no more will be done or said."

"Ho no..." chuckled Robert, shaking his head. "You'll not get off that lightly. I'm going to make you squirm."

"Leave me the regalia. Go, go to France, to Belvoir. You may be welcome there."

"I have no wish to go to Belvoir."

"Where is the regalia? Why did you steal it? What good could it do you? Just to prove my supposed incompetence?"

"You without your fancy regalia. It was like taking a stick from an old man, to watch him fall. If I could beat you with it, all the better."

"Where is it, Robert? Tell me and you can go..."

"Not before I have branded you a murderer and a traitor."

"Traitor? How so?..."

"Do you not remember how you and Quimper used to plot and write your little messages? Oh yes, it was you who passed on information from the castle to Quimper and his network in Brittany, wasn't it? I have a few little messages of my own in cipher" and he patted the pouch at his hip, "to give to John to explain a few things. When Quimper died...no when you murdered him, you carried on your felonious trade back and forth to the Bretons, didn't you?"

"I did not murder Quimper, why would I? You killed him because he knew that you had stolen his money. I don't think he ever knew what you were doing with it. But I know. You paid some of it out to Master Glover for the hawking glove. You also used his money to buy poisons, I think." I stared him out.

"While we are about it, tell me, how did you learn about poisons? After all, it's not a natural subject for a young lad, is it?"

He scrutinised my face for a while. I waited. Then his face changed and I saw he was going to tell me. "Quimper. He had books and he had learned a lot about herbs and plants and their properties. It was he who told me about walnut juice for dyeing the hair. Good disguise eh?" He lifted a lock of his own cropped thatch. "I have been within feet of you, out and about in the town and you did not know me. Yes, he was more than willing to pass on his knowledge to me. Silly fool, he had no idea I was actually going to use them to make poison. I couldn't stop laughing when he died and you gave all his books and papers to me."

"You killed Quimper to stop him talking to me. You knelt on top of him whilst he slept and you smothered him. His ghost will haunt you," I said, "and that of Piers."

"No ghosts will haunt me. I do not believe in such things."

"Quimper was not a bad man, Robert, misguided maybe, but Piers my steward was a good, good man. I could find no earthly reason why you would kill him. I believed his death was an accident."

I closed my eyes and I could see the scene before me, in my mind's eye. " But now I am convinced you killed him. It was you who brought us the news, you who spoke to him before he died. I can see his eyes, the look he gave you and it was your name he spoke as he faded. I couldn't understand why he would call to you. He didn't, did he? He was naming you his murderer."

"Utter nonsense."

"I suppose you planted the hayfork, positioned it well, lured him to the wall walk and pushed him. You seem to be quite good at pushing people where you want them to go. What did you do? How did you get him there? Tell him you'd found something? Ask him to look at something? Show him....."

Robert was suppressing a laughter that was inhuman.

"No, no something much more ingenious."

I shook my head. All I had to do, it seemed, was appeal to Robert's warped sense of pride in what he had done and out it all came.

He blurted out, laughing, "I told him that I had seen him rogering the kitchen boy and that I was going to tell you that he had had a go at me, tried to sodomise me. You should've seen his face. It was so comical!" He was giggling like a girl. "He couldn't believe it..."

I ploughed on, even though I felt such a repulsion, I could have been sick. "Then you pushed him off the wall walk, backwards when he was facing you, bewildered and hurt?

Why, Robert? What earthly harm had he done you?"

"Perhaps he had tried to sodomise me. You'll never know."

"Don't besmirch the good name of a fine fellow Robert. He was a good God fearing man."

"Didn't save him did it? God didn't reach out his hand and catch him as he fell. Piers made me sick with his perfect little manor, run so beautifully. Dotting every i and crossing every t." Robert grimaced. "I killed him to get at you, as you once said to me, to rid you of a support. I hoped you'd flounder and drown in it all."

I waited while my temper cooled. It was deathly quiet save for Robert breathing hard.

"So he was the first."

Robert's head snapped up at that.

"Oh no...not the absolute first. I am cleverer than that."

I looked at him carefully. "No, I think that was your first...we had no other deaths."

"You don't believe me? Well, then. Listen to this. You remember your dog Samson?"

I think I groaned. Robert had been but twelve then.

"Ha ha, yes, I poisoned him too."

I wanted to smash that beautiful face to pulp, but I clenched my fist instead.

"Yes, that was me. Well, of course I was practicing for..."

"Once more, Robert, I have to ask you why? Why did you kill a defenceless dog you hardly knew, in such a horrible way? He really suffered you know. What did his death avail you?"

Robert showed his teeth in a grin which was no real smile.

"But you suffered too, didn't you? I watched you grieving and you missed him for months."

"No, you're wrong there Robert," I said. "I miss him still. Every day."

"Hahahaha, good!"

"So poor Samson was a practice for...?"

Robert just grinned.

"I have it, Robert. For Cecily. You failed in your first attempt..."

"Not failure....she should have drowned but for that idiot Fisher. He was too quick."

"Ah yes....you must have been so cross when I took Cecily for my bride, Robert. Brides mean the possibility of children, don't they?" I shook my head. "If I took another bride, you'd do the same wouldn't you? Get rid of her."

"Well, I managed her the second time. Arsenic and yes, it was in her drops. That was easy." Robert laughed.

"Oh..." I'd had a thought. "Was that you at the wedding, the owl hooting? I know you are quite good at mimicry. Very clever if it was. It did unsettle quite a few people. So, when Cecily was wounded, people almost expected it. I have to give you credit Robert, that was a masterly stroke."

Slowly, with his eyes fixed on my face, Robert folded his hands into a ball and put his lips to his thumbs. The unearthly hoot of a tawny owl, not such a strange sound in the gloom of the night, echoed around the little stone chamber. I remembered it well from that happy spring day. It had not been well received in daylight, at a wedding.

"Very clever."

Oh, how I wanted to kill him.

"So you killed William next. I must confess, I am a little hazy on how that was achieved, save to say that you took the opportunity presented that night, to slide your knife up into his neck. Yes, we found the wound and we found knives which could have made the wound but never in God's Christendom would we think it was you. Why? What reason did you have to murder an elderly merchant who was nothing to you? Not even family. Again, the only reason was to get at me. To remove my support, my rock. To hurt me."

"He was a clever man. I thought he was beginning to suspect. I used to catch him looking at me askance sometimes. I don't suppose I meant for him to die then but it was convenient that night, I'll admit. I had to do it."

"The wolves never came that close, did they Robert? No wolf knocked down William. That was Bran. Poor, devoted, well trained Bran."

"Aye..." he looked away quickly. "That was hard for me, to use that dog and then kill him, make it look as if a wolf had mauled him."

"You killed your own dog to make it look as if he had been in a fight with a wolf? Why in God's creation would you do that?"

A wry smile came to Robert's lips.

"I had no choice. There were no wolves who came as close as I had said. I had trained Bran to knock down a man and maul him. I didn't know when I might use that skill of his, if at all, but it seemed a good thing to teach a dog as big and as fierce as Bran. He went for William on my command, and knocked him down. He mauled him and then, to make sure, I took my knife and slipped it into William's neck, in amongst the bites and gashes. I didn't think it would be noticed."

"Bran ran off at your command...what was it Colmar heard...?"

"Enough. That was my command. Enough"

I could see at last that Robert was exhibiting some remorse. He could kill my dog without a flicker of sadness. But his own? That had hurt him badly.

"Did you go back later that night and finish him?" I was shocked when a tear appeared in Robert's eye.

"Very early that morning." He wiped a hand across his face. "I had taught him to wait at a particular point in the forest. Of course he was unhurt. I hit him with a heavy rock, felled him and then set to, to make it look as if he had been fighting. Trouble was, I did my job too well. Only meant to wound him, killed him with the first blow. Worst thing I have ever had to do in my life."

"That beast trusted you, Robert."

"Aye, I know." At that moment my brother was almost human.

"And Colmar?"

Robert came back with a laugh, "Idiot. He thought he could approach me with a proposition. He had, he said, worked out that there was no wolf that night close to us on the hill. The more he thought about it, the more he believed that Bran had been incited to kill William."

"He wanted money I suppose, not to bring his new found knowledge to me?" I asked.

"That is what he said. I paid him at first."

"Quimper's money?"

"How clever of you, yes. He had to go of course. He got greedy. We shared a drink -you know I took the brandy wine?

"Yes."

"Aconite was easy to administer to him. He loved his food."

"Did you make the poison or was it one of Quimper's?"

"I made all my poisons," said my brother proudly, "Quimper just knew how to. He never made any."

Robert smiled "But in his case a few chopped up and pulverised roots in a decoction dropped into his dinner was all it took, when his back was turned. I followed him to the kitchen and we bargained as he ate. He'd consumed quite bit before he wondered what it was he was eating. He was going to start the food for us all but was suddenly taken ill. There was no one about just then. It was the quiet time before the evening preparations. It's not far from the kitchen to the privy and he was on his way there. I helped him stagger into the alleyway between the kitchen and the hall and then left him by the blocks, covered in wine so all would think he had drunk himself to death."

I nodded. "And you made the mistake of which I have already told you."

"Pah..Oh well. No one is perfect."

"So Colmar dies and cannot tell what he knows."

I folded my arms. "It was you dressed as a woman in Marlborough wasn't it? Mistress Avice of Bristol."

Robert simpered and pulled his face into a girlish posture, his head to one side.

"Oh Master Glover, that is such lovely work. You are such a clever man," he sniggered in falsetto. "Old man Glover was a lecher of the first order. Easy to fool him."

I nodded.

"The poison in the glove?"

"I stuck the needle I had stolen from old man Glover, when his back was turned, into some flyblown dung. Yes, I knew Johannes would know how to cure the effects. The rest was good acting on my part. Convincing, wasn't I?"

"You have already admitted to the killing of Geoffrey, my son"

"Aye, that was hard. But you must see that you can never have a son. I had tried to get at him when he was a young baby, you know; babies, they die all the time of this and that but noble infants are always watched so carefully, at all times, aren't they? It was difficult for me to get a moment with him alone or find a way, when he was very small. I wouldn't have been so attached to him then, would I?"

"You'd had two years of him running free about the manor. Two years of him coming and going. You had five years of, as you say, becoming attached to him."

"Whatever you think of me, I did grieve for Geoffrey, truly I did."

"You care for no one but yourself. You are truly evil, Robert. Your evil has blighted my life and there is nothing I can do about it."

The material around the bed shivered and a disembodied voice said, "No, but I can."

Through the red curtains, feet swinging to be planted together on the floor, came the figure of Johannes of Salerno.

At the same time, the door behind the painted panels opened and John strode in, followed closely by Petit. John's face was thunderous.

Chapter Sixteen

"You jumped when I said that, Paul. You did not expect it did you? No lad, neither did I, then."

The moment is frozen into my memory. Johannes stood and in one movement, parted the red curtains, walked and put himself between my brother Robert and me.

I do not know why he did that. Perhaps to save me from any murderous attack which Robert might plan, though I know that he had no weapon with which to strike me. All of us were searched well, friend and foe alike, before we entered the presence of our monarch.

The only weapon in the room was the sword worn at the hip of John, the ing. This weapon was now sliding slowly and deliberately from the royal scabbard.

Robert's face was white with shock. He stood stock still, his eyes never leaving the grip of John's sword.

"Aumary cannot put into motion the mechanism of the law but, by the Grace of God and the power invested in me by John our king, I can," Johannes said. "Robert Belvoir, you are a self-confessed felon, a murderer guilty of the most heinous crimes. Four people in this room have heard you confess. You are damned, Robert, out of your own mouth."

Robert turned to me, hidden behind Johannes as I was, absolute hatred on his face.

"It was a trick, a trick to catch me out. You bastard. Burn in your hell."

"Truly, not one of my making," I said.

John shook his head.

"Only ourselves and Johannes of Salerno knew, oh and of course, faithful Petit, what we had planned, Belvoir. You can absolve Aumary of any guilt."

"You have only your pride to blame. Though we have evidence, Robert we might use to convict you; had you remained silent, we might never have known the absolute truth of the matter," said Johannes with a tinge of sadness in his voice.

Robert's bombast suddenly collapsed and the bravado went out of him. With it, our watchfulness and the tension relaxed. He seemed to slump and accept defeat. His shoulders went slack and he hung his head but I knew my brother. This was not like him. It was feigned.

John came further into the room. I noticed, behind him, Petit had reached to the ground behind the cloth panel and was now carrying a small crossbow, spanned and with a bolt in place. The doorway behind stayed open and the cloth panel was partly drawn back. I could see Harold peeping round the door jamb.

"Sit," said John to Robert and gestured with his sword.

I watched as Robert moved slowly to the nearest stool. It had been pushed further towards the fire when we had risen earlier and now, in one fluid movement, Robert ducked behind it, reached into the flames of the fire, pulled out the unburnt end of a glowing brand and hurled it, fired end first, at Johannes.

Johannes turned away from the missile and knocked into me. Taken by surprise, I staggered and fell across the backgammon table, knocking the whole table awry and landing heavily on my elbow. Not before the table had cannoned into Petit and dislodged the crossbow from his grip. It skidded along the floor. Robert scooped it up.

John lunged with his sword for Robert as he skipped past him, but did not make contact.

My brother used his elbow to ward off the swing and caught John in the midriff. John doubled up, winded.

The door was closing. We heard a key turn in the lock.

There was a scuffle outside the door. Then silence. Poor Harold had fallen foul of Robert. I hoped he had not been too badly hurt. He was only a child but then Robert, as I knew well, had no scruples regarding the young.

Johannes was the first to recover.

He strode across the room to the larger door and pulled it open. I gave my hand to Petit who gratefully accepted the help and pulled him up. He, in his turn, went to his stricken king and patted and stroked him on the back. I have noticed this before. When people are bruised and battered, others pat and massage the back though the back is rarely the actual area of the hurt. I remember, strange at such a moment, wondering if it was something that helped.

Wheezing, John stood and re-sheathed his sword.

"Which way, Johannes?"

"Left I think. Careful my lord, he has taken the crossbow."

***

We all piled out of the door and down the stone staircase. At the bottom we collected an armed man who had been patrolling the next floor and had come to see what the noise was all about. The corridor at the base led to yet another stone stair and this time we crossed the room opposite, to reach the staircase one floor lower, down which my brother had fled.

Down again we went and came out in an inner courtyard. There, in the semi darkness, where there was only one flare on the wall, we stopped to get our bearings. All was silent.

John and Petit knew this castle well. It was John's principal residence when in Normandy and the king had known it from childhood.

"Petit, go to the gate, tell them to allow no one out. No one."

He ran to us and then turned back to Petit, "Oh, and as little force as is necessary - we want him alive."

We followed the King in the semi darkness through a covered walkway and then into yet another well-lit courtyard.

There we stopped here to listen. Faintly from ahead and above us came voices.

John turned to his man at arms.

"More men, to the east tower. Some to the west courtyard should he double back. All those on duty to keep their eyes to the walls."

Then we were off again, plunging into yet another staircase, this one a little wider than the last. John was up ahead. I called to him. Did he think it wise to forge ahead so careless of his person when Robert was known to have a crossbow? His answer was lost in shouting and the sound of the slamming of doors above us.

Over at the other side of the courtyard we could hear folk in the great hall, rising and milling about, woken by the unlooked for nocturnal activity. We were aware of lights here and there, small pinpricks reflected on walls and ceilings.

We reached a slight landing in a bend in the stairs. John looked out through the small embrasure which served as a window.

His voice carried into the night. "This is John your King. We want no one to follow us. The east tower is to remain sealed until you hear my voice again."

We heard a muttering way down below us in the courtyard we had just quitted.

One more flight of stone steps. At the top, lit by a flare fixed to the wall, we met a body, seated, doubled over and leaning against the wall, with outstretched legs. By that wall there was a small table with the remnants of food on platters. A large metal jug had been upended and had been used to render the guard, for guard he was, unconscious.

The man was groaning.

"Alive then," said Johannes, smiling.

John faced the door. I saw him brace himself.

He walked into the room.

I was not prepared for the luxury of the little apartment, for apartment it was. Three rooms, a reception room, newly panelled in wood, with a wood block floor and glass in the windows. We crossed this empty room. Another room, a bedroom with a garderobe off, on the outer wall overlooking the moat, again panelled and with glassed windows. The bed covers were flung open as if the occupant had left in haste. To the other side of the bed was a small chapel big enough for a couple of men to pray. All rooms were lit with one or two candles of good beeswax. Through another door we went. I notice John was more cautious now. This door opened onto a larger room, with a bigger window. A few books were scattered on an oaken table and here there were the remains of a meal taken some hours ago. It was here we found another body on the floor.

Johannes bent over and felt for a heartbeat. He shook his head.

"This one was not so lucky."

I craned my neck. A small eating knife protruded from the man's body where the neck met the shoulder. Suddenly we heard a splash below us. It sounded like a body had been tipped into the moat.

"Three guards," said John. "Now there is only Arthur."

Johannes looked fearful. "No, sire...he wouldn't..."

"There is only one way to find out."

He started for a small doorway set into a tower in the eastern most corner. I quickly set myself before him.

"No John, let me go first."

I climbed the circular stair with Johannes and John behind me.

At the top there was no door, just the turn of the last step and then open air and I stepped out into the cool of the night and a fine drizzle. Robert was there at the far wall, with his crossbow.

And with him, the breeze ruffling his already bed-tousled hair, a cloak tightly wrapped around his nakedness, was Arthur Duke of Brittany.

I stepped closer. "What do you hope to gain by this, Robert? Accept defeat. Come down with us."

The crossbow was lifted and pointed at me.

John moved out onto the little tower top behind me. Johannes was just to be seen on the last stair.

"Arthur, step away from him," said the King.

"He has come to rescue me. The castle will soon be overrun with my supporters."

"He has not. He is an escaped felon and he is hiding behind you, using you, Arthur."

"Pah...you are a liar, uncle. You lie to me constantly. There are more soldiers down there." Arthur pointed away across the moat, "rallied to my cause. Ready to rise up and fight for me as the true king."

"You are deceived."

"Move out of the way," ordered Robert.

Slowly John took a couple of steps nearer. How proud I was of John's bravery at that moment.

"Belvoir, leave him. Put down the weapon. This is the command of your King. We shall be merciful."

Robert grasped Arthur by the cloak wrapped round his arm and tugged him, meaning to pull him further around the tower top.

"Come sire, time is pressing. We must join the others."

"There are no others!" shouted John. "There is to be no rescue." We knew that his voice had carried to the men on the ground in the courtyard, for there was a collective hushed in-breath.

"You will never be King."

The light from the courtyard to the side of the tower flickered up to us as dozens of flares were lit down on the ground. I saw Robert's eyes twitch over the stone coping, watching his moment when he might make a dash for the door way.

Johannes stepped onto the last step. "Robert, you cannot hope to leave here alive, without surrender. Do not add to the tally of dead you have left behind you."

My brother laughed that slightly hysterical laugh I had heard before and inched nearer to the exit, and for the first time swung the crossbow at Arthur. He nodded.

"Go now, before me, or I will kill you where you stand."

Arthur looked bewildered.

"You tell me that I am to be taken to safety tonight by people of my party... and now..."

"Move before me to the steps."

"Why should I do as you say? I am your duke. You cannot command me."

"No one is my duke, or my King." Robert's eye flicked to John.

For the first time Arthur looked unsure. His gaze swung from Robert to John, John to Robert.

By inches they had reached a small gap between the coping of the tower and the stair, where the wall was slightly lower and which was roofed over with slate.

The King chose that moment to make his move. In one action he drew his sword and leapt into the middle of the roof. Robert swung round and released the catch of the crossbow.

I wasn't aware of doing it but I threw myself across the space and onto the body of my king, knocking him to the ground. The rest was accomplished by the slick stones of the roof space, wet with rain and debris. John fell and I fell atop him but not before I had grabbed him, taken the crossbow bolt through my left shoulder and been knocked back a pace.

They told me afterwards what happened then, though through the rushing of blood in my head and the sensation of being punched, I heard the eerie sound of a long drawn out scream, cut off with a sickening crunch, like an egg being dropped onto a cook's slab. Then I heard the pounding of feet.

I had taken the bolt intended for John.

***

My brother threw the now useless crossbow at Johannes and there was an short struggle on the rooftop between Arthur and Robert. In a trice my brother had grasped the legs of the Duke of Brittany and tipped the unwary and confused young man in one movement, over the waist high balustrade of the tower, to fall to his death on the flagstones of the courtyard beneath. Then Robert was off down the stairwell and away.

I felt John slide from under me. I heard him rush to the edge. There was a whispering of voices, rising in volume as thirty people looked up and saw, John their King looking down at them from the top of a tower. A tower from which, it seemed to those who stared up, he had thrown his nephew Arthur to his death.

For me, the rest was darkness.

***

They took me slowly back the way we had come to the room occupied by Arthur moments before and laid me on the bed. I was told later that John's men were leaping into the room from the stairs, called up by him when we arrived, and John gave them instructions, calmly and with authority.

The castle was tied up tighter than a miser's purse. Robert could not escape. He could hide but eventually he would be apprehended.

The rest was up to John. I could do nothing for I did not regain consciousness that night.

Johannes asked for boiling water and cloths and borrowed surgeons' equipment and extracted the barb from my shoulder. I was lucky. The arrow had gone into the fleshy part of the top of my shoulder where the arm meets the collar bone. It had shattered no bone, pierced no major blood vessel but it had made a mess of the muscles at the top of my arm and I have to this day a weakness there which no amount of exercise can drive out.

'Tis a good thing I am right handed.

John, Johannes told me later, went off quickly leaving me in his care, to recover the body of Arthur and to limit the damage done to him by his nephew's public death.

It was put about that Arthur had tried to escape that night and had, in a scuffle, fallen accidentally to his death from the tower. It was not entirely a lie.

There were many rumours flying about that spring about the death of Arthur. John had slain him with his own hand, in a drunken stupor. Some say that he died as a result of his wounds after John asked that his eyes be put out. It was said that the king had told a henchman that Arthur be drowned in the river and allowed to float out to sea. Some fishermen swore that they had discovered the body of Duke Arthur later next day, caught in reeds at the side of the river and had taken it for honourable burial in Rouen.

The story that Arthur had fallen from the tower remained just one of those rumours. Those who had witnessed the event, mostly castle staff and a few men at arms, were warned not to embellish the tale, on pain of dismissal, but how do you contain such a story?

I know the truth of it, for I was there and I know that Arthur was buried with all due respect shortly after April the fifth, in a vault in the cathedral at Rouen, and forgotten.

John seemed not to care that he had been blamed for Arthur's death. Perhaps he had been contemplating his politic removal after all. He kept silent to the end of his days on the matter, as have I and Johannes. The only reference to the event I ever heard John make, was a throw away comment (I know he also wrote to his mother, the selfsame words, for he told me so).

"God's Grace has stood me in better stead than I could possibly indicate." Make of that what you will.

"There. I have said it. It's out. I know who killed Arthur of Brittany. I have kept this secret for forty years. On the evening of April the third 1203, in fine drizzle on the top of a tower at Rouen castle, in Normandy, my half brother Robert Belvoir threw him to his death. He killed him as surely as if he had stuck a knife into him.

"Have you got that Paul....Paul...are you asleep? No. Well, read me what you have just written so that I may be absolutely certain you have it right. Good. Let it be known that John Plantagenet, King of England did not kill Arthur of Brittany."

I lay for two days in the large bed in that room with Johannes attending me. No word reached us about Robert.

Despite the wound in my shoulder, and I have no doubt I owe my quick recovery to Johannes' ministrations, I felt quite well and though the shoulder pained me, it was nothing I couldn't bear. In part this must have been due to the wonderful tisanes which he made me drink. The man was a genius and I am sure I owe him my life and my limb.

John came in a little under two days after Arthur's death, full of praise for us both, overflowing with bonhomie and good cheer. I could tell though that there was an underlying worry which was niggling at him and eventually we persuaded him to tell us. He was leaving the castle and us, he said. Philip had resumed his attacks on the fringes of Normandy; in Poitou the barons had broken out into rebellion, and the Bretons, distressed by the rumours about their hero Arthur, had assaulted Normandy from the west. John was finding it difficult to organise a resistance on so many fronts and was constantly on the move. For our own safety it was best that we return to England as soon as I was able to travel. It was clear to him that many of the Norman barons were no longer loyal to him. How true that was, for many castles had been treasonably surrendered to France and the list was growing.

I did not ask what he was doing about Robert. Were they still searching? Had he, against all the odds, escaped the castle?

On the night of April the seventh we had our answer.

John asked me to remove to his own room, the little room with the painted panels, for I could be cared for there better than here in this tower which was in an outer limb of the castle and not so easily served. He was off to Molyneux again and would not be in need of the bed. I argued. It was my king's room. As much as it was an honour, I could not accept.

Nonsense. After all I had done for him....No. I must be accommodated there, it was better for me, he said, and for his staff. Besides, I would be off for England soon. No doubt he would next see me there, in Marlborough.

The walk from Arthur's apartment to John's room tired me (we went by an entirely different route to the one we took on that fateful night on the third of April), so that I stumbled and staggered the last few steps and had to be revived when we arrived there, by a drink of brandywine, not a liquor I particularly like, but effective nonetheless.

They seated me in a porter's chair which John had had specially brought in, with cushions around me to prop me up and to insulate my wound from the hard wood at my rear and with a blanket over my knee like an old man. I had not seen a chair like this before and vowed to have one like it made for my solar, when I returned to Durley.

"Yes, Paul, I am sitting in it now."

It had not legs like an ordinary chair but a solid seat going down to the floor so no draughts could creep up at you from behind. The top was bent over like a priest's hood (some called it a priest's chair) and round the sides, so you were cocooned in a leather-clad semicircle. It was so comfortable that it was possible to doze all night happily leaning on the side panels. I found it less painful than lying in a bed to sleep.

The fire was lit and was most welcome. John's two dogs, Gog and Magog, the wolfhounds whom he had left in Rouen, were lounging by the hearth. As I entered, their tails thumped in greeting. How gratifying that was. As you know I am fond of dogs and I deemed it a touching gesture that John had left them here to keep me company.

Ha! Company? I was not lacking for it. There was no shortage of people coming and going, seeing to my wants and needs, not least Johannes, who had decided to bed down on the truckle bed in the room with me. I was relieved to see the small page too; Harold, still in the land of the living and sporting an almost closed and good black eye which must have elevated his status a few notches amongst the pages of the castle. Stephen and Peter, my armed men, were bedded down comfortably outside the door. Fulke was bedded outside the secret door with two more men.

That night was the first time I was really able to stay awake and to think and so it was the first opportunity I had to ask questions of Johannes.

First I had to know what he was doing in Rouen and why he had not made himself known to me.

He laid himself with ease back on the bed, crossed his ankles and put his arms behind his head. "Best I tell it from the beginning then," he said.

"Last I saw you, you had just locked your brother in his room and denied me an explanation. I felt I was owed some justification, some reason. I must say that, at that moment I felt hurt that you would not confide in me. It worried at me too, for I was beginning to have doubts about Robert myself. I returned the next day I was able, to have it out with you and to see the old priest. Of course, you had gone and so, God bless him, had Benedict. John Brenthall explained that Robert had been asked to leave Durley and that he had then somehow stolen the regalia and had attacked Hal. No one knew why or had any explanation. This set me thinking further.

He also told me that you had taken Robert under guard to see Benedict that last evening. I asked myself, why would you do that? Then it hit me. You were trying to obtain a confession. John told me that they had found some items in Robert's room and I went to look."

"Did you find the orpiment?"

"Yes, and several other items a young man of good breeding does not generally have lying around his room.The men you set to look through Robert's things did not find the money as you asked but they did find small vials of liquid. Solutions of aconite and belladonna - deadly nightshade. I found books with well-thumbed passages about poisons and equipment for making such things. They left some of them in your office for you to look at but I suppose you did not."

"I knew what they were. I had no need to look. Besides, I had left for Normandy by then."

"John Brenthall came to me later with the knife you had taken from Robert and the slingshot. Oh yes, and the length of twine, nail and knot. He wondered if they were important, for you had set them aside in your office with a rather cryptic note for me, had you not?"

"I did not finish writing to you. I was overtaken by events."

"I sat in your office and I puzzled and puzzled. I knew by then that Robert had killed. I was beginning to see why he had killed. What I did not understand was why you seemed so powerless to act against him. Yes, he was your own brother but he had killed your wife and uncle and your son. A man does not sit back and let the murder of his close kith and kin go unavenged in this way and I knew you were not craven. Especially so, if that man is law in those parts. I vowed to follow you."

"I am glad you did," I said shifting my bad arm and smiling. "But how did you know where we were going?"

"Ah, that was Hal. On my way home to collect my travelling gear and another horse, I stopped by the priory to look in on Hal. He was well cared for there and he told me his story. He felt that you were going to the King in Normandy for, on the trip to Marlborough, Robert had moaned about you incessantly and maligned you, and told Hal that he would go there to look for redress for the ills you had done him and seek justice from the King."

"So you followed?"

"I nearly didn't for, finding a ship to take me was a deuced hard thing." He smiled wryly. "Cost me a fortune. As I travelled, I pieced together the little fragments I knew. Those fragments became bigger more coherent chunks. Still I did not know why you did not act. You had followed, not because Robert had murdered but because he had the regalia. Peter Brenthall told me the tale of that. However what use that could be to Robert at that moment, before his unmasking, I could not see."

I nodded. "I think Robert plans so far ahead, he cannot sometimes see his own hand in it but he will have had a reason. No doubt, he felt that possessing the regalia gave him some power over me. After all, he used it to try to convince John I was not a fit warden. When he was caught - and yes, that night in the forest, he did try to kill me and make it look like yet another accident; he used the regalia to brain poor Hal. I think Robert had two leather panniers. One in which he put the regalia and which we allowed him freely to pack onto his horse and the other in which we found the poisons."

"Where did he hide the second pack?"

"Peter saw him going to the stables. Perhaps he had a hiding place there?

We allowed him to saddle and pack his own horse. That was my mistake, I own it. I should have supervised it myself but I was so angry with him I wanted no sight of him, lest I break my vow and his neck."

"Did we see where he retrieved it from?"

"That is not something we were watching him for. No doubt if we asked the grooms, they could tell us he fetched it from somewhere in their domain."

"I know now why you did not act of course."

"And what do you think of that? I suppose you heard me tell the King, or John told you?"

I recall that Johannes did not answer that question but came back with,

"I sent a letter begging an audience with John, telling him that I believed Robert a murderer and that your life and possibly his was in danger should he encounter the fiend. I told him what I knew and what I surmised. When we met, he told me what he knew. He asked me to wait for a while before making it known to you that I was in Rouen. Best keep it secret he thought."

"And so the two of you decided to unmask my brother, leaving me still true to my oath? Do you know, that night I first talked with the King here in Rouen, I felt that there was some other hand in this, some reason why John was so easy to convince, so pliable. It was you wasn't it, behind that door?" I gestured at 'Susannah and the Elders.'

Johannes shrugged, "John asked me to wait outside. I did. He would not arrest Robert there and then, even on your say so, though I supposed you would never be made to tell what you actually knew. We had to find a way of getting the truth from Robert's own lips; even just a part of it, to use against him."

"How did you know though, that he would damn himself out of his own mouth?"

"I didn't really," Johannes scratched his head. "But that sort often cannot keep their tongue silent in their head. They must crow about what they have done."

"It was a risk still."

Johannes chortled. "That little charade was John's idea. It worked better than we could ever hope."

"He's a wily player is our king."

"Aye, let's hope he's wilier than Philip Augustus of France."

Johannes climbed from the bed and built up the fire. Then he rolled himself up in his cloak once more and we allowed the silence between us to lengthen. The fire crackled, a log shifted. One of the great dogs, Gog I think, began dreaming and his back legs ran on some imaginary hunt. I smiled. I would be pleased to see my own dogs and my own home soon.

Johannes' breathing steadied and soon he was asleep. I followed shortly after, my head nodding against the side of the leather chair.

A slight noise woke me; it must have been a few hours later for the candles had burnt down and the only light left came from the fire. Enfolded in my comfortable chair as I was, I did not move. Gog and Magog stirred but did not wake fully from their pleasant dreams. I saw Magog's nose lift and twitch as if he were testing the air for a smell. If this indeed is what he was doing, he recognised it and slept again, happy that it was a familiar one.

A hooded figure slipped gently through the door behind the panel. I was instantly alert. No one was allowed to enter without our permission. We had guards on both doors. A voice said quietly, "Yes, Father - I shall Father...." A boy's voice.

Momentarily confused I wondered whose father this was. Then I realised. This was a Benedictine Father and no secular figure. As he quietly glided into the room, I saw the glint of a small cross worn over the scapular in the firelight. If I had been more awake and less muddle headed I would have wondered what the priest was doing here in the late hours of the night and why he had been allowed in to see us.

I was hidden from him by the curve of my chair. He did not see me. I leaned forward to speak as he approached the bed.

It was then I noticed that this Benedictine priest, this midnight visitor, his head covered by the cowl, his arms folded under his scapular into his voluminous sleeves as was proper, wore not sandals on his feet, but good leather boots and with a jolt I also realised that I recognised them.

Chapter Seventeen

With a yell which woke the two huge hounds from their slumbers and shook our visitor from his purpose, I reared up from my hiding place in the chair.

Johannes, warned by my cry and by the barking of the dogs, rolled from the bed and the knife which surely would have caught him in the heart, was driven harmlessly into the bed covers.

The hood fell back as the intruder pulled the knife out from the mattress and he stabbed in anger, again and again into the pillow, raising a cloud of feathers. He then picked up the pillow and threw it at me. Feathers flew everywhere.

Johannes had by now recovered and pulled off his swathing cloak, wrapping it around his hand as a protection from the next blow which was to come a moment later.

Now the men at arms had flooded into the room, two to each door. They hovered, uncertain how to approach and I yelled, "Take him alive...alive I say, the King's orders."

Stephen moved forward and drew his sword. Sword against knife was no contest but Robert - for Robert was our pretend priest, grabbed for Fulke who had entered by the secret door and he menaced him with the knife, drawing him close and driving the point into his throat, so that it raised a few red droplets. I saw Fulke swallow. The weapon looked like the sort of knife one used in the kitchen, pointed and sharp on one edge.

"Stay or I will kill him."

"Back Stephen, for he will do as he says." I cried. "I have reason to know it."

Robert gestured to my two guards and they came pliantly into the middle of the room, leaving the door free. Johannes was guarding the secret door. The other two guards stood behind him, short swords drawn. Robert would not go that way.

Edging his terrified prisoner closer and closer to this escape route, Robert crossed the edge of the room and was almost past the fire, when the two wolfhounds rose up as one and with an unearthly growl, leapt on Robert. He was unprepared for this and stepped backwards. As he raised his arms to ward off the bared teeth, Fulke slid down and scrabbled on his hands and knees away from the fracas.

The knife flicked towards the dog's face, Gog I think, but Magog's teeth had already bitten into Robert's wrist and the knife clattered uselessly on the floor. Robert screamed.

He stepped back again and fell over the stone hearth and into the fire, turning to save himself as he went.

The flames, which had been desultorily licking the almost burnt out logs, flared into life with the new material to catch at; the hood of Robert's habit which had again fallen over his head. Robert tried to turn over to rise to his knees but the heavy dogs ravaged and tore at his back, pushing his face into the flames.

The rest of the habit began to catch fire. I noticed his hair had begun to smoulder. He screamed incessantly. There was a terrible smell of charring flesh and hair.

The dogs snarled and tore, ripped and gouged. Neither of them seemed to mind the flames which licked at Robert's body from underneath them. I frantically searched the room for something to pour onto the flames but we had drunk every drop of liquid and no water was in any bowl or pot. Not even the chamber pot had anything in it.

Johannes was suddenly there with a heavy blanket, trying to beat the flames and the dogs away.

He succeeded in dousing some of the flames but the dogs were undeterred and they simply went for Robert again once he had crawled from the fire. We fell back. The castle men at arms behind Johannes did not attempt to control the dogs but stared wide eyed, for these were their master's beasts and inviolate.

Robert was by turns whimpering and crying, screaming and yelling curses. He pulled off, with badly burned and ravaged hands, what was left of the smouldering and smoking habit and rose to his burned knees. Peter and Stephen took their cue from Johannes and were then beating with blankets, the flames from the burning habit and the scattered logs which had set alight to the rushes, and which were threatening to spread and set fire to the room.

The dogs pushed my brother over again and with one movement Gog deftly went for his throat. I saw what was left of his devastated face as the dog fastened his teeth and ripped. Never again would I wish to see anything so horrifying. The pictures of the terrors of hell which my father had caused to be painted on the high wall of the chancel of our church at Durley, were as nothing to the blood-flecked, burned, half-destroyed, almost eyeless, noseless figure of my brother. The noise he made was prolonged, a high pitched scream falling to a bubble and a gasping, with a sobbing that was no sobbing for there was no throat to sob with. The dog, snarling and growling, backed off, sensing the job done.

Recovering his wits and crying, Fulke had clawed his way up from the floor by grabbing handfuls of Johannes' gown and leaning on him. He turned to the awful scene and shouted.

"Gog, Magog, to me! To me, now!"

Immediately, the two beasts shook themselves and sloped off to stand with Fulke, licking their chops and checking themselves for damage. They had one or two small burns and a gouged ear showed red where one dog had bitten the other accidentally in the fight. There seemed no animosity at that.

Magog was licking a paw. I think he had burnt it on the scattered cinders. Gog lay down, and breathing heavily, began to lick a small knife nick which Robert had given him on his front leg.

Robert was writhing on the ground, blood pumping from his wounds. His eyes, or what was left of them, were staring at me. It seemed to take an age though I suppose it was only a few heartbeats and then suddenly, the life went out of them. The twitching ceased and he was gone. So quickly. It did not seem right.

I remember saying into the slightly shocked silence which ensued, "The punishment has fit the crime."

"Aye...that was hell," said Johannes "And that is what he will endure now, for eternity."

Little Fulke collapsed on the floor beside his dogs and sobbed.

"Are you going to be sick Paul...? No? Good. I know it was not a pleasant thing to write but I do want to write the truth. Are you ready to go on?"

We raised Fulke up and sat him on the bed.

He blubbered that it was his fault, for he had let the priest into the room and he would be called to account for his death. We assured him that this was no priest but a felon sought throughout the castle; that his death would not be held against him; nor would the dogs, John's dogs, be punished.

"I saw his cross, the little silver one...I recognised it and so I thought it was Father Francis, but it wasn't was it? I let him in. He said he had been called to the hurt man, to you sir, to hear your confession. So I let him in. These two, Thomas and Roger, also thought it was Father Francis, so we are all to blame aren't we sir?"

"No one will call you to account for this Fulke, I promise." But we could not convince him that he would not be whipped for his error.

What was left of Robert Belvoir was lifted on a cloak and removed and I asked that he be taken to the nearest chapel, even though I knew that he did not deserve my care nor that he believed in any of the ritual we would lavish on him. The blood was wiped away by some sleepy eyed maids, who when they saw the devastation, were sleepy eyed no longer and chatted at their work as if clearing up the blood and gore of a murderer was the highlight of their year. They would probably eat out on the tale in a local tavern, for weeks.

Gog and Magog were taken off eventually by Fulke who said he had to attend their hurts. Before they went, I thanked them both with a pat on the head, for releasing me from my vow and for avenging my dead. Fulke's eyes were huge when he heard that. Heaven knows what he made of it.

As they went through, past 'Susannah and the Elders,' I asked Fulke why the dogs had attacked with such ferocity.

"They stay with my lord the king at night and are his bodyguards when he is here in Rouen, my lord. If he is attacked or threatened, or indeed if I am, (I sleep on the truckle bed you see) they have been taught to take down the attacker."

"I suppose they recognised the habit worn by the intruder," I could not bring myself to say Robert's name. "His smell would still be on it and until they were close to the man, they thought him a friend."

"Aye sir, they know Father Francis well. He has access to all parts of the castle. He often comes to talk to the King, at night."

"Have they ever needed to attack anyone before?"

"No sir. But when the man took hold of me, they did not like it sir and knew that it was not Father Francis. They would defend me, you see."

"Thank you Fulke. Take good care of them. They are a priceless weapon."

I thought of Samson, my faithful Samson, dead this few years now by poison at the hand of my brother and of Bran, his dog, crushed with a rock and used in such an ill way by an uncaring master. Yes, it was justice, the punishment had indeed fitted the crime.

Wine was brought for both Johannes and myself and we sat in silence sipping it, he on the bed and me in my chair. I had begun to shake with shock.

Johannes wrapped me in a blanket and built up the fire once more; the fire which had consumed my brother, only this was a different log, these were other flames. He was burning and burning in another fire now.

I stared at the hearth. There was the tiny silver cross worn by Robert, the string broken through.

I looked up suddenly, "So we must set ourselves to finding a priest without a habit, Johannes. We must do it now. Do you think he still lives?" I asked urgently.

"If God is merciful. We must put out the word that a search must be made."

Two hours later, we had word that indeed the luckless man had been found. Stripped to his drawers, knocked out cold and stuffed head first into one of the castle garderobes. It took almost an hour to get him out. I am told the smell was appalling and the poor man was almost asphyxiated.

We tried not to smile.

***

Two days later, my arm done up in a sling, I went to the chapel to see Robert one last time, when the women had finished cleansing him and when I had visited the castle carpenter for a coffin. Much as I would have liked to put him in the ground bound in nothing but his shroud, in the end I could not. The dogs and the fire had changed him beyond recognition.

Gone was the beautiful blond hair. The dark locks, coloured with walnut juice, were charred and frazzled, though I think I could just see some light regrowth at the crown of his head, where the bandages left a gap, for the throat was held in place by strips of cloth tied up over his ravaged forehead. His face was scarred and puffed, black and raw. The hands laid reverently over his chest were missing fingers and they too were charred and mutilated into nothing but lumps of flesh, where the dogs had done their work.

I turned away. I would remember him as he was that day when I first spied him, when he was twelve, like an angel, all brightness and gold, smiling and happy, and not the black and twisted devil he had become.

We buried my brother with as little fuss as possible in the churchyard nearest the castle on St. William's Day, the tenth of April. We did not stand vigil for him, nor did we pay to have a mass said for the repose of his soul. Many might think me remiss at that but Robert himself had no faith and his soul was as black as a carrion crow, the bird of death. Indeed several were wheeling around the sky that morning, calling with that raucous 'argh', one after the other, as he was lowered into the ground.

***

Then we turned our thoughts to packing and to home.

And to one more thing. To finding the Savernake regalia - we had no idea where Robert had left it.

We discussed how we might go about tracing it. It was no small thing to be easily hidden. Was it left in the leather pannier and lying in some hostelry in the town? How many of those would we have to search before we found it? Had he buried it somewhere out in the countryside where we should never find it? No, it had to be somewhere where he might retrieve it easily, for if he had been believed and the king had been taken in, he would have had to produce it as evidence of my malfeasance.

We were sitting in the hall one evening, after supper, Johannes, Stephen, Peter and I, discussing the trip home and the possibility that we should never recover it when a voice behind us asked our pardon and, squeezing between Johannes and Peter, laid a fresh jug of ale on the table.

"Sirs, I could not help hearing...."

It was Harold, the page, waiting on tables now that John had gone from the castle and he was no longer needed as a body servant in Rouen. I realised he was a little older than the other pages, perhaps by two years. Almost a squire then.

We smiled at him. His damaged eye was now more open, though still bloodshot, the skin around a mix of purples, yellows and blues. Stephen slapped him on the back and made room for him on the bench.

"I have heard you talking about your lost treasure. Might I be of some help?" Harold threw his leg over the bench and sat side on, facing me.

We all looked at each other, puzzled.

"Do you know where it is, Harold? I asked, "Have you seen it?"

"Oh no sir," He shook his head "You would have to draw me a picture of it so I knew what it looked like."

"A picture?"

"Yes sir, then, I know what it is I am looking for."

"You would help us look for it? Well, that is most kind but we have no idea where to start."

"Perhaps if you got me a map, sir, we could start with a search of the castle."

"A map…a drawing of the castle?"

"Yes, sir" he said, smiling, "I think the lord has one of those from when the new building work was done. You could ask him if you could borrow it."

I remembered my own building work and the 'map' which Phillip Carver had of the existing buildings and then of the planned extensions and changes, which was locked in a chest at home.

"How will this help us? Harold" I asked.

"I can dowse for it sir."

I saw Johannes' eyes narrow. He knew what the lad was on about.

"How would you do that?" I asked.

He went on to tell us that he and his father and his father before him, had all been gifted with the power to find water by dowsing for it. They were in great demand round-about whenever a well needed sinking or a spring needed locating.

I saw Stephen cross himself surreptitiously. Some still thought this sort of skill a thing of the devil.

"I have read of this talent but have never seen it in action," Johannes said in an excited voice. "It is a most exact thing. If it were possible it would save us days, even weeks of searching by hand and eye. It's not only water which can be found. Metal too, I'm told. Other things."

Harold beamed. "Yes sir, that's right. And your treasure is made of metal, is it not?"

"Some of it is made of silver, some of steel."

"It can do us no harm to try," said Johannes.

The next morning we approached the custodian of the castle and asked if we might look at the maps he had of the buildings, the plans. He scratched his head.

"Dunno. Better ask Ancelm, I can't read 'em anyway. Never learned, never needed to. He'll point you in the right direction." We laughed at that, for that was exactly what we were about.

Ancelm of Falaise, the archivist, turned out to be a tiny little man with ink stains on every part of him. He found the plan for us, a huge rolled parchment covered in calculations and notes. The main castle had been inked in black and the later additions and changes drawn in a blue ink. Then he bustled off about his own business. We cleared Ancelm's table of papers and books and secured the corners of the stretched out plan with stones kept for that purpose.

Harold fished in his scrip and brought out a polished black stone no bigger than a cherry. A hole had been drilled through this and he threaded a fine string through the hole and knotted the end.

Holding the free end of the string, he began to gyrate the stone over the map. Eventually the gyrations grew smaller and the stone, as if stopped by a physical force around it, hovered over the map in a tiny circle.

"I have, to make sure we can be certain of our answers. It is customary, when first asking questions, just to ask them in my head. For example, where on this map we are situated at present? You can see that the stone is pointing to the little room, here, which is indeed where we are standing."

Johannes grinned. I looked on not convinced. Well naturally Harold knew where we were and could influence the swinging of the stone.

"Now if one of you will draw me a representation of what we are looking for, I will try to picture it in my mind's eye and see where the stone takes us, sirs."

I looked around for vellum and found a small piece of graphite sharpened to a point.

I am no limner but I knew the regalia well and began to draw, in shaky lines, the pattern of the horn with its silver bands and roundels.

"First" said Harold, "I must make sure that what we are looking for is indeed in the castle and not somewhere else."

He held out his arm and said to himself, "Is the Belvoir Regalia of Savernake Forest in England, now in the castle of Rouen in Normandy?"

We watched fascinated as the little stone, with no help nor movement what so ever from Harold began to circle.

We all stepped forward. No, Harold was not moving the stone. He was standing as still as he could. Again Stephen crossed himself.

The stone eventually began to lengthen its swing and in a few heartbeats had begun to swing backwards and forwards from Harold's body, in a line about a foot deep.

He threw it up into his hand and caught it. "Yes, it's here," he said with confidence.

Johannes was bobbing his head, "It looks for all the world as if it's nodding its head Harold," he smiled.

"Aye and if the answer was no, it would have shaken side to side, like we do," answered the lad and gave us a demonstration by shaking his own head.

He stared at my scribbling. I had tried to make it as realistic as possible but my drawing skills were not the greatest of my accomplishments. However, there on the parchment was as good a likeness of the Horn of Savernake as I could make.

Harold turned my drawing this way and that and peered at it carefully.

He then stretched the stone out into the middle of our plan. He shut his eyes and we all held our breath. It began to move, as was its wont, in a circular movement. Gradually, the gyrating increased. It covered the main buildings and then passed out over them into the lesser buildings and courtyards of the greater castle. Within a few heartbeats the little stone had changed its movement and was now concentrating on a section of buildings in the eastern most corner. Gradually, stealthily, the stone circle diminished. Harold opened his eyes and stared. The stone came to rest over a small building built into the eastern-most wall, by the moat.

"There. It is in the laundry" he said triumphantly.

I had not been aware of holding my breath but I blew out air through my lips.

"That is.....well," I looked at the young lad, who was still grinning and was so confident of his pronouncement that I didn't have the heart to argue. ".... astounding Harold. If it is indeed in the laundry, I shall not know what to think, but that it's some kind of magic."

The grin went from his face. "No sir, it's no magic. Merely a skill. As I say we all have it, all us St. Clairs. Father and sons."

We rolled up Ancelm's map and left it on the table and quitted his domain for the eastern range of outbuildings by the moat. Harold led the way, as he was familiar with the castle. We should have got lost, for as in all these sorts of buildings, there was never a straight way to get anywhere.

The laundry was not much in use today, for the castle was depleted of its main host. Just a few cloths from tables and other napery were being washed by girls, leaning over large tubs, their arms up beyond their elbows in piping hot, soapy water. The air was steamy and thick.

The five of us entered and the girls did not cease their labours but watched fascinated, craning their necks and almost falling over into their tubs as they followed our progress through the buildings. We lifted every bale of washing. We searched every tub. We poked into the barrels of lye. We even searched the rafters, Harold balancing like a rope walker on the beams, hoisted up by Johannes, the tallest of our men. Nothing.

Harold came down then and brushing himself of cobwebs and dust said, "Let's narrow the search."

Out came his polished stone again. He stood in the middle of the laundry. This time, his request was, "Where is the Belvoir regalia?"

He circled, and when he had turned to the outer wall, the stone began to move in an outward fashion, away from Harold's body.

He walked slowly in the direction it pointed. At last he reached the wall.

There was nowhere else to go. I sighed.

We all followed and stared. There against the moat wall was a barrel. We turned it to the light. It was empty and the bottom had rotted in the damp atmosphere.

However behind it, cut into the wall, was a small gap. I traced it with my eye, backwards to the middle of the room. A runnel starting in the centre of the laundry ran all the way to the wall. This had been made so that water from the washing tubs could drain away into the moat and not collect in puddles on the laundry floor. I noticed there were several there on that wall, behind equipment and more barrels. They could all be covered with a sliding panel and locked when not in use.

The hole was about two feet square and to the side of it a peg had been driven into the stone's mortar. To this peg was attached a thin rope.

Peter dragged up the rope. There was a trickling of water as the thing rose from the depths of the moat. A cloth bag was pulled through the hole and as it hit the ground, there was an audible clank.

Water pooled out around it and much of it drained back through the hole. I noticed the laundry had a slight camber to the floor.

Stephen, down on one knee, opened the bag.

"Well, I'll be bug...."

Johannes cut him off. "He was clever, your brother, I'll give him that."

"As are you young man" I said standing up, and I patted Harold on the back. "If I hadn't seen it with my own eyes..."

"The stones never lie sir" he said.

***

That is the truth of how we recovered the Belvoir regalia. I do not know how that young man knew where to look, unless of course, he himself had found it elsewhere and put it there in the castle laundry. The accusation was levelled at him, but I had seen with my own eyes, as I said, how the stone had worked and I was inclined to believe him.

We now had no reason to stay in Rouen and within two days we had packed our bags, loaded our horses and set off for England. I did not look back at the little churchyard close by the castle walls where lay my brother...no, my half brother, Robert. I turned my nose to the north. I could almost smell the damp, red earth of the Forest of Savernake.

I was glad to be going home.

***

"What do we need to say more Paul, do you think? Is my tale done or do I need to add anything? What's that? My daughter, Hawise? Here? Oh send her in then if you must. You can pack your things away, I suppose. Hello Hawise, come here and let me kiss you. Yes, I have eaten. I do, I do feel better. Do you? Do you really think I look better?

"Paul, you can leave the papers on the coffer there. I will read it when I have time. Oh ,and thank you Paul. You have been the best of scribes. The most patient of men, for I'm sure it was tedious listening to the rambles of an old man, talking about things that happened a lifetime ago. If I have been short with you I apologise. What? Well, I'm glad you found it interesting.

"What my dear? Oh just a story I have dictated to Paul. It would not please you, Hawise. In fact, I feel so much better, I don't think I shall die after all. I think I might get up and sit in my chair for a while. Will you help me my dear? Paul, before you go, might I send to the priory for you again, if they will spare you? I have an urge to dictate some more. Do you think you might like to come again and write for me? Hmmm? Do you think they will let you?

"I think I shall sit by the window in my porter's chair and contemplate the forest. Don't fuss dear, I can manage. I shall probably doze a little and you will be very bored if you stay. Oh well then, stay and do your sewing, that's fine. You are a good daughter to me, aren't you?

"Now, tell me. How is that fine lad my grandson coming along? He's placed with the de Lacy's at Lincoln isn't he?

"Knighted? Already? But he's just a lad!

"How old do you say he is?

"Good Lord. Tempus fugit."

AUTHOR'S NOTE

Marlborough was an established settlement by 1204 but began to expand with the rebuilding of the castle, at both ends of the wide, long High St. The charter was indeed granted to Marlborough in 1204 by King John. The fair continues to this day but it has moved to October and is now a Mop Fair - once a hiring fair. There are still two markets a week - much shrunken, but still operating, as John intended.

Savernake Forest lies at the southern edge of Marlborough town in Wiltshire and can still be visited today. Access is along the A4 to Newbury or the A346 to Salisbury. It is much smaller now (46 square miles) than in the 13th century when it was at its most extensive, covering some 150 square miles. Today the Forestry Commission manage it but there is still an hereditary warden, and it is Britain's only privately owned forest.

Now, it's a forest of mixed woodland but in the days of the 13th century, it had, for example, few of the large beech trees, we see today. They were planted in the 17th century, and sadly are coming to the end of their lives. The oaks are of considerable age though. Big Belly (ied) Oak, is one of the oldest, already being about two hundred years old when King John rode past it! I have mentioned a few beech trees growing in West Baily simply because I wished to have a glass making industry in the forest.

There were many different people and officers in the Mediaeval forest; agisters, verderers and regarders to name but a few. Understanding the individual roles of these men and sometimes women is quite a feat, even with years of study so I have kept things simple and given the different roles, names which are easily understood.

Likewise, although surnames were not common in the early 13th century, for ease of reading, my characters have two names, in the main.

In the days of John, the L'Estourmi family were the wardens of the forest. It's true that Geoffrey L'Estourmi fell foul of King Richard, having to pay a huge fine for supporting Prince John in his uprising against the King. In my tale I have changed the name of the family. Unless we know who they really were and what they actually did, I'm loath to make them do anything, so I'd rather make it up and have fictional characters, though the names of some of the minor players are to be found in the annals, if you look. The name Belvoir IS pronounced Bell voir and not 'Beaver' as it is nowadays. The English pronunciation 'Beaver' was built up over many centuries through the inability of the Anglo-Saxons to master the French tongue. It is the name of a small town of eastern France and there is still a castle there owned once by a noble family of the same name. Aumary's family is a Norman offshoot.

Now to Aumary, (pronounced Aymery). He is a minor lord, not terribly wealthy and more a business man than pure aristocracy. As warden of the forest he has quite a practical job and needs to know about the forest and its trades. He is a knight - yes, but first and foremost, a forester. I have made him a sympathetic character as so many folk of his class in novels are portrayed as proud, haughty and nasty. I fail to see how many of them could be so. They were dependent upon their peasants for their livelihood. If the peasant didn't prosper, neither did they, at this level of society. Grander folk perhaps could be less amenable. Aumary takes every man as he finds him and isn't averse to rolling up his sleeves and getting on with it. His job as warden means he is very in touch with the lesser people who work with and under him

Durley, now a small hamlet on the edge of the forest, was once well hidden in the trees. The manor can no longer be seen but there is a farm and a house called Durley House though this manor wasn't founded until the 1400's. The manor most people know about of course, is the one in Hilary Mantel's Book, Wolf Hall, (originally Ulfhall), probably a timbered building very near Burbage. The manor belonged to the Seymour family in the 16th century (who were also the hereditary wardens of the forest) and was the childhood home of Jane Seymour; I didn't want to go anywhere near there.

The Regalia existed and was extant until the 17th century when it disappeared. It was very likely broken up and melted down in the Civil War of 1642-5. However the ivory and silver horn is in The British Museum but sadly it's not on display.

The manor I have invented is a walled courtyard house with a stone hall of two storeys and a mezzanine floor, accessed by a staircase of stone and an undercroft below, very much like Boothby Hall in Lincolnshire, the finest surviving mediaeval house of its type in the country. The village around it owes much to Sheila Sancha's portrayal of Gerneham, (Irnham near Grantham) village, again in Lincolnshire, in her wonderful children's book The Luttrell Village - Country Life in the Early Fourteenth Century.

This is a depiction of the home of Sir Geoffrey Luttrell in the thirteen hundreds, so wonderfully documented in the Luttrell Psalter (now in the British Library) considered one of the richest sources for visual depictions of everyday rural life in mediaeval England.

Salerno in Sicily was one of the finest medical schools in the known world from the tenth to the thirteenth centuries. It was the most important source of medical knowledge in Western Europe, both of the Arab and ancient world and people of both sexes flocked from all over to study there. Books were the mainstay of the school, hundreds being translated from Arabic, Greek and other languages. As a result, the medical practitioners of Salerno, both men and women, were unrivalled in knowledge and practicality.

Sadly the school declined in favour of Montpellier later in the thirteenth century and then as the church tightened its grip, medical research came to a grinding halt, not to be resurrected until the seventeenth century.

I have tried to follow the Patent Rolls (in the form of the Rotuli Litterarum Patentium) by Thomas Duffus Hardy in 1835, to show where King John was known to be on certain days in his reign. I hope I have it right.

As to King John's character, I have never thought the portrayal of this much maligned monarch quite fair. He did have bad press. He annoyed the church so they were less than kind to him in their writings. He annoyed his barons as well so they too were less than complimentary about him.

Many of his critics were hardly snowy white themselves. The thirteenth century is a very shadowy time and much of what is written is ambiguous. We know King John was good to his friends; he did have some. His half-brother William Longspee was a life-long supporter. William Marshall, that octogenarian, larger than life character who bestrode the 12th and 13th century mediaeval stage like a colossus, thought him worth backing, with a few reservations, and despite a few hiccoughs, kept faith with him to the end of his days. Life as a monarch in those days was a tough one and decisions had to be made which we would find utterly distasteful today. I know John was probably a bit of a baddie but he certainly was not the out and out baddie of the legend of Robin Hood, (which incidentally antedates the reign of John by almost a couple of hundred years.) I have tried to make him a little more human.

Little is known about the 13th century castle and town of Marlborough. Most historical work done, concentrates on the period of the later Middle Ages. Research tells us that the castle was an extremely large and important one even early in its history. The original market place of Marlborough town, may have been on what is now the Green. The castle I speak about in my book, consists of just the inner, kidney shaped bailey. There may have been a huge outer baily extending to the middle of the High Street, but nothing now remains. The motte of the castle keep is behind some buildings in the Marlborough College grounds and is a re-used prehistoric mound not unlike Silbury Hill, its big sister a few miles to the West. The town of Marlborough must have been important enough to have a charter and I have made it, perhaps a little bigger and grander than it really was.

The Gilbertine Priory of St Margaret of Antioch, the only completely English ecclesiastical foundation, was actually situated up the hill to the South. I have placed them on the High Street for ease of story-telling. The order whose buildings actually lay on the High Street were the Carmelites founded in 1316 and too late for our tales.

I have also straightened the river Kennet to make it easier to follow on my fanciful map and shortened the (present) High Street a little.

Some people might think my use of the pipette - Walter's pipe for feeding lambs, several centuries before it was truly 'invented' far-fetched. I cannot believe that someone, somewhere did not try this, long before it was patented in the early 20th century. We do know they were in use in the 1790's, so why not a humble Wiltshire shepherd with brains in the 13th century. After all, someone, somewhere had to slightly burn the first piece of bread to make toast!

To any who think that it is not possible for dowsers, like young Harold in this book, to find things lost or secreted away, I say, it is perfectly possible. I am a pendulum dowser myself.

Susanna M. Newstead October 2017

GLOSSARY OF MEDIAEVAL TERMS

abjure the realm — The person taking the oath swore to leave the country directly and promptly, never to return to the kingdom unless by permission of the sovereign.

aconite — Winter flowering yellow flower Eranthis hymalis.

gazehound — A medium hound rather like a modern greyhound.

apostate — One who has abandoned one's religious faith.

apothecary — Primitive dispensing chemist.

archivist — One who collects, organizes, preserves, maintains control over, and provides access to records and archives determined to have long-term value.

arnica — A herb, Arnica montana, a cream of which is used to treat sprains and bruising.

assart — A piece of land converted from forest to arable use.

bee skeps — Old word for beehives.

belladonna — Plant, deadly nightshade, often used in small quantities to dilate the pupils of the eye, by mediaeval women. It was thought to enhance their beauty.

Benedictine — Monk of the order of St. Benedict.

bliaut — Voluminous overgarment worn by both sexes (but mostly women) and pleated to the waist or under the bust.

bothy — Small, simple building often of daub and wattle, roofed with thatch and having a beaten earth floor.

Bran — Ancient god of the British.

burntwine — Brandy.

carding — Action of teasing the wool fibres straight with a carding comb, so it could be spun.

chamberstick — A candlestick which has a handle for carrying.

churching — The ceremony in which a blessing is given to mothers after recovery from childbirth, including thanksgiving for the woman's survival after childbirth.

cotte — A long sleeved shift or tunic. A coat.

coroner — The man appointed by the Crown to deal with unexpected deaths. The coroner was the man who drew up the jury of twelve men to decide the cause of death and if need be, impose fines.

demesne (pronounced domain) — Land belonging to and adjoining a manor house. Estate.

deodand — Some personal property, such as a horse or a spade, was considered a deodand whenever a coroner's jury decided that it had caused the death of a human being. In theory, deodands were forfeit to the crown, which was supposed to sell the chattel and then apply the profits to some pious use.

distaff — A wooden sticklike tool used in spinning. It is designed to hold the unspun fibres, keeping them untangled.

donjon — Another word for castle keep, the central tower of a mediaeval castle.

downs — Chalk hills with steep coombes and valleys, thin soils and few trees.

dowsing — To dowse is to search, with the aid of simple handheld tools or instruments, for that which is otherwise hidden from view or knowledge. A twig or a pendulum are the most often used tools.

embrasure — A small opening in a castle wall from which arrows might be loosed.

fief — The estate or domain of a feudal lord and the rights granted to it.

Gascony — An area of southwest France, noted for its wines.

Gilbertine priory — Conventual buildings in Marlborough. Founded around 1130 by Saint Gilbert of Sempringham, Lincolnshire, where Gilbert was the parish priest. It was the only completely English religious order. The actual priory was on the southern hill towards the forest and I have exchanged position with the Carmelite Friary on the High Street.

herbal — An illustrated book about herbs and their uses.

joint stool — A small stool with stretchers and turned legs.

Justices in Eyre — The highest magistrates in mediaeval forest law.

limner — Painter; artist.

lymer — large dog used for hunting.

malfeasance — Wrongdoing by a public official.

meadowsweet Filipendula ulmaria — A herb for strewing on the floor to release a pleasant smell.

megrim — migraine.

mummers — Seasonal folk plays performed by troupes of actors often known as guisers (from disguise).

orpiment — A yellow mineral consisting of arsenic trisulphide in mono-clinic crystalline form occurring in association with realgar. Old French from Latin auripigmentum gold pigment. An ore of arsenic.

page — A young male servant between 8 and 14 who may also have been used as a messenger, to wait on tables, to be a body servant, fetching and carrying and to look after armour, etc.

palliasse — Straw-filled mattress.

pannage — The practice of releasing domestic pigs in a forest to feed on fallen acorns, beechmast, chestnuts or other nuts. Historically, it was a right or privilege granted to local people on common land or in royal forests.

prie-dieu — A piece of furniture for use during prayer, consisting of a kneeling surface and a narrow, upright front with a rest for the elbows or for books.

privy — the loo or bathroom.

quarterstaff — Staff made from hardwood of a tree split or sawed into quarters.

reeve — An official elected annually by the serfs to supervise lands for a lord.

reliquary — A box or some other container, usually decorated with precious metals and gems, to house the venerated body parts of a saint.

sanctuary — A sacred place, such as a church, in which fugitives were immune to arrest recognised by English law. They had forty days to make up their minds to either plead guilty and go into the hands of the law, or to abjure the realm.

sarsen stone — Large sandstone blocks found in quantity in the United Kingdom on Salisbury Plain and the Marlborough Downs.

scrip — A pouch worn at the waist on a belt.

sennight — A week; seven nights.

solar — Generally on an upper storey, a room designed as the family's private living and sleeping quarters. The room was usually situated so that sunlight would be caught for the maximum amount of time in the day.

spinster — Person (usually a woman) who spins thread and yarn with her distaff, by hand.

squire — A knight's trainee/apprentice. Over fourteen, these boys received training as knights themselves and looked after the needs of their masters.

stomach rupture — Hernia.

stooks — Corn gathered together and bound into bundles.

tempus fugit (Latin) —Time flies.

threshing — Beating the grain to separate wheat from chaff.

tump — The little hill made by a prehistoric burial mound.

undercroft — Lower part of a house used as a storehouse.

vassal — A person who has entered into a mutual obligation to a lord or monarch. The obligations often included military support and mutual protection, in exchange for certain privileges, usually including the grant of land held as a fiefdom.

For a pronunciation guide to some words used in this novel
and for more information please visit:
www.susannamnewstead.co.uk
or The Savernake Novels on Facebook

TITLES IN THIS SERIES:

Belvoir's Promise
She Moved Through the Fair
Down by the Salley Gardens

Made in the USA
Middletown, DE
12 December 2017